A GREATER EVIL

Jeff Haws

A Greater Evil

Printed in the United States of America

First Printing, 2020

ISBN: 978-1-945768-12-5

Publisher: Shifty Squid, LLC

P.O. Box 170392

Atlanta, GA 30317

Visit the author's website at www.jeffhaws.com

This story is dedicated to Jeremy Haws, who always asked me about my books.

1

Crouching in a small tent, her toes wrinkled against the hard-packed dirt at her feet, Stephanie reached up and scratched her cheek with nails grown long and ragged.

She looked at the back of her hand, lines of dirt now gathered underneath her fingernails. Gray rags hung off her body like neglected drapery, torn and caked with whatever filth was floating around her.

How long had she been locked up in this pen, a one-person tent her only solace from the relentless summer sun and the roaring storms that blew in without warning? The weather was her only way of keeping track of time, and she wasn't sure the summer was over yet. That meant it couldn't be longer than about six months.

But that was six months without a life. Six months without conversation, without sleeping in a bed or drinking from a glass. It was six months of lying on the ground and lapping warm water out of a bowl outside her tent. Six months of her hair drying into ropes before George haphazardly chopped most of it off one morning with a pair of scissors. Six months of being cut off from the outside world.

She hadn't seen her ex-husband Michael since the day he'd voted against her, propelling Audrey back into power and dooming Stephanie to this fate. It was hard for her not to feel bitter and resentful. They'd been through too much together for him to turn on her then, at the most crucial moment. Too much was at stake. Whatever he thought she'd done, that wasn't the time to take some sort of principled stand. It was the time to beat back the forces that wanted to tear Alessandra apart. And Stephanie couldn't help but feel like Michael turned his back on that.

"Get out here!" William's voice bellowed, and Stephanie scrambled through the tent flap, squinting into the midday sun. "Jesus, Stephanie. You stink worse every time I come down here."

She crossed her arms and blinked.

"Don't worry. I can take care of that." He laughed and lifted one of the metal pails that were sitting next to him. "Strip."

Stephanie closed her eyes and took a deep breath, then shook her head. The humiliation never ended in this place. She liked to think of herself as being resilient, fighting back against whatever was thrown her way, defiant in the face of doubt. She'd overcome so much in her life to get where she had been, first a head of research at a major hospital and then leading her hometown through the aftermath of a pandemic and the iron grip of an authoritarian maniac.

But then there was *this*. The will to live was strong. But she was finding that, once it was broken, it could be hard to repair. There were times a bullet between her eyes sounded like a relief sweeter than a glass of rosé.

Stephanie yanked her stiff grey top over her head, then dropped it on the ground. She shoved down her shorts, stepping out of them and kicking them to the side. Expressionless, she stood up straight, naked, arms stiff at her sides.

The first several times she'd been ordered to do this, she fought it. No way she was going to strip. They could leave the water for her, and she'd bathe herself. But they said the pails could end up being a weapon, so they weren't going to let her keep them and set up a surprise attack. She thought it was bullshit—bringing a bucket to a gunfight didn't strike her as a winning strategy—but what she thought didn't matter. They didn't even have to give her a stupid excuse. If they refused to leave the water, she could strip in front of them or remain endlessly dirty.

It wasn't the stink that got to her. You got used to that after a while. It was the feel of having a second skin of dirt and grime that was hard to live with. Your body felt stiff and creaky, like it was covered with a thick crust it couldn't shake. It made it hard to sleep, hard to even move around comfortably. Bathing restored enough of Stephanie's dignity that she didn't care anymore how much stripping on command took away.

William tossed a small bar of soap toward her; she tried to catch it, but it tumbled out of her hands into the dirt, picking up a thin layer of earth she tried to quickly brush away.

"Gotta have soft hands on that catch, Steph." William snickered. "Let the soap come to you."

She ignored him and blew on the soap for a few more seconds before she was hit with a splash of cool water that sent goosebumps cascading up her arms as it lowered her skin temperature twenty-plus degrees. She shivered for a second, but it felt great. Like it was sent from heaven itself. Frantically, she started rubbing the soap everywhere—face, hair, down her torso, particularly over her now-bushy underarms and her thighs up between her legs then around to her butt. It was always a scramble to try to get as clean as she could before the second wave hit.

Just as Stephanie reached around behind her, the next big splash came. It almost took her breath away. She ran her hands all over her body now, watching brown water streaming off and pooling at her feet. It was an amazing feeling, almost like being freed from her own personal prison even while being locked in a larger one. It made her want to live, if only for one more day.

2

Unfastening the band from his waist and letting the steel ring clank at his feet, Michael leaned it against the wall and stepped inside the mansion. It hadn't taken him as long as he'd expected to reacquaint himself with lugging twenty pounds of steel around his waist. Still, it was always a relief to shed it when he came back home.

Living here had taken some getting used to. At first, he felt separated from the town, from friends and people he'd known all his life. But, especially as the threat of the virus continued to loom like a storm cloud over Alessandra, he came to welcome the serenity and isolation of the mansion.

Only a few more people had been infected since the election, making a lot of people believe Audrey's rings really did make a difference in preventing the spread of the virus, even as the means of virus transmission was still a matter of some debate. They'd known for some time that it could spread like wildfire through a community if left unchecked, but they still weren't entirely sure how, or why some people seemed either immune or asymptomatic. They also knew how it manifested itself—first, with a rapidly escalating fever and lethargy within a few hours after exposure, followed by searing boils on the skin and what was often an excruciating death within roughly a day.

If Audrey's rings could prevent that, whatever inconvenience it caused was worth it. And it was the brutalist solution they needed until a vaccine was ready. That was certainly the story she'd tell, anyway. Michael wasn't entirely sure what to think, though he had gained confidence they could contain the virus far better than they used to. The doctors at St. Francis knew how to handle it by this point, and they could keep it under control if it didn't spread too quickly.

Regardless of the rings' effectiveness, you could understand the people wanting to latch onto whatever solution was presented to them. When they wore rings before, the virus never infected anyone. They got rid of the rings, and the virus struck. So now, again, people were staying safe within the confines of twenty pounds of steel. At the very least, nobody wanted to jinx their good fortune by changing something that wasn't causing problems.

Although there *were* problems. They weren't entirely evident from a casual walk around the town. On the surface, everything looked relatively normal, or as normal as it could get in a small town scraping by in a world ravaged by a relentless virus that seemed hellbent on wiping out every last one of them.

But scratch beneath that veneer, and you could see a society that wasn't operating in the way it should. The same issues that plagued them during Audrey's previous administration—depression, isolation, lack of motivation to work, no sense of community—appeared to have returned. On occasion, someone would simply disappear and never be seen again, presumed to have wandered off into the woods to die, unable to go on living like this anymore.

The projects begun under Stephanie and Michael—digging a trench from the lake, regular water pickups, construction jobs—were languishing as people shut themselves into their homes. Once again, cohabitation was banned, and families were broken up into separate living quarters. Children had been taken to their own facility north of the mansion, where they were supervised by a few women who Audrey said were tested daily for signs of the virus.

Michael suspected people had been skeptical when Audrey reintroduced the rings, but she sold them as the protection they and their families needed, a temporary measure necessary only until St. Francis researchers could deliver a vaccine for the virus.

So everyone acquiesced, waiting, the pressure mounting on the researchers to come up with something, *anything* that Audrey could promote as her legacy—saving the world from this killer that many thought was unstoppable.

As Audrey's second in command, Michael got to walk to St. Francis each day to get an update. There typically wasn't a lot of news, but it had turned into one of his main duties in the role Audrey had given him.

He peeked his head into Audrey's office and knocked on the door.

"Ah, you're back," she said, looking up from a paper she was reading on her desk. "Any progress?"

"Nothing notable. Still trying to isolate the H6N1 strain from the material they have saved. And they reminded me again that they're shorthanded."

Audrey rolled her eyes. "That bullshit again?"

"It's true, Audrey. You know as well as I do that Stephanie was the best researcher they had. Having her down there could speed the process quite a bit."

"She's a *murderer*, Michael. Law and order has to matter more than anything else. If we let behavior like that slide, the virus won't matter because we'll kill ourselves off first."

"Do you really believe that?"

She stood up, her hands pressed against the desk. "I *know* that. I've seen it with my own eyes. We're all animals, in the end, trying to survive from day to day. You take away the deterrent factor, and it becomes every man for himself in the blink of an eye. These people aren't special. They're not different. You have to show them violence won't be tolerated in order to root it out. Let Stephanie go, and you lose everything."

"True or not, you don't let her go, and the virus may take everything anyway. It doesn't give a damn about your deterrents. It only wants to kill."

Audrey closed her eyes and sat back down. "Yeah. And of course I want the vaccine to happen. I just think she could be dangerous."

Michael shrugged and shook his head, then turned to walk

back out the door, but stopped.

"She never got the trial you promised, you know. You said we'd treat her fairly. Are we?"

"Of course. It just takes time to set this up. You know that, Michael. Come on. She's healthy, getting three good meals a day, has access to everything anyone else in this town does. She's fine. *More* than fine, really."

"You know all that?"

"I get weekly reports from George and William. I can show you the lists of everything they provide her, if it would help. Or if you want to go see for yourself, I can have one of them escort you down."

Michael looked at the floor, his shoulders slumping. "No, I… I don't know how to face her. What would I even say?"

"I understand. But rest assured, she's good. It's no Hilton penthouse or anything, but she's comfortable enough. And the trial is happening soon. Okay?"

"Fine. Yeah. And think about what she could do for the virus research. She could make a major difference."

Audrey nodded. "Sure. I'll take it under consideration."

3

Alessandra was quiet. Dew dripped off the grass, and the sun peeked over the horizon as George strolled the streets, William keeping step to his right. Even before the rings returned, this would have been a peaceful time of the day for the town, the world stretching its arms and rolling over in bed. It was when George most liked to get out, the mild bite of cool air reminding him that autumn was beginning to poke its head around the corner.

It was a different feeling taking his walks these days. Since Audrey took over, he'd quickly gone from being what seemed like an outcast, that guy staked out at the gate every day, to being a prominent member of the town's leadership. He'd always felt like people didn't respect his job, that he didn't do a whole lot—it's not as if they had a steady flow of visitors, and he merely followed orders when they did. There wasn't much use in trying to explain to people how essential his role was, and how he'd kept it through two administrations because he was good at it.

But now they understood. Now the people could see that he wasn't sitting on a wall picking his nose. He was out here, walking the streets with the authority to do as he pleased. He came with the blessing and trust of Audrey, a woman of whom most townspeople had a healthy amount of fear—and for good reason. Unlike Stephanie, Audrey had proven repeatedly that she wasn't someone whose boundaries you wanted to test. And the fact that people knew George was out patrolling on Audrey's orders meant he got the respect that she got.

He liked that. Maybe more than he anticipated.

Audrey didn't come out here much. She mostly saw herself as the orchestrator of what went on in the town, and she directed a team of people to execute her plans. George had been able to recruit much of Zac's old group of followers—Andy and Benjamin most prominently—to help with some of the grunt work. Audrey was giving the orders, but execution was George's responsibility. And to him, that meant this town was *his*. He owned it now. He was the highest authority walking the streets of Alessandra, and everyone had to respect that. If they didn't, he could stash them away up at the compound, and nobody was going to say a word.

He had no intention of hurting anyone, of course. He only wanted what was best for the community. But they'd learned well the lesson that a soft touch only led to chaos and rebellion. Order was the only way forward. Audrey was the leader this town needed, and George was going to make sure her vision for Alessandra was realized.

So these walks weren't just therapeutic for George now; they had a real purpose. Not only did he want to be Audrey's eyes and ears out on the streets, but he wanted those eyes and ears to be seen and felt by the townspeople. He wanted them to know they were being watched, that there wasn't anything they could sneak past Audrey's team. He and William could make an intimidating pair, walking the scraggly pavement of Alessandra's streets. If anyone considered having a visitor without authorization, they'd be afraid of getting caught. If they thought about going outside without their ring on, they were taking a risk with their lives. There were no surveillance cameras anymore, but Audrey had eyes and ears everywhere. Break the rules at your peril.

George had also been able to give William back what he wanted—a job in law enforcement, and some fleeting glimpses of authority. William was never going to be a leader, and they both knew that. But he liked being *close* to the leader, taking direct orders from someone, and being granted power over others. That was a role he was comfortable in. George made sure he felt like his talents were being utilized.

To this point, George could walk through the town with his head held high. There was plenty of progress still to be made, but he was confident they were going in the right direction. Audrey's plan was taking shape. The rings had been re-implemented with a minimum of resistance, and there had been virtually no new cases of the virus since the election. They knew it was probably still lurking, and was always a threat until they got the vaccine, but it hadn't ravaged the population as many feared when it showed up in the spring.

Alessandra was quiet. He hoped it continued to be. It meant people were calm, and staying to themselves. It meant that any contagion that found its way into one person would likely die with him right where he stood. They'd effectively isolated everyone. And their fear was going to keep them that way.

4

"Michael, can we talk?" Audrey said, walking into his office and sitting down in front of him. He looked up from his desk.

"Of course. What's up?"

"I've been thinking about what you said about the researchers at the hospital. About how they need Stephanie's help to succeed in creating a vaccine. Do you really believe she's *that* valuable?"

He sighed. "That's the impression I get. I mean, I'm as far as possible from an expert in medical research, but I think she was great at it. She's got a Ph.D. from one of the best schools in the country. And she returned to Alessandra because she cared about giving some of that expertise back to her hometown. Without her leadership when the virus first struck, who knows where we'd all be now? I have no doubt she'd be an asset."

"Right." Audrey adjusted in her chair and folded her arms across her chest. "But what I mean is…are they—"

"Yeah. No. I get it." Michael waved a hand in front of his face, then ran it through his hair. "Are they *exaggerating* their actual need to help an old friend?"

Audrey nodded. "So are they?"

Michael turned his eyes toward the ceiling, pausing for several moments.

"Maybe a little. They *are* friends. Whatever Stephanie's done, it wouldn't be shocking to find out they wanted to extend a hand to her. I'm not gonna deny that. But I've also known these doctors for a while. I've been to their houses for barbecues, chatted with them in the hospital cafeteria, even been their patient from time to time. It's been a little while since I've spent a ton of time around them, but when I was married to Stephanie, our lives revolved around Saint Francis. We used to joke that the hospital was her second husband. It's the way working in a place like that goes, I guess.

"Anyway, all that is to say, I think I have some experience that helps me be able to read the staff there a bit more than a lot of people in the town. Maybe that's even part of the reason you're sending *me* over there rather than George or William or whoever. Are they wanting to help Stephanie? They almost certainly are. Hell, I wouldn't even be surprised if they don't believe she did anything to Zac. But do they *also* actually need her help if we're going to beat this fucking virus?"

Michael scratched his forehead, then sat forward in his chair, arms pressed against the desk and his eyes boring into Audrey's.

"Absolutely," he said. "Not a doubt in my mind."

"So you'll vouch for them? The doctors and Stephanie?"

"Me? Oh, um, yeah. Sure. Everything will be fine."

"I'm counting on that. They can come here and ask questions, collaborate. I recommend you work it out so they don't ever see or talk directly, in case they try to pass along some sort of code or whatever. Maybe have a go-between. I'm skeptical, but I'm open to trying it if it pushes this process forward."

"Okay, great. I'll make it happen. They'll be thankful for the chance to get her help."

"Good. But remember, I'm putting my trust in you here, Michael. You're to watch *everything*. You suspect the slightest thing is up, call it off. If anything happens, it's on you."

Sitting not far from Doctor Frank Lawry but out of Stephanie's line of sight, Michael half listened to their conversation in the mansion's courtyard. Stephanie was behind a fence, and Frank was tucked in against a wall so that they couldn't see each other.

Michael had only gotten the briefest glimpse at Stephanie, enlisting Benjamin to bring her over to the fence and let her know the ground rules—no discussion of anything other than the virus and its vaccine, keep all body parts inside the fence at all times, no looking at one another. Michael still couldn't bear the thought of actually being face to face with Stephanie.

Was that guilt eating at him? Shame? Or awkwardness he didn't know how to deal with? It had been months since they'd exchanged so much as a nod. It seemed like there was so much to say and so few ways to say it. Had he made the right decision in flipping his vote to Audrey? He still felt like he did. The reinstatement of the rings was disheartening, but he couldn't deny the results—the virus had slowed, they were surviving as a community and even making progress toward a vaccine. Michael wasn't sure he was convinced yet that his ex-wife had been involved in Zac's death, but he didn't have a better explanation, and the knife he found in her house still bothered him. If it wasn't Stephanie, then who did it?

Regardless of what she'd done, he worried about her out here alone. He didn't know how she could take it, sitting down here by herself, the summer sun beating her down for months, tucking herself into a tiny tent for shelter. Seeing her, even if for a moment, was a bit of a shock. He was trying to keep himself from thinking about her emaciated face, tightly cropped hair, and dry rags hanging off her body like old, dingy curtains. That person behind the fence was barely recognizable as Stephanie at all, the sharp cheekbones and skin tinted to a brown that could have been a suntan or a layer of dirt.

Audrey claimed that Stephanie was being taken care of, that she was comfortable. Michael wanted to believe that. He wanted to convince himself everything was fine. Her mind was still sharp, with terms like "adjuvants" and "split virion" being tossed back and forth between the doctors. And he wasn't sure she looked *un*healthy, just thin. Maybe that was understandable. He couldn't think she'd be given enormous amounts of food up here. She was a prisoner and a murder suspect, not a family friend crashing on their couch.

Still, he wondered if Audrey had been down there to see her at all. Did she actually know the conditions Stephanie was living in? Did she know what Stephanie looked like? If not, why was Audrey avoiding seeing it for herself? And if so, why did she keep inviting Michael to go on his own?

It occurred to him that it could be a test of loyalty. Sending him down to see her would accomplish one of two things—confirm that Stephanie was being taken care of perfectly well, or show him she wasn't at all. And if it was the latter, he was going to have to decide which road he wanted to take. Would he demand change to see his ex-wife treated humanely while in custody? Or would he turn a blind eye to what was going on, sticking with Audrey through another atrocity?

Would he be complicit? Was he already?

5

"You're sure that's what you saw?" George asked, breaking into a half-jog through the town square and onto the streets of Alessandra, still not wanting to believe William. "It's still a little dark. This better not be a mistake."

"I'm tellin' ya. I saw a shadowy figure dart between the houses toward Derrick's back door. We didn't make eye contact, but I saw enough of her face to know that was Leslie. When I hustled around the edge of another place two doors down, I got a plenty good enough glimpse at her before the door opened and she went inside."

"Son of a—" George could feel the rage welling up within him. Hank's ex-wife flaunting the ring rules—any unauthorized visitation was prohibited, but visits of a sexual nature were strictly banned until the virus wasn't a threat—to mess around with a non-Alessandran, some random immigrant who didn't even deserve a place in this town. George didn't even care that Derrick was black. He didn't *think* he did, anyway. No, it wasn't about race. He'd tell you he didn't even *see* race. This was about the law, and this man being from somewhere else. Leslie was being wildly irresponsible, and there would be consequences.

How long had this been going on? Maybe they'd been sleeping together even before the rings were brought back, and hadn't been willing to stop. Had they been able to keep it a secret all this time?

"You think…it's locked?" William asked between gasps for breath, catching up to George on Derrick's front porch.

George looked at the door and frowned, then reached for the doorknob. He turned it slowly, trying to stay quiet. He felt the handle catch, turned back to William and nodded.

William was still bent at the waist, his arm across his gut.

"You gonna be all right?" George asked, his voice low.

William sucked in a deep breath and exhaled forcefully. "Yeah. Yeah. I'll live." He stood up straight, his face bright red. "What do we want to do here?"

"Okay. If you can get some oxygen in you, I want you to bang on this door and yell. Loud, man. All right? I want the fucking devil to hear you. Whatever you've got."

"Won't that scare her off?"

George smiled. "That's exactly what I'm counting on."

Once Leslie arrived, Derrick was ready, pulling the back door open enough for her to slide inside. She'd only been out there for five seconds or so, long enough to step out of her ring and prop it against the wall. Surely not long enough for anyone to spot her. When she left later this morning, he could go outside and make sure no one was around before she slipped out.

Were they taking a risk? Of course. But others had pulled it off. It didn't seem too tough to get away with, especially under cover of the morning darkness. Derrick wasn't even sure they were seriously enforcing this rule. The virus didn't seem all that active anyway.

Derrick and Leslie didn't really meet until she brought him a tray of grilled vegetables she'd made when he was recovering from being attacked while working in Father Hayden's back yard. He was still having a hard time getting around, experiencing frequent dizzy spells and headaches, so she wanted to make sure he had enough to eat. She brought him that first dish, and they began talking. She started bringing over food nearly every day, and eventually they started having meals together. One evening, they barely touched the food before heading to his bedroom, and he was pretty sure he was falling in love.

But Audrey had won the election, and would soon re-institute the rings, banning visitations and physical contact, at pretty much the height of them craving it more than ever. For a month or so, they tried to work within the rules, meeting occasionally outside their homes while wearing the rings, discreetly brushing fingers to whatever extent they could so they could feel the electricity of each other's touch. Instead of satiating the hunger, though, those clandestine meetings only caused it to grow inside of them until there wasn't any reasonable way to contain it anymore.

They started meeting at each other's homes either late at night or very early in the morning, first going with Leslie's house because she was neighbors with Stephanie and Michael, and neither was in their homes at this point, so they felt like there were fewer eyes on her. But they worried about her first-floor bedroom and someone seeing their shadows or hearing something, so they started trying Derrick's house for his large bed on the second floor.

This was their third time meeting there, and the first two had been easy. And, at least for him, there was something exciting about the danger of it, however unlikely it was they'd be caught. Thinking about the fact that there'd be real consequences to being seen added an extra allure to the sex, and had him craving it even more than he might normally in the honeymoon phase of a relationship.

"You think we're okay?" Leslie asked, as the door shut behind her. Derrick kissed her and pressed her body tightly against his, arms wrapped around her shoulders.

"We're perfect," he said, pulling back for a second and smiling before kissing her again. Her fingernails ran up and down his back. "I think we're getting good at this."

He reached for her hand and led her to the stairs. At the top, he pushed his bedroom door open, and she came in behind him.

"Oh, Derrick. It's beautiful!" she exclaimed when she walked in, a dozen lit candles lined up on the windowsills and shelves above the bed. "Where'd you get these?"

"Been scavenging them for a while. Found some in abandoned homes. A few people left one or two out on their front porch for me to grab. I thought it'd be nice to be able to really see each other this time."

She smiled and kissed him. "That's sweet. It makes me think of the old world a little bit. How candlelight created this romantic moment, rather than just being the only means of light. With all the huge stuff we lost, sometimes you miss the little things, ya know?"

Derrick nodded. "There's still hope we can get back to something resembling that. The world hasn't ended yet."

Leslie looked at Derrick, then back at the candles.

"How long do you think we can keep this up?" She took off her coat and laid it on top of the dresser behind her. "Are we pushing our luck?"

"No, don't think like that. They're getting closer to a vaccine all the time. And once they have that, we won't have to worry about any of this sneaking around nonsense. We can walk down the street holding hands, kiss by the old courthouse in the square on a beautiful spring day. People will smile and wave. They'll be happy for us."

She started to grin, but Derrick thought it seemed a little bit forced.

"I wish I were as confident as you about that," she said, looking away from him, toward the bed. She paused for a few moments, silence hanging over the room. He was about to speak when she began again. "I want to be. I really want to believe things are going to work out all right. For us. For Alessandra. For the *world.* Ya know? It's just hard. It's been so long, and we've lost so much about who we were, and how everything used to work."

Leslie reached over and touched a light switch on the wall.

"You remember being able to walk into a room and flip one of these switches? You wouldn't have to scavenge anything. There was no rationing of electricity. You did it without a thought. It was magic."

"It was," Derrick said. "There was a lot we took for granted back then."

"Sometimes, I feel like I dreamed it all. Like, it couldn't have been real—light switches working, taps flowing with water at the flick of a wrist, grocery store shelves brimming with more food than we could ever possibly consume. Everything was so easy. So simple. But the memory fades, gets harder to hold onto with every passing year. We get further away from it, and it feels less real. If we're ever allowed to have kids again, they'll never know any of it. They'll think we *must* be exaggerating at least some of it. Hell, I find myself wondering that too."

Derrick stepped close to her and pressed both hands to her cheeks, bringing her face to his and kissing her softly.

"I understand how you feel. This world is different, and there's no telling what the future will ultimately bring," he said. "But all that matters right now is you and me. *Here*. Together. Not knowing what the future holds is all the more reason to cherish these moments we have."

She smiled and nodded, her eyes bright, meeting his. They embraced and then kissed again, lips wet, tongues dancing together. Leslie began to unbutton his shirt, her fingers feeling for the right angle to twist the buttons without looking. When they were all undone, he yanked his arms through the sleeves and dropped it to the floor.

He pulled her closer and tugged at the shoulders of her dress; she raised her arms, and he pulled it up over her head. She wasn't wearing anything underneath. She slid her feet out of a ragged pair of loafers, and stood before him, her bare, pale skin luminous in the candlelight. He smiled and wrapped his arms around her waist, lifting and kissing her as he carried her to the bed and laid her gently on her back.

Derrick unbuttoned his jeans, sliding them down his legs to the floor. He leaned over and kissed her stomach, running his tongue slowly up her midsection, hands crawling up to her thighs, spreading her legs apart. He laid on top of her, kissing her neck, teeth grazing the skin as he moved his tongue toward her earlobe, electricity coursing through his body.

Five ear-shattering bangs on the door shocked them both, and Derrick's heart leaped in his chest as he turned away from the bed back toward the front of the house.

"I know you're in there with Leslie!" the voice rose up through the dark morning, barreling into Derrick's home like a wrecking ball. "Come the *fuck* down now!"

6

"Is this what you expected things to be like?" Benjamin paced along the platform on top of Alessandra's gate. "When we got the right people back in power, I mean. Is this what you expected?"

Andy looked down at his ring and drummed his fingers on the steel for a second.

"I didn't see these things coming back, that's for sure," he said. "I don't think Zac would have done that. But it's tough to complain about the results. I think we're safer. Smarter. I feel more in control. Everything isn't bright and sunny, but fuck feelings. None of that matters. Freedom is bullshit."

Benjamin flexed and stretched the fingers of his right hand, still painful after never quite healing correctly following his fight with Nick at Walt's Bar several months earlier.

"Yeah." Benjamin grimaced and leaned against the wooden railing. "Do you ever wonder what would be different if we could have gotten Zac elected instead of Audrey?"

"If that Stephanie bitch hadn't killed him, you mean?"

"Right. Because if Audrey beat her ass, surely Zac would have too."

"Easily. Wouldn't have been by one goddamn vote, that's for *damn* sure. With everything Stephanie had done, it was an embarrassment that Audrey could *barely* beat her, and only because Michael finally grew a set and stood up to her for once in his cuck life. Zac wouldn't have needed a murder on her rap sheet to take her down. Hell, the tide was already turning before that.

Her stupid-ass decisions would have been plenty for him to hammer her on. And that's why Stephanie killed him. She fucking *knew* she couldn't beat him in a fair election."

"We'd be up in that mansion if Zac would have won," Benjamin mused, looking up the hill at the massive house looming over the town. "Not sitting here at the gate watching the grass grow."

"Damn straight, we would. We'd be making real decisions, making Alessandra great, man. Instead, yeah. Here we are. It's *something*, I guess. But there's not a whole lot to actually *do*. What I'd love to do is get my hands around Stephanie's throat for a few minutes. Pin her down in that tent and fucking squeeze the life out of her."

"Or blow her head off with Zac's gun there."

Andy looked over at the FN-FAL they'd taken from Zac's house after he died.

"There'd be something fitting about that, wouldn't there?" He continued looking at it for a few seconds, then snapped back to Benjamin. "But no, there's something very personal about killing someone with your bare hands, ya know? Something *deserving*, in this case. I mean, look, I'm not a cold-blooded killer. I don't go around murdering people for no reason. An eye for an eye, though. I think it's ridiculous she gets to live while Zac's in the fucking ground."

"Using up resources too. Food, water, time to take care of her."

"Fucking *right*," Andy said, smacking a hand on his ring. "It's not like this is a goddamn utopia, overflowing with riches, a land of milk and honey here. We're fighting every day for our lives, trying to survive as a colony at the end of the fucking world. Stephanie isn't contributing shit, she's a murderer, and yet we're spending some of what little we have toward keeping life going in her worthless body? Why?"

"Well, I did hear something about her helping the hospital with research into a vaccine for the virus."

"Oh, for fuck's sake. If they need the help of a murderer to get that done, maybe it was never meant to be."

"That is a big deal, though," Benjamin said. "If they can figure that out, everything changes. We can start really building toward something. We can all be immune, and that'd give us a hell of a lot of power to wield in this world. We could venture out if we wanted to, socialize more, have more of a real community. It could be great."

Andy scratched his forehead, then ran a hand through his hair. "Well, look…If Audrey and George actually think she's helping with that, fair enough. I'll respect their wishes for now. But ya know what? The day they do find that vaccine, Stephanie's on borrowed fucking time, I'll tell ya that much. The first chance I have to get the justice Zac deserves, I'm taking her out. You with me?"

"Try and stop me."

7

"I think that's Officer Greene," Derrick said, barely above a whisper. Leslie was still lying naked on the bed, clutching a blanket to her chest. "Shit. He must have seen you come in. But *how*? You were out there for the blink of an eye."

Leslie's mind was swirling. Had she not been careful enough? She thought she'd been discreet, avoiding streets where possible, weaving between abandoned houses with sun-baked paint flaking loose on the outer walls, weeds growing unchecked up to her waist. But whatever she'd done hadn't been enough.

In the back of her mind, she'd always known this was a possibility, but only in the abstract. Audrey's team hadn't taken anyone away except for Stephanie as far as she knew. So they'd figured maybe the rules weren't being enforced with the vigor they were last time, when Paul was making a lot of those calls.

She should have known, though. Even if they weren't being as strict, she knew there were risks to being with an outsider. So there was always the chance that she and Derrick would be treated differently.

Had they been planning this ambush for days? Weeks? Months? Waiting for the right moment to catch them in the act, here in bed together? She had no way to know. Nor did she know what the consequences would be. What had Stephanie's fate been? No one seemed to have much clue, and Audrey's team never said anything except that Stephanie was awaiting trial for the murder of Zac. Seemed like a long wait.

But it wasn't like there was a Constitution anymore. No Bill of Rights. No tradition of how the government was supposed to treat people—free speech, freedom of religion, due process, all that. This wasn't the United States of America anymore. There *was no* United States of America. The borders and common understandings from the previous world died alongside virtually all the people who enforced them.

As Leslie's heart pounded, her breath getting short, she knew they were at the mercy of whatever George and his men wanted to do to them. Unless she could get out before being spotted.

"I need to go," Leslie said, scrambling off the bed and shimmying quickly into her dress, then stepping back into her loafers. "How many ways are there out of this house?"

"What? No. We can hide you. Under the bed, maybe. A closet. He'll see you if you go outside, and then we're dead."

"Derrick, you heard the man. He's a big guy. He's gonna start kicking that door in if you don't open it, and that's gonna piss him off even more. We don't have time to find the perfect hiding place. My best bet is to get the hell out of here before he sees me. What are my options?"

Stunned, Derrick swung his head toward the front of the house as more banging echoed up the stairs from the door.

"The, um, front and back door," he said, eyes wide looking back at Leslie. "That's really it. And you obviously can't use the fr—"

Leslie shoved past him and ran to the end of the hall as William's voice reverberated through the house again. She stopped in front of the window along the back wall. Derrick came up behind her.

"You're not thinking—"

"Help me get this open." She pushed up on the latch, but it wouldn't budge easily.

"No. You're *not* going out a second-story window. This is madness. I've got an attic with lots of old crap in it. Tons of places to hide. Or you can use the back door to leave. Officer Greene's in front!"

"Look, we don't have time for this. They'll expect me to go out the back, since it's the only other real exit. That's why this window on the side of the house, and well away from the front door, is the best option. Help me get this thing open, then go let Officer Greene in while I make a run for it. Okay?"

Derrick rubbed his temple and sighed. "I don't—"

"Hey." Leslie put her hands on his shoulders. "It's okay. I appreciate your concern. I really do. But we need to do this *now*." She kissed him softly. "All right?"

He nodded and went to the opposite side of the window from Leslie; they both pushed, and it lurched upward. The screen behind it was brittle, and it nearly crumpled as soon as Derrick yanked on it. He pulled it inside and tossed it into one of the side bedrooms, then lifted Leslie onto the window ledge, her legs dangling inside the house.

Derrick leaned over and kissed her, his hands resting delicately on her waist.

"Wish me luck." She smiled and swung her legs around to the outside, then rolled over on her stomach, grabbing onto the windowsill and holding tightly as she carefully slid out the window. After a few seconds, her body was stretched as far as it could go, pressed against the side of the house, hanging on by her fingertips. She looked up once at Derrick and saw the concern on his face, then nudged off the wall with her feet and let go.

Leslie landed on the balls of her feet, then let herself tuck into a crouch, falling backward and crashing her butt into the ground, her legs flying up. She shook her head and paused for a moment, feeling for any pain. She wiggled her arms and legs but didn't notice any problems.

She looked up at Derrick and smiled, giving him a thumbs-up sign as she heard the first kick hit the front door. He shut the window and quickly disappeared down the hall. She stood with her back against the wall, waiting to hear Derrick let William inside before she made her break. She was thinking about what the best route would be when she remembered: *My fucking ring. It's still outside the back door.*

Leslie closed her eyes and looked up at the sky. In the urgency of trying to escape the immediate danger, they'd both forgotten about her ring. Could she leave it there and come back for it later? It might be okay if she could get home without being seen, then stay inside the rest of the day, retrieving it in the dark of early morning. But that'd be risky. If William saw it—and it wasn't like it was inconspicuous, leaning against the wall next to the back door—it wouldn't take much detective work to figure out it was hers. The waist fit would be *far* too small for Derrick.

No, that wouldn't work. Leslie was going to have to get it now. But this was doable. She needed the timing to be right. She heard Derrick and William talking. She couldn't make out all the words, but the shouting and banging had stopped. That was good. The last thing she needed was rubbernecking neighbors seeing her.

Leslie took a peek and saw William step through the front door; she started quietly moving toward the back of the house, staying low so she couldn't be seen out of any of the first-floor windows. Would William check out the back door? Derrick wouldn't know not to let him, because he wasn't thinking about the ring either. The worst thing would be to get her hands around the ring as that back door opened, William standing there smiling down at her with that crooked grin of his.

Ideally, she'd wait until they were upstairs, but she didn't think she could take that chance even if she could hear enough to know where they were. She needed to get the ring as soon as she could, then get the hell out of there.

Leslie looked around the back yard and saw nothing in the early-morning light, the sun's rays beginning to flood out the darkness. Everything was quiet and covered in dew, a mild cool breeze tickling the short hair of her arms. She made her break for it, around the old, rusted air-conditioning unit that had stopped working years earlier, then streaking to her ring, clutching it in both hands and turning to go back when she heard a familiar voice.

"Hi, Leslie," George said, stepping out from the other side of the house. "It's been a while. How have you been?"

8

Lying in her tent, Stephanie pulled her knee toward her chest and heard it make a satisfying crack. The tent wasn't big enough for her to fully stretch out—her knees always had to be bent a bit when she was lying down—but she often found herself splayed out in there for hours at a time.

What else was there to do in this barren plot of dirt? During the summer, at least the tent protected her from the sun's unrelenting heat all day, though it got stuffy enough that she'd have to unzip the opening to get some fresh air moving through. She'd usually keep it all the way open at night if she wanted to have any chance at all of sleeping; even after six months of practice, it was hard to sleep in a pool of your own sweat. Lots of her nights consisted of fitful rest.

This tent had become her home, her sanctuary from the world outside. The only place she had any privacy in this awful place. Lying there, staring up at the blue top, the early-morning sun's light casting a dark spot on the tent's right side, she heard the now-familiar sound of the gate being unlocked.

The sound made her cringe. She never knew what—or who—to expect. It was a rotating cast of men who came to visit her, some who wouldn't even say a word as they dropped a bowl of food and water, picked up any old dishes, and left. Other times, she'd get beckoned out of her tent for one reason or another, maybe to get clean, maybe to be whipped, beaten, or stripped and shoved back into her tent to be raped from behind, her face turned sideways and pressed hard against the tent floor.

That was always Andy. At first, she'd resisted. But he always came armed, brandishing a long-bladed knife. She'd felt the blade pierce her back more than a few times as she tried to scream and writhe, wanting to buck him off of her, but he had enough bulk to eventually pin her down every time, then leave her bleeding on the tent floor when he went back to the mansion. Every time, she'd lie there afterward, shivering and curled up on the tent floor as if instinctually protecting her body from further trauma. She'd try not to replay the event in her mind and admonish herself for not fighting back, for letting something like that happen to her. And she'd wonder what would happen if she got pregnant. It was hard to guess what they'd do—force her to bear the child in secret? Put her through some crude, unsanitary abortion procedure? Kill her so they didn't have to deal with it?

It always left marks on her, mentally and physically. Each time. She couldn't see the scars, but she could feel them with her fingers as she traced her back. The scars of battles fought and lost.

What each one of those taught her was that they might be willing to hurt her, humiliate her, or drive her to the edge of insanity, but they weren't willing to debilitate or kill her. It had been at least six months. If they were going to take her out, they'd have done it by now. There had to be orders coming down from somewhere—Audrey? George?—that they could have their way with her as long as she was kept alive and mobile. She was still getting three meals most days, along with enough water not to get dehydrated. It was a long way from comfortable living, but they could have done worse.

There was a reason they didn't. And now that Stephanie was having occasional conversations with Frank from the hospital, she was getting an idea of what it was Audrey still wanted—the legacy of being the leader who oversaw the eradication of H6N1 for her community. Audrey was smart enough to know that eliminating one of her best medical minds didn't make any sense for her long-term goal of finding a vaccine. She had probably been hoping they could do it without Stephanie, but was keeping that insurance policy. Now, they were starting to cash in on that.

Stephanie wanted that vaccine as much as anybody. But she also wondered if finding it would be the end for her. Once that was done, she'd be worthless to Audrey. There'd been talk about a trial, but Stephanie had no expectation of that ever happening. Due process was barely a whisper from the past. For most of the people of Alessandra, Stephanie was out of sight, out of mind. Keep her locked up long enough, and people will move on with their lives. Then you announce she died in captivity, say a few mildly kind words, and the world marches forward.

No one had said anything for a few minutes since the gate had opened, but there was definitely someone inside the enclosure. Stephanie could see through her tent well enough to spot a silhouette moving around. The man looked like he was building something not far from her; it was making noises she didn't recognize. She tended to stay shut inside unless she was called out because she didn't see any reason to have a confrontation if she could avoid it. But she was curious what was going on.

Then she heard voices, first George yelling at someone to walk, and then a woman shrieking as she hit the ground. Was that Leslie? Stephanie thought so as she huddled against the side of her tent, trying to make out what was happening from the blurry shadows moving outside.

"Stephanie!" George yelled, and she closed her eyes. "Come on out and meet your new roommate."

Stephanie's back stiffened, and her shoulders were suddenly very tight. A roommate? Was she really not going to be alone in here anymore? It seemed impossible after all this time. She unzipped the tent and climbed out into the light.

Walking toward her, knees scraped and wearing the same drab, gray outfit as Stephanie was Leslie, hair matted to her dirty face, a dark circle starting to swallow her left eye.

Stephanie pursed her lips and nodded to her. Leslie turned her eyes to the ground.

"I believe you ladies know each other," George said, nudging Leslie a little bit closer as William finished setting up another tent a few feet away from Stephanie's. "You're going to be sharing this pen for a while until we can see if there's a more suitable place to keep Leslie. Hope you enjoy the company, Steph."

William drove the last stake into the ground, then followed George out. The gate slammed shut, and everything was quiet. Stephanie stood, arms stiff at her sides, Leslie still looking down.

"What the hell happened?" Stephanie asked.

Leslie sighed deeply and looked up at her, then shook her head and walked to her tent, climbing inside and zipping it up behind her.

9

"What can I do for you, Michael?" Audrey said. She had been talking to one of her men but stopped abruptly when Michael appeared at her office door, both of their eyes swinging in his direction.

"Oh. I don't want to interrupt anything. I can come ba—"

"Don't be silly." Audrey sat down in her chair and slid it behind her desk, motioning for him to take a seat across from her. "I've always got time for you. What's on your mind?"

"Well, first, I wanted to give you an update on the situation with Leslie and Derrick. I'm told it's handled."

"Excellent." Audrey clapped her hands, then laid them on the table. "I knew it wouldn't be a problem. And this is going to have positive effects. It's a good example of consequences, and showing people they can't flout the rules. Perfect. Was there something else?"

Michael looked down, crossing his arms and then un-crossing them, shifting a bit in his seat.

"Um, yeah. It's just…when we distributed the rings several months ago, you told the town that the people like us who weren't wearing the rings as often would be tested regularly for the virus. You remember?"

"I do. It's roughly the same speech I gave the first time I introduced the rings."

"Right," Michael said. "So…I mean, I haven't been tested even once. At least, not since everybody got their tests six months ago when it looked like it was spreading."

"The word 'regularly' can mean a lot of different things."

Michael frowned. "Sure. But, in this case, what *does* it mean? Because I'd think it would mean more often than every six months."

Audrey stood and walked slowly around her desk until she was standing next to Michael. He started to stand, but she held her hand out toward him, and he carefully lowered himself back down.

"Look, Michael…There are some things you need to understand about politics. There are a lot of things you have to *say* that are merely performative. The people need to hear certain words to justify living their lives and forgetting you're out there working in the background. So you tell them what you know they need."

Michael's shoulders stiffened. "Even if it's a lie?"

"Words are a tool, Michael. Lies? Truth? Irrelevant. It's the wrong question to ask."

"Then what's the right question?"

She smiled and put a hand on his shoulder. "Does it get us what we want?"

Michael heard a succession of loud noises coming from somewhere in the town. Everyone looked in the direction it came from.

"What was that?" he asked, startled.

"Sounded like gunshots," Audrey said. "We need to go check that out. Both of you, come with me. Nathan, bring your handgun just in case. Michael, grab yours as well. Let's hope we don't need them."

The sound of a few more shots helped them trace the source to the town gate, where Michael could see Andy pointing his gun into the woods and sweeping it slowly across his line of sight.

Audrey climbed the ladder ahead of Michael to get to the platform where Andy and Benjamin were staked out. Andy lowered his gun and leaned it against the railing.

"What are you guys shooting at?" Audrey asked, as Michael reached the landing. Nathan was climbing up behind him.

Andy looked at Benjamin, then nodded out over the gate. Audrey and Michael both looked to see two bodies on the ground, one man and one woman, blood pooling underneath them among the pine needles.

"Shit," Michael said, grabbing ahold of the railing, feeling the color drain from his face. "Why did you kill them? What were they doing?"

Benjamin sat back down, and Andy shrugged.

"I don't know," Andy said. "Just walking, I guess."

Michael felt something approaching rage. "You *guess*? Were they some kind of threat? Are they armed?"

"Maybe."

"Doesn't look like it from here."

Andy shrugged again, and Michael was struggling not to grab him by the throat. How could they fire on unarmed travelers who were likely seeking a bit of help? They probably saw Alessandra ahead and thought they finally found someplace where they could survive. Like Derrick, Emily, and several others who'd become part of their community over the past couple of years.

"Well, if this is how you handle the responsibility of watching the gate, you're done," Michael said. "Leave the gun and get the hell out of here."

Benjamin didn't budge. Andy crossed his arms and sat down, looking at Audrey.

"Did you *hear* me?" Michael said, anger rising in his throat, scarcely believing what he was seeing. "Audrey, wanna chime in here?"

"Look, Michael…This is a complex situation," she said. "Now, these are good men who are doing a difficult job for us. It's a lot of responsibility. I know they wouldn't fire on anyone without justification. Isn't that right?"

Andy looked at Benjamin, and they both nodded. Michael wanted to punch them both in the face.

"This is fucking ridic—"

"Michael, you shouldn't judge them," Audrey said. "We're sitting safely up in that mansion. They're down here in the line of fire. Who knows what might be coming out of those woods?

Immigrants are often violent, lazy, entitled, and many of them carry diseases that could take out our entire town. What if those two had H6N1? What if they were hiding weapons, or they meant us harm? This is a tough time, and we need to trust the people we know, right here in Alessandra. We need to band together as a community. Trust no one who doesn't have Alessandran blood."

"Including your beloved men?" Michael snarled as he said it, then looked at Nathan standing nearby before turning back to Audrey, whose eyes narrowed.

"Don't be ridiculous," she said. "Everyone knows they've done more than maybe anyone ever has to earn their spot here. I won't even entertain that nonsense. You owe Nathan an apology, Michael."

Michael closed his eyes, shook his head, and climbed back down the ladder without saying a word.

10

Leslie hesitantly allowed her eyes to begin opening. Little by little, the world revealed itself, a blue tent surrounding her as she lay on its floor, hard and lumpy against the packed dirt. It was hard to tell for sure from within the tent, but it looked like it was probably dusk; she'd slept most of the day, it seemed.

She'd needed an escape, and that had been it. Her body didn't know what else to do, how to process how her world had disintegrated beneath her. What was supposed to be a passionate early-morning tryst turned into her and Derrick being dragged away at gunpoint, neighbors gawking and their future uncertain.

Leslie didn't know what they'd done with Derrick. Once they arrived at the mansion, William took Derrick off in one direction while George led her in another. He shoved her to the dirt and screamed at her, calling her a slut and a whore before punching her in the face, her hands helplessly tied behind her back and a rag stuffed inside her mouth. There was nothing she could do but take it.

There was something different about the George she saw that morning and the George she'd known a bit prior to Audrey taking command. He had a confidence, a swagger that she hadn't seen in him before. Like the world could do nothing to him. Like he knew they were scared of him, he could have his way with them without consequences, and he was enjoying it. It all had the air of the kid who's always been beaten up finally getting the best of the bully, and soaking up the spoils of being king of the playground. All you could do was nod condescendingly and hope for an opportunity to put him back in his place.

Feeling like her throat was lined with sandpaper, Leslie pushed herself into a sitting position and took a deep breath, finally reaching out to unzip the tent. She figured she should get the lay of the land, and maybe see if there was some food and water.

She crawled out and stood, looking at a desolate landscape before her, patchy weeds and grass poking up through a field of barren dirt surrounded by what looked like a six-foot metal fence. They were caged like animals.

The flap to the other tent slumped open, and Stephanie crawled out, but Leslie had never seen her with such short-cropped hair, her face crossed with lines of dirt. It had only been six months, but Leslie thought Stephanie looked like she'd aged years. Was that what this place did to you? Leslie wondered how she'd be able to handle it.

"Hi, Leslie." Stephanie stood up straight, stiff, keeping her distance. "I'm sorry you ended up here. As you can see, it's not much."

"You've been…*here* ever since they took you?"

Stephanie nodded. "Where do people *think* I am?"

Leslie looked at the ground and scratched the back of her neck. "I think they're afraid to talk about it. I mean, what are you gonna do? We've still got a life to live, even if that life is pretty shitty."

"What's it been like out there? With Audrey back?"

"Well…" Leslie looked around, over both shoulders. "Did you know she brought back the rings?"

Stephanie closed her eyes and exhaled loudly, turning her head to the darkening sky.

"So yeah," Leslie said. "It's not good. Everyone's on edge. I think people are trying to bide their time until they find a vaccine, and then hopefully everything can go back to normal."

"Or as normal as they can be with that crew running things."

"Right." Leslie took a step forward. "I voted for you, ya know."

"Oh, I know." Stephanie smiled slightly. "I remember pretty

much everything about that morning, as hungover as I was."

"I don't think you did it. Audrey told everyone about the knife and all that, but I just can't see you killing Zac. You shouldn't be locked in here. It's not right."

Stephanie lowered her head and nodded. "Thanks. I appreciate that. So, what did you do to get tossed in here?"

"Derrick and I…we…"

Stephanie's eyes got big, and she smiled, walking closer to Leslie. "*You and Derrick*? Wow. I can't say I blame you. That's awful, though. And they…caught you? *Together*?"

"Yeah. At his place. I don't know how they saw me, but they did."

"Shit. And where's he?"

"No idea." Leslie shrugged. "I hope he's okay. He doesn't deserve this either. He didn't do anything wrong."

"Neither of you did," Stephanie said. "The way Audrey runs this place is through displays of power and control. That's what the rings and all these rules are about. They're looking to psychologically beat us down to the point that we feel like we can't survive without her. We become dependent. I saw it the last time, and that's undoubtedly what she's doing again. The benefits of it were all bullshit then, and they're bullshit now. It's a device of control. It really is that simple. And you're caught up in the middle of it. We need to take that control back."

"How are we gonna do that from in here?"

"We need to survive until the opportunity arises. Keep going. And when we see an opening, let's drive a fucking truck through it. You with me?"

11

"So, are you really worried about him?" George asked.

"I think we need to keep a close eye on him," Andy said, pounding his fist against Audrey's desk. "Michael's not one of us. We had to offer him something to get his vote, so I get why we let him in. But I don't appreciate him disrespecting me like that. I was just following Audrey's orders."

Audrey leaned forward in her chair. "He doesn't know that, Andy. And he's not *going* to know that. All right? Look, we all knew Michael wasn't the perfect loyal follower for our cause. He was the main reason I got kicked out of here the first time, so I know full well what he's capable of. But he also brings us a level of credibility with the rank and file out there. They know him and respect him. Yes, we could strong-arm everyone like we did last time and rule with an iron fist, but having Michael on our side gives a lot of people who would be on the fence a reason to trust us. And, believe me, this shit is a lot easier when they trust you."

That was important to Audrey, especially after the way everything fell apart during her first tenure as leader. The truth was, she felt like she'd squandered a lot of goodwill with her choice of Paul and how he ruled over the town. She'd let that happen. She allowed a bad person into her regime and then didn't act quickly enough to curb his violent tendencies. She was somewhat blinded by him being family, but probably also by confidence in her own good judgment. Being wrong wasn't an option.

Now, she knew she was fallible, and so did everyone else. There was a chink in her armor. So having that credibility boost that Michael brought mattered to her. When he voted for her, that was the first step. Him joining her administration in a prominent role meant people could move on from Stephanie, and accept that Audrey really had changed, or Michael wouldn't sign on to help her. There could be no doubt that she was the good guy, that she only wanted what was best for Alessandra and its people. Every single thing she did was to make life better for them.

"That's all well and good," George said. "But how much pushback is gonna be too much for us to accept? He keeps leaning on you about the trial. Now he berates Andy over taking out a couple of clearly dangerous outsiders? Isn't he supposed to be a native Alessandran? Why does he care so much about what happens to people from outside these walls? Fuck 'em. We have to protect our own at all costs."

"Damn right!" Andy said, pacing around the room. "This is our *home*. We can't let *anyone* penetrate these walls. That was one of the biggest mistakes Stephanie made. You don't know what they want from us. It's nothing good, though, I'll tell you that damn much. They want to take from us, and not give back a goddamn thing. They want to suck us the fuck dry—that's what they want. They want a piece of what we have. So yeah, fuck 'em. We built this. Go create your own town with all your dirty people, and leave us alone!"

Audrey nodded. "I get it, guys. I really do. And you're right. Hell, Zac said the same thing. That's one of the reasons Stephanie killed him—he was saying too many things that made sense, and contradicted Stephanie's policies. He made her look like a fool, and she couldn't handle it. But remember, Michael recognized that, and signed on to be a part of our movement. He's entitled to get frustrated from time to time."

"*Frustrated*?" Andy stopped and stared at Audrey, mouth agape. "He tried to fucking *fire* me for doing exactly the right goddamn thing!"

"I know, Andy. I know. I'm with you on this." Audrey waved

her hands in front of her face and motioned for Andy to sit. "He overreacted. It's important to remember he's not hardened in the same ways we are. He hasn't witnessed a lot of death. Seeing people gunned down can be traumatic for some people. He probably had an emotional reaction; it's understandable. Not *acceptable*, but understandable."

"So what are we gonna do about it?" George asked. "How are we gonna make sure he's totally on board? We can't have people with one foot in and one foot out of the pool. We need him to jump in with us."

"I agree," Audrey said. "I need to make sure he's committed. I'll have a talk with him. And I actually have a good idea for a loyalty test for him. It's something I've been pondering for a few days now, and this might be the time to do it."

"What's that?" Andy asked.

Audrey turned to George. "How long would it take you to get Stephanie cleaned up and presentable enough to go out in the town?"

12

Stephanie watched William walk out through the pen's gate, still not believing what she was seeing.

"Is that normal?" Leslie asked, climbing out of her tent.

Stephanie's head slowly swiveled toward her, and she silently shook it, then turned back to gawk at the large tent and table William had erected at the back of the pen, complete with two padded chairs and plates set up with what looked like grilled trout and boiled white potatoes. It was more food than she'd seen in months. As she stepped closer, she noticed a large wooden bucket next to the table. When she looked inside, she saw it almost full of water and two bars of soap sitting on clean towels next to it.

"What the hell?" Stephanie whispered to herself. She spent six months living in squalor, barely eating, being splashed with cold water to achieve some semblance of cleanliness, and then *this* happened when Leslie showed up?

On the surface, it was nothing to complain about. She wanted to devour the food, and Leslie had hurried past her to start doing that.

"No forks?" Leslie said, looking around the table. "I guess this fish is finger food."

Stephanie laughed at the absurdity of it all, Leslie halfway complaining about not having the proper silverware. After eating on the ground with her face in a bowl for so long, Stephanie had almost forgotten forks were an actual thing.

As Leslie dove in, shoveling flaky pieces of fish into her

mouth, Stephanie knew she should be thankful and eat, but something was holding her back. Why would they suddenly do this after all this time? Did they just intend to treat Leslie a lot better than her, so Stephanie was catching the trickle-down spoils of that?

Or could something nefarious be going on? She sure as hell didn't trust them. Was the food poisoned? That seemed like a weirdly elaborate way to kill them when there was nothing stopping the men from putting a bullet in their brains. Was this some sort of "last meal" ritual, giving them a nice plate of food as a humane gesture before finally ending it all? It was possible. But if that was the case, there was nothing Stephanie could do about it, so she might as well eat it while it was warm.

She sat down in the chair next to Leslie.

"How is it?" Stephanie asked.

Leslie licked her fingers and picked up a potato. "Could use some Old Bay. But otherwise, pretty good."

They both laughed, Stephanie remembering those boxy cans of seasoning that had seemed like magic on seafood. Earthy. Salty. She tried to think when the last time was she'd had it; she could remember a trip she had taken with Michael to Maryland. They'd flown into the airport north of Washington, D.C., picked up a car, and driven to the beach. They rented a cabin there and did nothing for three days except swim in the ocean, lounge on the beach, and eat fresh seafood from local markets—delicious blue crab, scallops practically the size of her hand, perch that turned into butter in her mouth. The last day, they'd driven to Baltimore and gone to a baseball game, wandering down to the Inner Harbor after it was over, dancing, drinking, and eating all the crab cakes they could stand until past three in the morning.

Sometimes, when she thought of other places in the past, she wondered what they looked like today. That area had been so full of life, and so had they. Was that gorgeous ballpark crumbling, grass and weeds beginning to overtake it? Was the harbor dark and abandoned, seagulls having picked at the last remaining crab shell lying on the ground? It was easy to mourn for the world they'd lost, the society humans had spent thousands of years building only to see it befallen by bugs invisible to the naked eye.

Stephanie jabbed her fingers into the fish and started tearing off chunks. She didn't want to eat too quickly. Having eaten only small scraps for months, she didn't want her stomach to reject a full meal, tempting as it was to scoop up handfuls and then lick the plate clean.

When they were done eating, they walked over to the bucket of water. Stephanie didn't hesitate to remove her clothes and grab a bar of soap, dipping it into the water and starting to rub it over her body, her fingers feeling the bumps of her rib cage as she scrubbed the dirt from her midsection. After being forced to rush so many times, it was amazing for her to be able to take her time, massage the soap into her skin, feel it seeping into her pores, like layers of grime were finally being shed from her body.

At first, Leslie seemed unsure what to do. But seeing Stephanie strip down gave her permission to do the same. When Stephanie sufficiently lathered up, she took the bucket and dumped some water carefully over herself, a cool rush running down through her toes as it hit her. She shivered a bit as she handed the bucket to Leslie and then picked up a towel to dry off.

Stephanie pulled on her clothes, and Leslie followed suit, both of them stepping out of the shadow of the large tent to catch the heat of the early-fall sun.

"The short hair's a good idea," Leslie said, her long, stringy hair tangled and soaking wet. "May have to go with that look while I'm here."

"I'll be sure to let the stylist know. Mention my name, and she'll give you twenty percent off."

Stephanie heard the gate rattle, and she turned in that direction. Unconsciously, she held her breath. She'd suspected this had been too good to be true. It'd had to be a prelude to something terrible. And here it was. Who was that coming through the gate, and what did they have in store?

But quickly, she realized that wasn't one of the familiar shapes entering their pen. Not as big as William or George. Not as skinny as Andy. She wasn't sure at first, but there was something familiar about that sandy brown hair. As he took a few steps closer to them, she gasped, her hand covering her mouth.

"Hi, Steph," Michael said, his voice catching. He bit his lip before lifting his head in what looked like a show of confidence. "I'm gonna need you to come with me."

13

George climbed the ladder and hoisted himself up to stand on the platform above the wall's gate, a familiar perch from his time manning this station himself. He took in the view of the world outside their little town; it always made him wonder how many other people were still out there somewhere. They knew they weren't alone, but how scarce were humans? Were there a couple million remaining, spread across the globe, clustered in small towns here and there in Europe, Africa, Asia? Or maybe a few hundred, and they weren't even at the top of the food chain anymore?

From the ground, the wall cut off that perspective. It was easy to become insular, thinking only of the day-to-day survival of yourself and your neighbors in Alessandra. From here, though, you were reminded there was more.

"You wanted me to come?" George said, still staring out into the woods.

"Yeah," Andy replied. "We need to talk."

"Do we?"

"About this Michael and Stephanie bullshit."

"Not my call, man," George said, turning and walking closer to Andy. "You've got a problem with it, take it up with Audrey. She's making the decisions around here."

"Oh, sure. Take it up with Audrey, huh? Well, I'm sure you and her are all chummy, and you can walk into her office unannounced and start popping off about what a fucking boneheaded idiot she is, and she'll thank you for your refreshing honesty." Andy stood up, hands balling into fists. "I don't know if you noticed, though, but I'm stuck down here where your stupid ass used to be, relegated to being stared at by fucking trees all day, trying hard every minute not to pick up that FN-FAL there and blow my and Benjamin's goddamn heads off out of pure boredom. I don't exactly have her ear, if you know what I mean."

"Fair enough." George scratched his forehead. "I've been there. What's your problem with the plan?"

"*Everything*, man," Andy seethed. "*Come on.* Surely you see how crazy this is. Michael and Stephanie, walking alone back and forth to Saint Francis every day? Everybody knows they were married and were fucking right up to when Audrey tossed Stephanie's murdering ass in that pen. Too good a fate for her, if you ask me, but at least she's got it rough, and we get the chance to make it rougher. But those two took Audrey out before. They're gonna scheme their little asses off if given the chance to talk that much unsupervised."

George frowned. "I don't know what to tell ya. I mean, I hear what you're saying. But Audrey thinks it's a good way to see if she can trust him. She's probably right. And what can they really do? If they deviate from the path, it's easy enough to see that."

"Yeah, but…how are we gonna *really* know what's going on with them? I, for one, don't think we can afford to let them walk around out there with no one else around. We need eyes on them, if not ears."

"Well, we can't exactly bug their conversation. Following closely behind them seems a little obvious."

Benjamin pushed his chair back and stood. "We need to go up there and tell Audrey that it can't be only Michael with her. We need someone else to be there. I could do it. Andy can handle the watch here when I'm gone."

"Is that what you want?" George turned to Andy. "You want me to try to convince Audrey to add another person to 'supervise Stephanie' duty?"

"I guess it's probably not necessary."

"What do you fucking *mean* it's not necessary?" Benjamin

yelled, his eyes bulging. "You said it yourself…we've got to keep an eye on them. We can't let them plot out their next coup right out there in the open. I can stop this!"

"George is right; she's not gonna go for it." Andy seemed like he was calming down, almost as if Benjamin's explosion prompted him to go in the opposite direction. "Not for *that*, anyway. She learns nothing about Michael if he knows we're watching. Of course he's gonna be on his best behavior then. The key question is what will he do if he *thinks* they're alone, but they're not? Not *really*, anyway."

"Okay," George said, as Benjamin sat back down, his face still red. "What do you have in mind, then?"

"Well, none of this is gonna be perfect. We can't bug 'em, like you said. To hear them, we'd have to be in earshot, and we fucking can't be without them knowing it. I mean, look at the path they'll be taking."

Andy walked toward the town side of the platform, leaning against the railing and pointing.

"Starting from the mansion up there, they'll come down into the main town area and cross through the square. From there, it's a couple more blocks to the hospital. The square's completely open. Few trees along the route, just some houses after the square, and there's no good place to hide there. My point being, while I might be able to round up a crew to help, there's no good place to stick them to reliably hear the two of them talk.

"So, here's what I'm thinking…From this vantage point, we can see the vast majority of their walk every time, and I've got binoculars to be able to get a good look. I say I watch them closely from here. They'll never even think to *look* up here. And if they do, I could just as easily be checking out something else inside the town. We're far enough away that they won't notice."

"But you can't hear anything," George said. "What will you be watching for?"

"Shit they shouldn't be doing. Huddling too closely together. Lots of conversation. Holding fucking hands. I'm watching body language. You can tell a surprising amount from the way people physically *act* when they're together. This is strictly business.

There's no reason for them to be too friendly. That'll be our canary in the fucking coal mine."

George turned and looked out over the town, scanning the route Michael and Stephanie would be taking. Andy was right. This was a good spot for keeping an eye on them, albeit a relatively far-flung one. He'd estimate it at not quite two football fields of distance at its closest point, where they'd cross the square. It was far from ideal surveillance, but it might be their best chance to keep some tabs on what they were doing.

"How will you know when they're starting their walk?" George asked.

"If you can find a small mirror or something else reflective, you could use the sun to alert us from up at the compound when they leave," Andy said. "Flash us a few times, assuming the sun's out."

"Sure. I can probably do that. What about from the hospital? Stephanie's got friends there. You're not gonna find many allies to help you."

Andy looked toward St. Francis. "We'll have to keep an eye out. They'll probably develop some patterns with the sun after the first few days. I don't think we'll miss 'em."

George nodded. "What happens if you *do* see something suspicious?"

"Depends on *how* suspicious. But I'd probably hold out as long as we felt we could before telling Audrey, so we gathered enough intel that he couldn't fucking deny it. We'd have him dead."

"And if Audrey refuses to do anything?"

Andy walked across the platform and picked up the FN-FAL, patting it lightly and smiling.

"Then I'm a damn good shot."

14

They began the walk down the stairs from the mansion toward the rest of the town, the square not far up ahead, Michael allowing Stephanie to go first. They walked down the crumbling old driveway, weeds forcing their way up through cracks in the cement, retaking the land from human hands. Near the bottom of the hill, they skirted the old metal car gate, rusty, vine-choked, and falling off its hinges, a victim of the elements and a lack of care. Stephanie still hadn't said a word, not after he entered the pen and told her to come with him, not as she walked past him with her shoulders stiff, and not as he gave her directions on where to go. She never even attempted to make eye contact.

He wondered what she was thinking. Six months later, was she still holding a grudge over him voting for Audrey? Could she not see that he had no choice? Once he found that knife, what was he supposed to do? Vote for an unstable woman who likely murdered her chief political rival and tried to banish the other in the middle of what was supposed to be a fair, democratic process? That would have set a terrible precedent for Alessandra, not to mention potentially placing an authoritarian murderer in charge of the town. Even if Stephanie hadn't killed Zac—he thought she probably did, but he was still willing to hear her side of the story if she wanted to tell it, feeling like he owed her that much—she'd still tried to send Audrey and her men to their death when she was threatened by them, and that made him question where Stephanie's head was. Had she been losing it? Was she even worse now?

Or maybe she was more embarrassed than angry, at this point. Maybe she didn't know what to say, knowing how badly she'd blown everything, and that Michael had ultimately been right. Wallowing in self pity in that pen for this long could accomplish that. Watching her walk a couple of feet ahead of him, Michael thought about how he'd be willing to forgive her everything if she apologized. If she could find it in herself to admit her mistakes and say she was sorry, he had too much history with her not to accept it. At times, he'd even fantasized about it, her breaking down on her knees, sobbing, begging him to forgive her for what she'd done, maybe try to get Audrey to let her work in the hospital again.

Without hearing any of that, though, it was hard for Michael to justify sticking his neck out for Stephanie. He still cared for her—maybe even loved her, somewhere deep down—but she needed to know what she did was wrong, and acknowledge that. Forgiveness that isn't asked for can't be granted, and Michael felt like he needed to hold that line. If she wanted to be completely silent on these walks, that was fine with him. His priority right now needed to be on what was best for Alessandra, not idle chit-chat or reminiscing about the past. He was doing this because Stephanie had knowledge and skills that could be put toward accelerating the development of a vaccine that could literally change the world.

If they could achieve this, it would open up so many possibilities for the people of Alessandra. It was an exciting time. And if she could be a real asset to the St. Francis research team, he was completely willing to put up with whatever discomfort and awkwardness he had to in order to deliver her there to do the work, then take her straight back to the pen. He could tell she'd been reasonably well cared for. She was clean, and seemed to have suitable strength. Besides the short hair and some predictable weight loss, she looked fine.

He hoped this was going to work. He knew medical research was what she loved; it was always what she was most passionate about. If she could get Alessandra to the finish line, she'd earn some goodwill going forward.

* * *

As they walked through the town, Stephanie was still seething. Michael doesn't say a word to her the entire time she's been locked and tortured in that pen, and then marches in and tells her to come with him. No checking on how she was. No apologies for betraying her. Not a damn thing beyond a command.

And that's what it was—a command. What choice did she have in the matter? He knew the power structure here. Hell, he was probably enjoying it, the power trip of being able to push her around, to tell her where to go and what to do. But to get there, he'd had to side with a violent despot, blithely throwing Stephanie to the wolves because…why? Because Stephanie wanted to slightly shorten the stay of Audrey and her men, who clearly threatened the future of Alessandra? Because Michael found a fucking knife in her house? The knife could have been from anywhere. He had no way of knowing that had anything to do with Zac. After all their years together, how could something so small shove him into the arms of a woman he'd helped to get the hell out of that mansion not that long before? It was baffling.

Stephanie had expected Michael to stand by her. He should have. After everything they'd been through, after she'd given him the benefit of the doubt when he came to her and begged for her to help him chase down his wild conspiracy theory about Audrey, he should have extended her the same favor. He owed her that much, at the very least. Instead, he'd turned his back on her. He knew Audrey wasn't going to treat her fairly, but he backed Audrey anyway. He did as much as anyone to put Stephanie in that pen, and now he wanted to wield his new power over her.

She'd comply. She wasn't in a position to challenge it. She'd seen what those people did to her when she mostly followed instructions; she wasn't about to go against anyone at this point. It was easier to do what she was told while biding her time, waiting for a better opportunity. But she certainly wasn't going to forgive him for what he'd done. Michael had made his bed. Stephanie was ready to let him lie in it with Audrey for as long as he wanted.

15

Wiping her forearm across her brow, Emily slid through the small side gate in the wall, stepped back into her ring, and headed toward home, the sun beginning to dip beneath the horizon. It was about the end of the summer season for the town's vegetable garden, and she'd spent most of the day trying to make sure they got the most out of the tomatoes, cucumbers, and pole beans they'd planted several months earlier.

When Emily arrived with her husband, Xavier, at the gates of Alessandra, the first question Stephanie asked her before she let her inside was what skills she could utilize to earn her place in the town. She'd had to think fast. Over the months of wandering the woods, she'd learned some things about scavenging food, building shelters, and general navigation. But she wasn't sure any of that would be useful in a place that looked as organized as this one did.

So she thought back to her time tending to a small garden at their family home in Suwanee. There hadn't been much space that got sunlight, so she'd squeezed a narrow garden into the area between their driveway and the west wall of their house. It wasn't much, but it was her little plot of land, and she looked forward to getting it going each spring, first starting the plants with a light kit inside, then gradually transferring them into small pots and then the ground in elevated beds.

While it was Emily's project, Xavier and their two daughters helped wherever they could, watering when the rain didn't come, trimming leaves the aphids had gotten to, and picking the tomatoes at initial blush before the squirrels could snatch them away. It ended up being a family project that everyone got excited about, especially when she could turn those fresh vegetables into family meals. Not only did they save a lot of money, but there was a sense of accomplishment she got from taking the food from seed to the dinner table, and she liked knowing what went into her family's bodies.

When the virus took the girls, that had been devastating; she and Xavier decided to leave their home two days after burying them. There had been a real possibility, she thought, that they wouldn't be able to work up the will, that it'd be easier and make more sense to lie down and wait to die rather than try to go on without them. And they might have done that if Xavier hadn't pushed himself to his feet one morning and held out his hand to her.

"We have to live," he insisted, "because they can't."

And so they marched. For days, weeks, however long it had been until they saw the walls of Alessandra rise out of nothing in the North Georgia wilderness. And when she stood before Stephanie, her home was what came back to her, and she started to cry thinking of her girls with dirt all over themselves, laughing and spraying each other with the hose. But she choked out, "I know how to garden." Xavier said he was good with his hands, and project management. Stephanie nodded and welcomed them inside.

The town had changed quite a bit since then, though. They both voted for Stephanie because they felt like she'd been good to them, and had given them a chance. They'd heard stories about what it had been like to live under Audrey, but none of it had truly prepared them for the reality. Having to separate had been especially hard for Emily and Xavier, who had relied on each other so much since leaving their hometown, and now had to live on their own.

But, at least for Emily, the work hadn't changed much. Audrey knew the importance of the garden, so she hadn't made any impactful changes to that. When Emily originally got to the garden, she'd found it running pretty well already, but she was able to make some recommendations based upon what she'd done at her home. Most of the people had been fairly receptive, and she'd quickly taken on a sort of leadership role there. She could tell it wasn't a group that was especially experienced, and they welcomed what ideas she could bring; all of them were doing their best to keep the townspeople fed with something more than fish from the lake.

It was rewarding work that was going to get tougher—and cooler, she reminded herself as she rounded the corner onto her street and wiped her forehead once more—very soon. Ahead, she could hear yelling, but she couldn't make out what they were saying or who was saying it. She picked up her pace a bit and, a couple of houses away, it became clear one of those voices was Xavier in their backyard. Emily ran the rest of the way.

Coming around the side of the house, she saw Xavier standing outside his tent and pointing at George, William next to him.

"That's *my wife* in there!" Xavier screamed, flailing his arms wildly. "Where do you expect me to go?"

"*Was* your wife." George sneered. "Marriages aren't recognized under the current rules, Mister Pellico."

"I don't give a *fuck* what this shit town *recognizes*! Emily is my wife, and she's gonna stay that way no matter what you and your twisted people try to say."

Emily ran up beside Xavier, breathing heavily.

"What's…um, the problem, officer?" She wanted to defuse the situation and get them out of their yard. If she had to be the polite one, she'd try to play that role.

"Well, ma'am, your former husband is violating multiple codes living in a tent in your back yard. There are plenty of unoccupied homes, and we need each resident to choose one to live in for quarantine purposes. He's also violating the spirit of the family separation laws by being this close to you."

Emily could tell Xavier was getting angrier with every word George spoke. She wanted desperately to reach out for his hand, but she knew she couldn't.

"Thank you for bringing this to our attention, officer. We

weren't totally familiar with all the rules. I don't mind him being back here, though, and there are no empty homes nearby. We looked around, and he'd have to move two blocks away. We're used to being closer than that. He doesn't come inside. We only interact out here with our rings on. Is it really that big a deal?"

"I'm afraid it is, Miss Pellico. He's going to have to pack up his tent and find an actual home, or we'll do it for him."

Xavier shook his head and turned away from them, taking a few steps, looking up at the sky.

"This is *bullshit*!" He turned back and pointed at George, aggressively moving closer to him. "I've seen other people do this! You're targeting us because we're not from here! I know what's going on."

"Sir, you're going to have to step back," William said, putting his arm out as Xavier got within a few feet of George. "If you attempt physical contact of any kind, we'll have to take you away to full quarantine."

Emily's heart skipped a beat. She couldn't bear the thought of having him taken away and held somewhere.

"No!" she yelled, stepping between Xavier and the men, her arms up in the air. Xavier stopped before their rings hit. "Please don't do anything we'll regret, X. Let's figure this out peacefully, okay? Maybe you will need to find a house for a little while. It'll be more comfortable. You'll even get to sleep in a bed. Won't that be nice?"

"A fucking *bed*? I don't care. We're a *married couple*! We should be *together*. This is madness, Emily."

She looked into his eyes and nodded almost imperceptibly.

"I know it's hard. It'll be just as hard for me. I love you. I want you here. But it looks like we don't have much choice. And it's only temporary. Go pick out a house you like. You won't even have to put up a down payment."

Emily forced a smile, a tear dripping onto her cheek. She'd never wanted more in her life to take him in her arms and squeeze him tight. Having to stay four feet away right now was unbearably difficult. Their rings clanged together lightly as they stood.

"That's gonna have to be enough," George said. "Go ahead and gather your stuff, Mister Pellico. We'll escort you wherever you'd like to go and make sure you get set up with a key to the house you choose."

Xavier sighed loudly and looked at the ground, then turned and began breaking down his tent. Emily found his knapsack and started stuffing his belongings inside as George and William looked on. She thought she could hear them laughing, but she wasn't sure.

16

When Stephanie walked out to the hospital's lobby, Michael was sitting there reading an old *People* magazine they still had sitting in the waiting-room bin.

"You ready?" he asked, and she nodded, then slid into her ring. He put the magazine back, and they went out the door.

Now on the fourth day of doing this, they were starting to settle into a routine: Michael would come get Stephanie out of her pen after breakfast, walk to the hospital with her, keep an eye on the research for a bit, then go back to the mansion to take care of any other work that might be of importance, then return as the sun began going down to walk her back. It was taking up a lot of his time, but he hoped it would be worth it when they solved the virus, and hopefully it would only be temporary.

As they left the hospital on Day 4, she still hadn't spoken more than a few short words to him. Being around her had never felt so awkward. It seemed like they were in a sort of cold war, and someone was going to have to swallow their pride to thaw it. Michael knew that since he'd be held accountable for ensuring something was getting done with Stephanie at the hospital, he was probably going to have to be the one to make the first move. Audrey was going to want a detailed report soon.

"So, we're almost through the first week," Michael said, shingles curling on the roofs of the houses they walked past. "Any forward momentum now that you're working with the team?"

Stephanie turned her head, avoiding eye contact.

"This is a big deal," he said. "If Audrey doesn't see tangible progress soon, she's gonna pull the plug, and you can sit in that pen all day again if that's what you want."

She rolled her eyes.

"I'm serious, Stephanie!" Michael raised his voice, frustration building. "This is too important for you to throw one of y—"

"Tell her whatever the *fuck* you want, Michael." She stopped walking and turned to face him. "Yeah. Seriously. I don't give a fuck. It's not like there's any semblance of fairness or justice in this goddamn place. Audrey's gonna do what she wants to, and you can keep being her lackey if you want. But I'm not about to sit here and play this game as if anything I say is going to change her mind about shit. She wants to slap her name on a vaccine and trademark it The Audrey, so everyone knows she saved the fucking world. Gag me."

Stephanie started walking again, and Michael stood frozen to the pavement.

"You coming?" She looked back with an exaggerated shrug.

"I know you're still bitter about the election," Michael said as he caught up to her. "But she won fair and square."

"Oh, Jesus. Are we going there now?"

"She did!"

"Yeah. Because of your traitorous ass."

"If I'm a traitor, then I guess more than half of Alessandra are traitors too."

"You're not a *traitor* for voting for that power-hungry despot," Stephanie said. "That just makes you dumb, not traitorous."

"*Dumb*? Oh, so more than half of the town you supposedly love is dumb, then? That's not elitist at all."

Stephanie sighed. "People fell for the propaganda. They got freaked out. You included, apparently. You all knew how awful things were under Audrey before, but you all voted to put yourselves through it again. That certainly doesn't make you *smart*."

"You want to talk about *smart*? You're a doctor who won't even admit that these rings have some logic to them. You want to pretend like they're evil, just because it was Audrey's decision and you refuse to support anything she does. But you should know that they enforce keeping people apart, which is sound science when there's a killer virus raging—"

"But at what cost, Michael? Jesus. Has she gotten you this brainwashed? Now you're *for* the rings? There are ways to encourage distancing without strapping twenty pounds of fucking steel to everyone in town, if we want to talk about science. What about the family separations? You for that too? And the people she's killed? What about that?"

"Who? Name one person she's killed. Seriously. Give me a name."

Stephanie stared, wide eyed, and Michael met her glare.

"We both know I'm probably next," she said. "That was cinched the moment she stole that election."

"Stephanie, you really need to take some fucking responsibility. This victim mentality is ridiculous. You made a series of decisions that you know full goddamn well led people to turn against you."

"People *including you.*"

"Yeah. That's right. *Including me.* You think I did that shit lightly? You think I didn't stay up all night trying to decide if hanging that red banner was the right decision? I must have gone back and forth a hundred times over the course of the night, thinking about the pros and cons, thinking about what each one would mean for the future of Alessandra...thinking about *you.*"

She glanced over at him as they walked.

"Well, I'm glad to hear it was hard for you. It *should* have been hard."

"It was heartbreaking. Honestly. By the time I did it, I was confident it was the decision I had to make, but that doesn't mean I was happy about it. I took no pleasure in it."

"But you still did it. Why?"

"I think the hospital is where you belong. You were *made* for that work. That's your element. You're a leader, but you're not a politician. You...*care* too much, if that makes any sense. Everything eats at you, and it leads to either paralysis or drastic action. That mansion up there, that's Audrey's element. That's where she's at her best. I've grown convinced most of the bad decisions from last time were largely Paul's. She truly has the best interests of Alessandra at heart."

"Me being locked in a pen is in Alessandra's best interest? The rings are in our best interest?"

"Say what you will about it, but the virus seems to be at bay, and we're making progress toward a vaccine that could eradicate it completely."

"And you don't think that would have happened under my leadership?"

He frowned. "Under *our* leadership. And it *hadn't*."

"So you're really buying into Audrey's bullshit now?"

"No. I'm not buying into any bullshit. I know she's not perfect. And I know she'd be the first to admit she's made decisions that she regrets. She's told me as much. But I do think she's trying her best. And that her best is probably better than ours, for this town at this time."

"Well, for all of our sakes, I hope you're right," Stephanie said. "But be careful."

"What do you mean?"

"She's an authoritarian, Michael. You can see it in everything she does, in the control she wields unquestionably, in the way she neuters her enemies when she has the opportunity to do so. The only language she knows is that of power. And she's not gonna give it up easily for a *second* time."

"Everything will change once the virus is gone."

"Will it? Maybe. But mark my words: you're gonna have to cross her at some point. This isn't going to get easier. The more entrenched she gets, the harder it'll become. And when you cross her, let's hope you don't end up like me."

"That won't ha—"

"Or worse."

"Come on."

"I've got a real skill and a use. Why do you think I'm not dead yet? What's yours? What's your unique set of skills that she can't replace? She'll use you, Michael. Audrey looks out for Audrey. Nobody else. Watch your back, because I guarantee she's got a knife pressed against it, whether you know it or not."

17

"You wanted to see me?" Michael peeked his head into Audrey's office, and she looked up from her desk. "I can come back later if this isn't a good time."

"No, it's perfect. Come on in. Sit down."

He settled into a chair, and Audrey folded her arms.

"It's been several days with Stephanie. How are things going there? Any problems?"

"No, it's been fine. She's been very cooperative. Goes to the hospital, gets her work done, and we head back up here."

Audrey nodded. "Have you guys talked much?"

"Not really. We've kept it pretty straightforward. A little bit about the work. And she's wanted me to pass her thanks along to you for letting her do this. She thinks it's really helping."

"Well, that's terrific. I thought she could be of some service, and it's nice to hear that's working out."

"It really is." Michael smiled and leaned forward in his chair. "You were smart to make it happen."

"So, the big question, of course, is where are we with the vaccine? What sort of progress have we made? Would you say we're closer?"

This was a question Michael had anticipated, and he'd had some time to prepare his answer. The truth was, he hadn't gotten much of an update out of Stephanie; she hadn't wanted to talk about it a whole lot. From what he could gather, though, it was slow going.

He knew that wasn't the answer that was going to satisfy

Audrey, though. He'd finally gotten Stephanie talking again and, even though it wasn't entirely friendly, there was something so familiar and comforting about it, like stepping into a pair of old, soft slippers. He'd almost forgotten how much he loved her and still wanted her to be a part of his life. In this cold, merciless world, she was the one connection to his old life that still kind of worked, that reminded him of truly good times. He'd let that slip away from him once, losing touch with her for a while after the divorce. He didn't want that to happen again, and these walks to and from the hospital were his chance to rebuild that rapport and trust they'd lost. He needed to keep them going, which meant he needed Audrey to hear a story that would give her no choice but to stick with the plan.

"Oh, most definitely. Stephanie says they've made real, tangible progress. Closing in on a breakthrough. No doubt. She wants to put her head down and keep working. She'd stay there all night if you'd let her."

"I'm sure she would," Audrey said, laughing. "That's more really good news. And I guess that makes my mind up about something else I was considering."

"What's that?"

Audrey shuffled some papers on her desk, then looked up at Michael.

"I'd like you to help spread the word to the townspeople that I'll be giving an important speech tomorrow at daybreak in the square. Have George and William help you. Everyone needs to be there."

Michael's head was swimming. A big announcement? Was he the only one who hadn't known about this already? What did this have to do with Stephanie and the vaccine research?

"I'll get on that as soon as I leave here," he said. "Can I ask what the announcement is about?"

Audrey stood and walked around to the front of the desk, leaning back against it and grinning widely.

"You can ask all you want, but isn't it more fun for it to be a surprise?"

"I...well, with all due respect, I'm not sure if this is the time for surprises. People are going to ask us what it's about."

"And you tell them they'll find out tomorrow."

Michael had never been huge on surprises to begin with, and this definitely wasn't a situation where he felt like it was appropriate. But there wasn't much he could do to sway Audrey if she had her mind set on something.

"Okay, then. We'll see what you have in mind tomorrow. I'm sure it'll be great," he said. "Any hints or whatever I can give people to tease them about it?"

Audrey looked up at the ceiling and rubbed her chin, looking like she was thinking, but Michael suspected it was mostly a show. This whole conversation was about trying to keep him off balance.

"Tell them it's going to be transformative for the future of Alessandra," she finally said. "It's going to motivate us to even greater heights. I can't wait."

Michael found George near Alessandra's main gate, coming down from the platform.

"George, you got a second?" Michael said. "I'm gonna need your help with something."

George had been about to walk in the other direction and stopped, his back turned to Michael, then slowly turned toward him.

"What do you need help with?"

"Audrey wants to make an announcement to the town tomorrow morning. We need to spread the word so that everyone knows to be there. I figured we could split up the houses."

"You and me?" George asked, his eyes narrow.

"Well, William too, if you know where he is. Then we could knock it out more quickly."

George sucked in a deep breath and exhaled. "I've got things to do, Michael. So does William, I'm sure. Can't you handle this by yourself?"

"This isn't a negotiation, George. This is an order straight from Audrey."

George crossed his arms and said nothing.

"*And* from me." Michael stepped forward, jutting his chin out, his jaw set.

"Oh? From *you*, huh?"

"Yeah. Don't forget that I outrank you around here. I'm Audrey's number two in command. When the two of us give you an order, you goddamn do it. Got it?"

"Is that right? Look, Michael, you're a good enough guy and all. You did us a solid in voting for Audrey and turning your back on Stephanie like that. But let's get something straight: you're not commanding *shit*. Okay? I don't know what sort of smoke Audrey's blowing up your ass about having authority around here, but nobody gives a damn. You get her to tell me to my face to do this menial bullshit, and I'll get on it. Otherwise, I'm not taking second-hand orders from a guy who was Stephanie's lapdog before he was Audrey's."

George turned to walk away, and Michael grabbed him by the shoulder, spinning him around.

"What do you think Audrey's gonna do when I tell her you refused a direct order? You think she's the kind of person who fucks around? You've seen how ruthless she can be. You really want to invite that on yourself?"

"She wants to deal with me, she can deal with me." George laughed. "But what? I'm supposed to be afraid of *you*? With your face all messed up, trying to look tough? I've been in law enforcement and security for decades. I've dealt with nothings like you for practically my whole life. You say you 'outrank' me? Why? Because Audrey bribed you with a bullshit assignment to get your vote? She's putting you up there so she can keep an eye on you. You don't have authority over *shit*. So back the fuck off."

Tucking a red patchwork quilt underneath the edge of her mattress, Emily heard a noise from downstairs; it sounded like someone knocking on the door. She wasn't expecting Xavier, but she smiled thinking he might be stopping by out of the blue. She'd put a couple of benches in the back yard, where they could sit with their rings on and chat on nice days.

She left the bed half made and hurried down the stairs to

answer the door. Her heart sank when she saw who was standing in front of her.

"Hi, Emily," George said, with William behind him, peering over his right shoulder. She noticed neither one of them was wearing a ring. "Mind if we come inside?"

Emily had been wary of anyone associated with Audrey ever since she took over command of the town. Under Stephanie's leadership, she'd felt mostly safe and happy, at least until people started being attacked and then the virus returned. But she never felt targeted, and she had Xavier by her side. The world made sense.

Since Audrey took over, she felt a dark cloud hanging over her life, as if she didn't belong in Alessandra. Like, even with all she'd done to help make the garden a success, she wasn't a genuine resident because she was originally from somewhere else. Something about the way George and the others looked at her and Xavier made her uncomfortable. And now this was the first time she'd seen them since they kicked Xavier out of her back yard, where he'd been living for weeks without any problems. They both felt like it was discrimination, but there was nothing they could do about it if so. They had to make the best of it.

Looking up at him now, Emily was trying her best not to let her emotions show, forcing a smile that she worried looked a little too much like a grimace.

"The place is a mess, and I know we're not supposed to have visitors very often," she said. "Is there something I can help you with?"

George laughed and pushed the door open, then squeezed past her inside the house, William following him.

"We're not visitors. We're law enforcement doing our job. Not like your husband," George said. "Where is he, by the way? Have you seen him much lately?"

"Not…really." Emily saw William going up the stairs and wanted to follow him, but George was holding her gaze in the living room. "Where is he going? Should we go up with him?"

"No, no. It's fine. We should talk here. He's looking around. So you say you haven't seen…Xavier is his name, right?"

She glanced up the stairs a couple of times, worriedly, then back at George. "That's right. Xavier. Um, no. Not much since he moved into that house a couple blocks away."

"He doesn't come over to see you? Maybe stay the night every now and then?"

"Well…no. He definitely doesn't stay the night. You all have made it clear that's not allowed. He has come over at times, but we both work a lot, and it's hard to sync up our schedules when we're living apart like this, and we always just meet outside with our rings on instead of being in the house."

Emily heard noises from upstairs. Maybe drawers opening? Something hitting a wall? She took a step toward the stairs.

"Stay with me, Emily. I need to talk to you."

"But…I don't know what he's—"

"It's okay." George held out a hand toward her. "Don't worry about him."

"Maybe I could help him find whatever he's—"

"He's fine, Emily. Trust me. If he needs help, he'll come ask for it. Tell me, when was the last time Xavier was inside this house?"

"When…what?" Emily shook her head, confused. "He was forced to move out when Audrey gave us these rings. We never got any visitation rights, so that was it. That was the last time."

George stepped toward Emily. "You're *sure* about that? I mean, come on. A happily married…well, *previously* married couple? You never snuck him inside to get out of the heat? Never went upstairs for an afternoon quickie?"

Emily heard her bed drag across her room's wood floor.

"A quickie? What are you talking about?"

"You know what I'm talking about. Tell me what you two have done. Being honest about it will help."

"But I…we…" Something heavy hit the floor upstairs, and a door hinge squeaked loudly, followed by footsteps pounding across the hall. "We've done everything you asked."

"You knew him staying in the back yard wasn't in the spirit of the law, right? You knew that was flaunting the rules. Don't treat me like I'm stupid. You *had* to know that."

"No. We wanted to be near each other. Other people did something similar, so we thought—"

George's face contorted into a frown. "Are you calling us hypocrites?"

Glass shattered upstairs, and Emily's heart beat faster.

"No! Of course not. We were trying to be as close as we could while still honoring—"

George stepped forward within touching distance of Emily. It had been a long time since she'd been this close to someone, Xavier included. She squirmed as he peered down at her.

"We know what your kind is like. If we give you an inch, you'll take a mile. It's all about *you*. Not about the good of Alessandra, just what feels good to you in the moment. So be aware, we've got our eyes on you. And everyone else who doesn't have Alessandran blood. All right? We let you get away with shit for too long. The line is drawn. So much as sniff too loudly, and we'll put you the fuck away. Goes for your boyfriend too. Clear?"

Hearing him called her boyfriend was a knife dig in the gut, but she stood firm and nodded quietly. Heavy boots came clomping down the stairs, William with his sleeves rolled up. She moved aside so he could go past her and to the front door. George followed him out and stopped to look back before he closed the door behind him.

"Thanks for your time, Ms. Pellico. Enjoy the rest of your day."

18

Audrey climbed up to the stage in the square, holding a bullhorn to address the crowd that was gathering. People were shuffling into the square, with the occasional steel-on-steel clank that came with rings hitting, but they were mostly keeping their distance from one another. Audrey smiled as she thought of the social engineering marvel those rings were, forcing order and focus for Alessandra's people. And that made them feel safer, whether they truly were or not.

Once she thought the vast majority of the people had arrived and the sun peeked above the horizon, Audrey lifted the bullhorn.

"Thank you all for coming on short notice. We haven't done one of these in a while, and I want to catch you up on the amazing work some of your neighbors are doing, along with making a major announcement. So, to begin, I want to commend the work of Lucas and Dennis in the garden; they've done a tremendous job keeping it going with minimal interruption over the course of the summer, and they've ensured fall and winter crops are planted for the coming season. So get ready for baskets of cauliflower and Brussels sprouts, whether you like them or not.

"Also, some of you may have already noticed that the big canal project was completed recently, led by the three strong men I brought here with me to serve you, who are showing their worth every day. With the new canal dug from Lake Chatuga, fresh water is going to be quicker and easier to access for everyone in the town. It's all our responsibility to make sure that water flowing into the town remains clean for drinking, so please take care to not let contaminants get into the stream. If you wouldn't drink it yourself, don't put it in there.

"My men were also joined by Nick, Lucas, and some others... forgive me for leaving off any names of contributors...to repair the fire damage to the old Kites' house. We never were sure what caused the blaze, but it had taken out much of the northwest corner of the roof before we were able to stop it. No one wanted it to sit damaged like this, and those men thought they could patch it up well enough to where no wildlife or rain would get inside. And they say that work is done. It looks much better. Thank you, men!

"Now, with all that out of the way, it's time for what I know you all *really* came here for: my announcement. First off, I want to extend a thanks to all the hard work being done by Doctor Frank Lawry's team at Saint Francis. Many of you may be aware that they've been working day and night, testing and trying to find a vaccine that can protect the town forever from H6N1. It truly is groundbreaking work they're doing, trying to succeed where so many medical research teams failed. But I think we know they're smarter and more determined than those others. This is their chief focus, and I'm extremely pleased with the progress so far.

"On that note, I'm proud to announce this morning that they're closer than ever to finding that elusive vaccine. It's right at their fingertips, and is only a bit of refining away from being a long-awaited reality. Within a week from today, ladies and gentlemen, Alessandra will break through as the first place on the planet to wipe out the terrible H6N1 virus for good. Within a week, each of you will be able to line up to get vaccinated, and we'll start moving toward a new chapter in this town's history, one where we can stand side by side as brothers and sisters, husbands and wives, and raise our fists into the air to say when the gauntlet was thrown down by Mother Nature, we fought and eventually conquered."

There were gasps and then thunderous applause rising up, filling the air, Audrey looking out over the crowd and soaking in the adoration. She wanted this moment to last forever, the jubilation of her subjects expressing their love and appreciation for her.

There was one more key point she needed to address, though. She held her arms out, motioning for the crowd to quiet down.

"The doctors have also made a recommendation that I'm determined to follow, to further preserve the safety of the people of Alessandra. They've informed me that they've been able to confirm something I think many of us have always suspected—other than the very strongest among them, the people from outside Alessandra are weak, and will continue to silently lay waste to us as a community if we allow them to remain here. They're unclean. They brought H6N1 back through those walls when Stephanie let them in, and that's an error I have the ability and responsibility to correct. So, over the next twenty-four hours, those without pure Alessandran blood will be sent away from here. Peacefully, we hope. But with force, if necessary. I encourage them to begin gathering their things and preparing for departure. If they show up at the gate on their own and leave without making a scene, we'll even provide them with some food and supplies to help them in their transition.

"Thank you all! We're going to make Alessandra the greatest civilization in human history!"

Across the crowd, Stephanie's eyes met Frank's, and she shook her head, mouthing the words "No. It wasn't me." Then she swung back to Michael, standing next to her.

"What the *fuck*?" She bit the words off hard. "What did you *tell* her?"

"I…nothing. I mean, just that…things…are going well," he stammered. "I don't know."

Stephanie couldn't believe it. Either Michael had lied to her to inflate his importance, or Audrey was making things up to justify her policies. Stephanie didn't know which one it was, but either way, Audrey had placed their backs firmly against the wall, and pointed the finger at them for this monstrous idea of kicking out anyone Stephanie had allowed inside. Assuming Audrey wasn't going to suddenly become patient and understanding, they were going to need to produce *something* Audrey could call a win within the next week, along with trying to talk her out of throwing good people to the wolves outside the walls.

On the vaccine, the truth was, they *had* made progress. More than Stephanie had wanted to let on to Michael or Audrey or anyone else. They'd decided there was nothing to be gained from overpromising or letting them think something groundbreaking was within reach, so they had been vague about the specifics when asked. But having the fresh carriers from six months earlier had given them something real to work with, and having a mostly empty hospital had provided them with plenty of time to devote to the cause of testing, trapping a dozen or so mice—they were never hard to find—that could be rotated around as analogs.

In an ideal world, of course they would have gone through human trial phases, soliciting volunteers for double-blind tests that would allow them to fully understand if what they had could be effective across a population. But this was far from an ideal world, and they knew they didn't have those resources available. That was even more reason, though, to be measured in their promises, as they couldn't be sure there wouldn't be setbacks once they started administering it to humans, and it was counterproductive to get everyone's hopes up only to quickly dash them.

That's also why the research team never would have given off the impression that a week was remotely doable, even if they thought it was. That meant way more pressure than there was any reason for them to have, and Stephanie didn't want to see how Audrey would react to being wrong.

"You don't *know*?" she said. "Seriously, Michael? Well, *somehow*, she got it in her head that we can solve the biggest crisis man has ever faced in one goddamn week, and that travelers I allowed in brought the virus with them. I'm not the one reporting to her. That's you. And you have *no idea* where she got that?"

"*Really*. All I did was tell her that you felt like the team was making progress, and that it was good you were there. I had to tell her *something*."

Stephanie rolled her eyes. "Yeah, well, whatever you said really fucked us all over."

"Look…maybe if you had been more forthcoming with me instead of starting an argument, I would have had something real to report. But no. You couldn't give me any actual update for four damn days. I didn't push you on it for the first three. Figured you weren't ready yet. Fair enough. But when I finally tried to pin you down, you changed the fucking subject. Gave me *nothing*. So when Audrey asked me for an update, what was I gonna do? Tell her I don't know? Tell her you guys weren't accomplishing shit? Then you're back in that pen faster than you used to be able to flip your hair back out of your eyes. And what good does *that* do anyone? So yeah, I embellished a little. But not like *that*. And I sure as hell didn't say anything about immigrants being a problem."

Michael had a point. She knew she hadn't given him much to work with, but that was by design. She never anticipated that even Audrey would be so impulsive as to do something like this after just four days.

"Fine." Stephanie was trying to hold her anger in check, especially in the middle of this crowd. "Nothing we can do about it, anyway. What now?"

Michael looked up toward the stage and then grabbed Stephanie's ring, pulling her through the crowd. She felt like she was being towed, shuffling her feet ahead as their rings plowed a path in front of them.

They reached the side of the stage as Audrey was coming down the stairs.

"What was *that*?" Michael asked, his arms wide as he looked up at Audrey. "I never told you any of that."

Audrey smiled. "I know. But it's genius, isn't it?"

"Genius?" he said.

"Sure." Audrey reached the bottom of the stairs and stopped in front of Michael. "Stephanie would have dragged all this 'research' out forever if she needed to because she knows that's where she's valuable to us, and the aliens would have stayed here, continuing to infect the town. But now there are firm dates. There's no excuse for going longer than that. Everyone knows the aliens have to go, and the researchers need to fucking deliver something. Either they do it, or I have good reason to pull Stephanie off the project. She wanted to make this into her 'job' again. But she's not gonna play me like that. *Nobody's* gonna play Audrey like that."

Stephanie could feel a knot forming in her stomach with every word Audrey spoke. She took deep breaths, her eyes pressed tightly shut until Audrey was done.

"This is *bullshit*, and you know it!" Stephanie yelled, pointing angrily at Audrey. "You're gonna start a fucking *war* with all this. Is that what you want?"

Audrey looked at Stephanie with something approaching pity. "I didn't want any of this, Stephanie. Remember, they're only here because of you, and that means so is the virus. All of this is on you. You said you could help. Well, you've got your deadline now. So go fucking *fix it*."

"*You* put these impossible dates on us," Stephanie said, "and then if we don't impossibly hit it, no matter how much progress we've actually made, you're gonna stick me back in that pen to rot? That's insane!"

Audrey raised her chin, a wide smile crossing her lips.

"Oh, don't worry," she said. "Your time in the pen's almost up no matter what. You can rest assured of that."

"So, over the next twenty-four hours, those without pure Alessandran blood will be sent away from here."

Emily heard the words but could barely process what they meant in the moment. It was as if her brain refused to put them in the proper order and apply them to the reality she knew. She had felt some harassment, particularly since Audrey had taken over, and she knew from some brief conversations with Derrick, Grace, and others that she and Xavier weren't the only outsiders to face it. But she never imagined they'd go this far. She couldn't believe this edict actually came from the doctors. It didn't make any sense. Because Tyrone was the first to contract H6N1? It wasn't a slow-acting virus. However he got it, he was infected after he was already within these walls, unless they knew something about the virus Emily didn't.

She looked at Xavier standing next to her, his face ashen.

"They can't send us back into the wilderness, can they?" he asked, his voice pleading. "Can we talk to her, get her to change her mind?"

"I wouldn't count on it. There aren't a lot of us, so it's easy to turn us into an 'Other' she can rally everyone against. I'm not sure who we can trust except each other. We need to meet together."

"Where? When?"

"*Now*. With this crowd, it'll never be easier and less conspicuous to organize this. That old abandoned warehouse on Juniper. It's barely standing, but there are only a few of us, so we can find a bit of cover there. I'm guessing Morgan and Grace are together somewhere. I'll find them and make sure they come."

Xavier started to jog away from Emily.

"X!" she said, her voice raised an octave. He stopped and turned around. "Don't run. We don't want to look frantic, like we're up to anything. Walk like normal. Take a route like you're going home, then divert to the warehouse once it looks like you're clear. I'll meet you there."

He nodded and started off again.

"Oh, and X…" He stopped and turned once more. "Love you."

19

Stephanie approached the entrance of St. Francis, with Michael next to her, both walking at a near-frantic pace.

"Look, I don't know exactly what all this means, but it's nothing good," Stephanie said, stopping outside the hospital. "What I do know is you've *got* to get me more time over here. If this is gonna happen in a week, I need to *stay* here. I need to fucking *sleep* here. This is all hands on deck, if Audrey sincerely wants to have *any* chance of getting this done that quickly."

Michael rubbed the back of his neck. "I hear you. And I agree. I don't know if she'll—"

"Then you fucking *make* her, Michael! You talk to her and make every argument you can until you're blue in the goddamn face. Don't take no for an answer. I need more time, and so do Derrick, Emily, Morgan, Grace, and the others who came here and are contributing to our future. Get that for us. You're supposed to be number two in charge, well fucking *act* like it!"

"Yeah." He nodded quickly. "Yeah, I'll do what I can. Seriously. Whatever I can come up with."

Stephanie took off her ring and leaned it against the wall inside the door, then stepped back out and grabbed both of his hands. It was amazing how much you missed simple gestures like this when you'd been denied them for so long. The two of them alone in front of the hospital, she figured there was little risk in it, and she wanted to get his attention.

"You can do this. Okay? We've been over it. You know what to do. Be confident. Chin up. I'll see you later."

She turned and went inside, then headed down the hall to the research lab when she heard quick footsteps coming down the stairs behind her.

"Doctor Sloan! Doctor Sloan!" It was the voice of Victor Davis, one of the nurses. Stephanie stopped as he scrambled over to her. "All that stuff about a week for getting the vaccine done, is that true? Did you tell her that was gonna happen?"

"I've really got to get to work, Victor. There's a lot to be done, and not a lot of time to do it."

She started walking again, turning her back on him. Then he called after her.

"Because I don't think you did."

She stopped, closed her eyes, and then spun her head around.

"And if I'm right," he said, "I think I may have made a huge mistake."

Stephanie closed the door to her old office, turned the lock and closed the blinds into the hallway.

"Okay," she said, sitting behind her desk with Victor in front of her. "We should be good here. What mistake did you make?"

"Well…" He sighed. "It's not like I really had a choice, I don't think. They threatened me *and my family*. What was I gonna do?"

"Who? Who threatened you? What are you talking about?"

Victor scratched his forehead, twisting his neck sideways and grimacing. "I'm not supposed to tell anyone. They said they'd make me watch them kill my wife and son if anyone found out."

Stephanie leaned forward. "Okay. I understand. Whatever you did, I get it. If someone threatened me like that, I'm sure I'd do whatever they wanted too. So I'm not blaming you. I'm not gonna think any less of you. But you really need to tell me what you did, and maybe we can start trying to make it right."

He looked at the floor and took a deep breath, pausing for several seconds. Finally, he lifted his head to look at Stephanie.

"All right. Just…keep all that in mind. So, as you know, we've had H6N1 specimens for a while. Since the initial outbreak, anyway. Kept them in cold containment in the basement. Those massive solar panels on the roof, that's what most of that energy goes toward maintaining."

Stephanie nodded silently, trying not to get impatient.

"A few days before the election," he said. "The one you, well, ya know..."

She stared at him, unmoved.

"Right," he said, meekly. "Anyway, Audrey's men show up, but I had no idea who they were at the time. I'd never seen them before. Which is weird around here, ya know? I hadn't even heard yet that Audrey was back, so I had no clue where these guys came from. I guess I was the first person they saw when they came into the hospital; I happened to be walking through the lobby. I asked if I could help them, and they lifted me off the ground and carried me into the men's room there. One of them shoved me into a stall while the others stayed on lookout duty or something. He pushed me down on the toilet and stood over me. I swear the guy looked like he was seven feet tall. He was a giant. Massive chest. Weird scars on his face. I was terrified."

Stephanie could feel her stomach and shoulders tightening up, and she squirmed a bit in her seat.

"He asked me where the virus was. I didn't know what to say. Obviously, that's not information we share outside the hospital. People in the town don't even know we've had it. We didn't want to panic anyone, ya know? So it was strange to me that he'd even ask, as if he *knew* we had it. Which, looking back, must have come from Audrey. But, at the time, it was confusing. The whole episode was baffling. So I told him I didn't know what he was talking about, and he grabbed my shoulders and lifted me in the air. I swear, I thought he was gonna throw me across the room like a rag doll and go find someone else to tell him what he wanted to know. Because we *all* knew. Right? Everyone here. If it hadn't been me, it would have been someone else. I didn't do anything wrong."

"What did you *do*, Victor?" Stephanie was nearly standing out of her chair. "You've got to tell me what you did before I can help you."

"He slammed me back down on the toilet seat and demanded again to know where the virus was. I told him it was in the basement cold storage, and he said that was where we were going. He lifted me to my feet and jammed a gun in my ribs. Or it felt like a gun, anyway. I never really saw it. Then he whispered right in my ear. I'll never forget it. He said, 'Sally and Harris. I have access to them. Try anything, and they're both dead.' He *knew their names*! And I still had no idea who this giant was! So I was scared to death. I went down the hall to the elevator. Figured nobody would be back there, and I didn't want to know what would happen if someone saw us. The other three guys followed behind us, and he kept the gun pressed against my side.

"When we got down there, he made me go back to where the virus was, and I showed him. They're behind glass, ya know? I said, 'There they are.' He said he wanted a vial of it. I said I can't do that, and he smacked me hard in the face. I swear, my whole jaw rattled. Felt like I was gonna see my teeth flying across the room. Then my head started *pounding*."

Stephanie shook her head. "You didn't. Tell me you didn't give him a vial of H6N1."

"What the heck was I supposed to do? They were gonna kill me *and* my family if I didn't do it. So yeah, I unlocked the case and got one for him. I was thinking, what's he even gonna do with it? It's not like anyone wants to risk letting it get out. It could wipe *everyone* out. I'd probably never even see the guy again. But then it turned out they were connected to Audrey, and I got a little concerned, but I didn't want to tell anyone what I'd done. I was hoping nothing would happen, and it'd be fine. And then the Brownings came down with the virus, and Hank too. We were pretty frantic, but we contained it. I convinced myself it was a coincidence. Little flare up. Doesn't have anything to do with me.

"But I heard Audrey today, and I thought she was lying. They're playing games with this virus, using it like a tool. It made me think they don't even *want* it to be cured, because it's too useful for them. It allows them to keep everyone tight under Audrey's control. She *needs* the virus."

Her heart racing, Stephanie stared at the wall, trying to process what she was hearing.

"And they had the means to bring it to life again," she said, her voice hollow in her throat. “Maybe still do.”

“I’m sorry. Maybe if I had known…” His voice trailed off as tears started streaming down his face.

Stephanie buried her head in her hands, no idea what her next step should be.

20

Coming through the front door, Michael saw Audrey walking down the hall toward the back of the mansion.

"What *was* all that?" he said, his voice louder then he wanted it to be; she stopped and turned around. "*That* was your announcement? You need to at least give me a heads up before you spring something like that on me."

Audrey's eyes narrowed. "I *need* to?"

"Look, Audrey, it's you and me now. Stephanie's not here. Can we talk like equals?"

"Yeah, Michael. See, we're *not* equals." She stepped forward and stood very close to Michael; they were roughly the same height, and their eyes met. "I don't *need* to tell you a goddamn thing. All right? Show some fucking respect. I make the decisions around here. You want to do something? Come to me and talk about it first. I want to do something? Well, then, that's what I do. That's how being in charge works. You've been an irrelevant number two before, so you should know something about that."

Michael felt like he was losing control of the conversation, and he wanted to steer it back. He was trying to remind himself what Stephanie had said earlier.

"Fine. Sure. You can do whatever you want. Got it. But we can't kick all those people out of the town for no reason. They're valuable parts of the community. Lots of them are helping to do the work you were praising in your speech this morning. We *need* their contributions to keep Alessandra running. We don't have so many people that we can lose several of them overnight and expect not to have a drop-off."

"What are you asking me, Michael?"

"Let them stay. Monitor them if you have to. Make sure they're tested at the same frequency as the caretakers in the children's building to ensure they're fine. They're already alone in their homes and wearing their rings. That should keep everyone reasonably safe. But don't—"

"It's not enough." Audrey clipped off the words, her face expressionless. "Our standard shouldn't be 'reasonably safe,' but 'safe.' This virus doesn't fuck around, Michael. Once it's loose in this town, there's no telling if we can get a handle on it. And, as the leader of Alessandra, that's not a chance I can fathom taking. The people of Alessandra are my priority. They're who I'm pledged to protect and defend with my dying breath. I didn't let these other people in here. That's on Stephanie. I feel bad for the Browning family, but it's no coincidence that a non-pureblood family was the first to come down with the virus. We acted quickly and were fortunate enough to contain its spread, though we lost Hank in the process. We were extremely lucky then. But if we're going to get a fresh start with a vaccine to move forward into the future, we need to be absolutely certain that we're clean. I've been pondering this for months, and this is the time to do it."

"But how can we—"

"The decision is made."

The face that first flashed into Michael's head was that of Derrick, lying in a hospital bed, bandages wrapped around his head, wires criss-crossing away from his body. He had been one of the victims of a rash of mysterious attacks on the people of Alessandra, and Michael and Stephanie were desperate to find out who was behind it. Derrick wanted to help so badly, but Michael and Stephanie could see that first visit that he wasn't up for much. It was too soon, but that didn't stop him from trying whatever he could to tell them. And, eventually, he provided the key information that allowed them to figure out Zac was at least *involved* in the attack.

But regardless, Derrick had been through a lot since he made it to Alessandra, and he'd been nothing less than a model citizen. The thought of pointlessly forcing him to go back out into those woods he nearly died in to get there seemed incredibly cruel. And Michael worried this was going to be anything but peaceful.

What could he do, though? He'd thrown his lot in with Audrey, thinking it was his best play. And he still thought that, given what information he had to work with around the time of the election, it had been the right call. She appeared to be more stable and capable than Stephanie. Didn't she? Had he been seduced by the idea of a new leader delivering what Stephanie never could—a chance for Michael to make real decisions that would help the people of Alessandra? Had that blinded him—or at least distracted him—from all of Audrey's flaws?

Because they were all coming back now. He saw them clearly. She didn't share power easily, which made Michael wonder how Paul had been able to wrest what authority he'd had previously. Maybe he was even crazier and more stubborn than she was. And maybe she'd learned from that, not to ever truly let power escape her hands. But what Michael knew was he again felt sidelined, a figurehead in a fancy mansion with an office he didn't need. And while Stephanie didn't always make the decisions he would have, she never would have done something like this.

Michael felt stuck, though. He still needed Audrey's ear if he was going to get Stephanie the time she needed to deliver something on the virus in the coming week, and maybe keep Stephanie alive. Turning on Audrey now, taking the side of the immigrants, was as good as killing Stephanie outright.

"Okay." Michael nodded solemnly. "Fair enough. You make a good case. I understand you're trying to do what's best. Speaking of which, one week is a *tight* timeline for the vaccine. I talked to Stephanie and the research team after your speech, and they said any extra time would be helpful. But if you absolutely need to have it within a week's time, Stephanie can't be going back and forth from here to there, pulling half days at the hospital; she needs to stay there for the duration."

Audrey sighed. "You think she can handle that? Let's remember that she's still a prisoner and a murderer, not the respectable doctor you married."

Michael cringed at the idea of Stephanie being called a murderer, and wanted to again remind Audrey that no trial had taken place, that Stephanie had never been afforded the opportunity to speak in her defense. This wasn't the time to make that point, though.

"I think she can. She's gonna be laser focused on that vaccine. She knows what's at stake here. No one wants to finish this more than she does, believe me."

Audrey ran her hand through her hair, yanking on the strands and pulling them back off her forehead. The gesture reminded him of Stephanie, back when she had her long, flowing hair that he'd always loved.

"All right. I'll try it. But she's *your* responsibility. Twenty-four hours a day, seven days a week. I don't care if she's here, there, or on fucking *Mars*. Whatever she does is on you, Michael. If she plays a role in them delivering this vaccine within a week, you'll get some good credit for that. But if she fucks up, if she makes me regret this, that's on you too. Got it?"

Michael nodded. "Yeah. I'll check in down there as much as I can, and keep an eye on what they're doing. You won't regret this. You have my word."

Xavier kept glancing back over his shoulder as he approached the old warehouse, expecting someone to be back there, his heart pounding in his chest. It occurred to him Audrey and her men may very well not be very concerned at this point. There were only five "immigrants" to deal with. And Audrey had what? George, Andy, Benjamin, Michael, and those three massive goons she brought back here with her? It seemed pretty clear they were going to be exempt from this deportation. Why, though? Because they were "strong"? If non-Alessandrans were "unclean," their bulging muscles weren't going to stave off the virus. Last Xavier had checked, you couldn't win a boxing match with H6N1.

But this was Audrey's show, and she was going to make up any excuse she could to keep her men here. In fact, they'd be among her enforcers to eject the rest. So, Xavier knew, the count wasn't going to be in the immigrants' favor.

He rounded the corner into the warehouse and looked around. Sagging hay bales were draped in early-morning shadows, sunlight peeking through the slats in the wood, which had separated significantly over years of neglect. Looking up, he could see what used to be a second floor, but it didn't appear stable enough to stand on now; there were several holes in what was left of the wood, perhaps made by bullets.

"X!" He heard Emily's voice from a darkened corner. He spun in that direction and could barely see her arm motioning him over. When he got there, he saw Morgan and Grace with her and nodded to them both.

"So," Xavier said. "I guess this is it. Do we have a plan?"

"We're hoping to have one before we leave here," Emily said. "I'm not sure how long we have. They may be watching us, expecting something."

"Or we're so outnumbered that they figure there's not much we can do," Xavier said.

"That's true," Morgan said. "And they might even welcome a fight. Let us start it, and then they figure they could justify killing us here and not have to look like the bad guys who kicked us out. Accomplishes what they want in the end, which is to be rid of us."

"But why?" Grace asked. "Why do they want to get rid of us? We're all doing our best, like everyone else. We're no different from the people who grew up here."

"Because it's easy," Emily replied. "Because despots who rule by force need to constantly create friction and some foil to turn the people against so they don't turn against her. It's the virus. It's Stephanie. It's us. Once we're gone and the virus is buried, she'll find something else to distract them with. She doesn't need or even want the people of Alessandra to be happy with their circumstances. She needs them to think she's on their team against a greater evil somewhere. And that she's the only one who can protect them from it. She wants them to think the wall and rings are shields when they're really prison bars."

Xavier looked around the group and saw heads bowing, eyes

staring at the floor. Everything Emily was saying was true.

"So what do we do, then?" Xavier asked. "I think it's all of us take a stand together, or we walk out voluntarily together. There's no middle ground here. If anyone's not ready to try to stave this off, let's take our parting gifts and make the best of it. What does everyone think?"

Emily nodded. "Yeah. I agree. Let's take a vote. It has to be unanimous to stay and fight. If even one of us votes to go, that's what we do. So, show of hands, then. Who says we fight this?"

Emily's hand quickly shot up; Xavier was always going to stick with his wife, so he raised his too. They both turned to the Vicarys, who seemed unsure. Just as Xavier thought they might call it for leaving, he saw Morgan's arm start to move forward, then up. Slowly, he raised it above his head, and Grace was the only one left, arms stuck to her sides.

Morgan was still looking at her, and their eyes met. Without saying a word, he nodded. Xavier could see him mouth the words "It's okay." Grace sighed heavily and raised her arm straight above her head.

"I guess it's decided," Emily said. "Now, who has guns?"

All four hands shot back up.

Emily grinned. "You all hid them instead of giving them up? That's good, because we're probably gonna need 'em. But there are some other challenges. Right now, the four of us are split up into four different homes. A big part of why she likes these rings and the virus as a pretense for isolating us all is that it divides up our defenses. Makes it harder to consolidate resources against her. The thing is, though, those rules only work when there's a threat of punishment behind them. But what do they have to threaten us with now? Not a whole hell of a lot. If they're kicking us out anyway, we might as well say fuck their rules. If they catch us, the worst they can do is try to kill us. And we'll be ready."

"So what's our plan, then?" Morgan asked.

"The place Xavier moved into on Front Street has a second story with a nice view up and down the street in front of the house, backs up to the woods and has a fenced-in backyard we can barricade closed. That'll give us the high ground and make it hard for them to flank us. Let's meet there."

"Morning?" Grace asked.

"Dead of night. Less likely for them to be patrolling. If anyone's still got a working watch lying around, head over between two and three a.m. Otherwise, think mid dark. Don't let it get anywhere *near* light. That cover's gonna help. Then we wait."

"We'll still be outnumbered," Morgan said. "What do we do when they come?"

"We kill them all," Emily said firmly. "Whatever it takes. Stake claim to our place in this town."

21

"You're sure about this?" Michael said, sitting in Stephanie's office at St. Francis.

"That's what Victor told me." Stephanie stood from behind her desk and paced over to the wall, adjusting an Emory University diploma that hung there, a relic of a distant past she couldn't bear to let go of completely. "Which means they had the virus in their possession before anyone started getting sick again."

Michael could feel sweat begin to gather on his forehead, his hands becoming clammy.

"Do we really think they would have infected Hank and the Brownings, though? I mean, I know you don't think much of Audrey and her crew, but doesn't that seem like more than they're capable of?"

"No. In the name of gaining power and pushing me out of the way? No. I believe Audrey would do literally anything for that. That's who she is, Michael. I'm not sure how you've forgotten that."

"But weaponizing the virus is risking…*everything.* They couldn't have known it would be contained like it was. What if her men had been infected? What if it had gotten out and wiped out the whole town?"

"If she can't have power," Stephanie said, settling back into her chair. "I think she'd just as soon there not be power to have."

Michael didn't want to believe it. Could Victor be making up a story to impress Stephanie? He'd always had a crush on her, hadn't he? It did seem plausible, though. Maybe Audrey wanted the virus as a sort of insurance policy against another coup. After all, she saw what happened last time.

But would she really order people to be infected with the deadliest virus in the history of mankind? The virus that nearly destroyed human civilization, just to thrust herself back into that mansion? He *really* wanted to say no. He wanted to say that the woman he worked alongside—the woman he voted for—wasn't capable of such an act. That, despite some of the decisions she'd made before, she wouldn't do something so reckless to turn voters against Stephanie. Michael didn't want to think he was such a poor judge of character.

"I just..." he said, his thought drifting off. "I have a hard time picturing it."

"A hard time *picturing it*? You helped to push her out before for a *reason*, Michael!"

"But not for something like this! You forget, she ultimately led the group that took out Paul, and then surrendered power."

"After she *had no choice*! She slinked away, refusing to face any consequences here, blowing town so she didn't have to look anyone in the eye after everything she'd done."

"She has her flaws, no doubt. And does she enjoy being in charge? Absolutely. But H6N1 is nothing to fool around with. Audrey knows that as well as anyone does."

"Look, Michael, I'm not saying it's a sane thing to do. I'm saying she has a lust for power, and she would have seen that letting the virus loose would allow her to both undermine my leadership and generate a pretense for bringing back those rings that let her encase everyone in their personal cocoons. You've seen how they change people. How they change *the town*. That's what she wants. Would she be willing to risk it? I'm not sure that Alessandra being wiped out would be that big a downside for her when compared to the alternate scenario of being shut out of power and then the town itself. So yes, I think it was a risk she was willing to take."

"But even if you're right, why the Brownings? Why Hank?"

"I can't answer that. But the Brownings were a family I let inside, and we've seen she has no love for outsiders. That might have been reason enough for her."

"And Hank?"

"I don't know, Michael. There's someone who very well *might* know, though. And you have pretty good access to her right now."

"Did you see the looks on their faces when she said she was finally gonna give all those aliens the boot?" Andy laughed, joined by George, William, and Benjamin in their perch on top of Alessandra's gate. "I thought so many people were about to cry. Especially fucking Emily. I looked over at her, and I swear she looked like she'd scream. It was so awesome."

"I can't wait to see them marched the hell out of these gates," Benjamin said. "We're gonna reclaim this town for those of us who belong here. We can't keep pouring what little we have into propping up people who are bringing in disease and crime."

George stood and looked out over the town and the lake glistening in the midday sun out in the distance.

"What do you think will happen to them once they're gone?" he asked.

"Ya know what? I could give half a fuck," Andy said. "You know how they talk about us when we're not around? They don't respect us. And not just the aliens either. There are still lots of bleeding-heart assholes around here who feel bad for the poor aliens, and they look down on people like us. Benjamin and I heard it ourselves. You remember what Nick and Hank were saying about Zac over at Walt's?"

Benjamin laughed. "Before we beat their asses, you mean?"

"Damn straight. And they earned every bit of that ass beating. How do you talk like that about someone who's trying to make your life better? Are you that delusional that you don't see how shitty everything was under Stephanie? Zac said it: 'Freedom's a placebo for the human condition.' Some people weren't ready to hear it. They want to live in their fantasy land, where everything's fucking puppies and rainbows. Popping that bubble's gonna be so damn sweet."

"You know what the elephant in the room is, though?"

William lifted a pail of water to his mouth and drank, then laid it back down. "Those men Audrey brought with her. They're just as much an alien as Emily or Derrick or any of the others. What do we do with them?"

Andy laughed and rolled his eyes. "Well…Good luck making those fuckers do anything they don't want to do. Especially with Audrey protecting them. I don't quite get what the story is with them, or why they're so loyal to each other. Clearly, they've got a past."

"So is it wrong for them to stay?" Benjamin asked. "Should they go with the others?"

"If I were in charge…" Andy paused for a moment to gather his thoughts. "I mean, I can see the argument, right? They're big and strong, so maybe they can fight off sickness better. They're physical assets who have contributed a good bit to the town while they've been here, so they'd be tough to lose."

"There's no reason to think being big and strong helps when H6N1 comes calling," George pointed out. "If that hits them, they'll fall like everyone else."

"That's probably true," Andy said. "And if I were in charge, they're aliens, and they'd have to go like the others. But the bottom line is that I'm *not* in charge. That's Audrey's call to make. And she's made enough right decisions, I'm not gonna challenge her on this. It's not a hill I'm willing to die on."

22

Leslie took her last bite of steamed cauliflower and pushed her plate across the table, sipping at her glass of water before standing up. She was eating alone, with Stephanie assigned to the hospital.

This setup hadn't been nearly as bad as she'd feared, but it was still difficult being locked within this small area, at the mercy of the elements. She hadn't even been camping since she went up to Hiawassee as a little girl with her dad. Watching him set up the tent and start a fire, then break out the food, handing her a flaming skewer of flaming marshmallow to stick between two chocolate squares, she thought he seemed so capable. So strong. But he was over 50 when she was born, and he seemed to get old so fast. That was one of the last fun memories she had with him. And she'd never spent another night outdoors until she arrived here.

She worried about what the winter would bring. They didn't live in a particularly harsh climate, but she'd been in Alessandra long enough to know how cold the wind could be in the North Georgia mountains. Would they supply her and Stephanie with appropriate winter clothing? Or would they move them to a better shelter? If Leslie knew what she'd have to face, maybe she could better prepare herself for it, if only mentally. But they weren't saying anything, and had ignored her when she'd asked.

As she opened her tent to climb inside, she heard the lock on the gate rattling, and she stopped. They didn't usually come to collect her dishes from one meal until they brought the next one, so this couldn't be that. And she wasn't expecting Stephanie back any time soon. An unscheduled evening visit was unusual, from her experience.

The gate opened, and she saw immediately it wasn't one of the usual men. She squinted to look closer at him, and finally recognized the boyish looks and sandy brown hair—Michael.

"Hey, Leslie," he said as he approached, then nodded his head toward the table and bench. "Can we sit down for a minute? I don't have long."

Leslie didn't know what to make of it, but she shrugged and walked back there, sitting on the back side of the table; Michael settled in opposite her and looked back over his shoulder as if he was expecting to see someone there.

"Did you hear about Audrey's announcement this morning?" he asked.

"Is that what that was? I thought I heard a lot of noise from down there earlier. But no, I'm afraid I don't get out much these days."

Michael explained the vaccine guarantee and the banishment of any non-native Alessandrans, and Leslie could feel her heart sinking in her chest. This wasn't what their community was supposed to be about. This wasn't something Hank would have stood for. They'd divorced years earlier, but they both stayed in town and remained fairly close. The relationship hadn't worked as they'd hoped, but they still had a good deal in common and spoke regularly. After his death, she'd gotten closer to Derrick, seeking to fill that void in her life, and now she might lose him too.

"That's insane, Michael," she said, her voice rising. He leaned forward and motioned toward the table, his palm down, telling her to keep the volume down. "What are we gonna do? We can't let this happen."

"About the immigrants, I'm trying to talk her down from that. So far, no luck, and time's almost up. But where I need your help is with Hank."

"What about him?"

"We know Audrey had access to the virus before the

Brownings and then Hank contracted it. Her men forced one of the nurses at the hospital to give it to them. It could be a coincidence, but Stephanie and I think it's possible they weaponized it to create a panic that would help get people to vote for Audrey. We can come up with a motivation for them to target the Brownings, since they were outsiders. Do you have any idea why they might target Hank, though?"

Her mind was reeling, but she took a deep breath and tried to focus.

"I might," she said, feeling like she might hyperventilate. She swallowed hard. "A few months after Audrey left, you may remember I convinced Hank to move into one of the open houses on our street. The Brownings hadn't been here long, but they were the first ones to volunteer to help him with the move. While they carried things a few blocks or wheeled it on wagons down the street, we all got to know each other a bit. Tyrone and Cherie were terrific people. We both loved spending time with them, and their kids seemed so happy. They didn't know anything other than this world, and there's always something amazing to witness about that.

"So it was pretty devastating when they got the virus and died. But one thing Hank told me…He was walking with them back toward their house after Father Hayden's funeral; that was the day before Tyrone came down with the virus. It was kind of late and I was tired, so I'd broken off to head home earlier. They said their goodbyes at the end of the block, and Hank started to continue home. But out of the corner of his eye, he saw something strange near their house. Some shadows lurking. When the Brownings got closer to the house, the shadows moved, and they were unmistakable as Audrey's three men. Then Hank said he saw them all going up to the porch, Audrey's men behind the Brownings. Hank called out to ask if everything was all right. Tyrone looked back and waved, then went inside."

"Why didn't he say something?" Michael asked. "He could have told me or Stephanie."

"What was there to tell? There was nothing illegal about them going in the Brownings' house. You guys had so many bigger things to worry about, with the assaults and murder. And that was also the day people called for a vote against Stephanie. So I'm sure she was upset. The next day, Zac was found dead, and everything seemed to fall apart from there. He didn't have any reason to think the men at the Browning house had anything to do with them getting the virus."

Michael nodded. "Right. But now it seems like it did. And he saw them there, which made him a loose end to tie up. Do you have anything that would prove any of this?"

"I...don't know. I'm trying to think. Um, well, one thing was kind of strange. He had this old wooden trunk he kept in the bedroom. It was his grandfather's, and passed down to him when he moved out. It's not like he talked about it all the time, but I knew it meant something to him. After he died, I felt like he'd want me to keep it, as the closest thing to family he had left. When I went into the room, though, I was surprised to see it locked. As long as I lived with him, he never locked it. I'm sure of that. There must be a reason he locked it."

"Maybe he started using it for personal stuff he didn't want Audrey's people getting their hands on?"

"Well, yeah. That was more or less my first thought: *I wonder what he's keeping in there now.* But I was also thinking about how I was gonna lug that big chest out of the house, across the street, and get it to my house. What was even stranger, though, was that when I went to move it, it wasn't even heavy. I jostled it a little, and it seemed like nothing was in it. I couldn't hear anything moving around. I know it used to be close to full. But now it's virtually empty, and he still took the time to lock it, then put the key somewhere else before he died."

Michael frowned. "So why would he lock an empty trunk?"

"Exactly."

"Do you have any idea where a key might *be*?"

"I looked around, but I couldn't find one. So it's just been sitting in my attic."

"We need to look inside and find out if there actually is anything there. It could be the evidence we need."

"Oh, god. I can't believe this is happening. And how do I

know you're not gonna tell them what I know? Aren't you working with them?"

"I thought I was." Michael rubbed his forehead, looking down at the table. "I don't know what to do. I never would have thought they were capable of *this*."

"Michael…" Leslie stared hard at him, trying to lift his chin by force of will. After a few seconds, he looked up to meet her eyes. "Whatever you do, if you want to be part of the solution now, do whatever you can to make them think you're still with them. You've seen what they're willing to do. Stay on the inside. If you don't, they'll kill you. And if we're going to beat this *again*, we're gonna need you."

"Yeah." Michael sniffed and looked like he was struggling not to cry. "You're right. I can't believe we've gotten to this point."

"I need to know one thing." Leslie choked down tears of her own and looked up at the sky. "What's going to happen to Derrick?"

Michael stared back at her. The answer was written on his face.

"I'm gonna do everything I can, Leslie. I don't know if it'll be good enough. There's not much time."

23

"Are you sure nobody saw you?" Emily asked, holding the gate open as Morgan slid past her into the back yard, carrying his ring in one hand and a Remington 870 shotgun in the other.

"I assume they would have stopped me if they did. But here I am. Is Grace here yet?"

"Been upstairs maybe an hour or so. She's sleeping. We're all gonna need as much rest as we can get between now and daylight. If this deportation is supposed to happen twenty-four hours after that speech, we don't have much time left."

Emily opened the back door, and Morgan went inside, leaning his ring up against Grace's, along the wall in the laundry room, brown rectangles staining the floor where the washer and dryer used to sit. She walked past him and hit the stairs to their right, going up into the hall and then veering into the first room on her left, with a window facing the street. Some strips of wallpaper still dotted the walls, featuring the smiling faces of puppy dogs looking down on them. A small desk and chair sat in the corner of the room, the wood nearly gray with dust and other debris that accumulated in recent years.

Xavier was sitting on the bed with a disassembled rifle across his lap, rubbing it with a white cloth.

"Welcome to the battle station, Morgan," he said, looking up. "Glad you made it okay."

Morgan nodded toward Xavier's gun. "What's your weapon of choice?"

"Ah. Marlin three-thirty-six. Used to be my dad's. Came in

handy for hunting when we were making it…out *there*. Easy to clean, lightweight, and works well with a scope."

"You a good shot?"

"Not bad at maybe fifty yards out. This thing isn't super long range or anything, but it'll get the job done."

"Let's do it, man." Morgan gave Xavier a one-armed hug, and came back to Emily.

"Next door on your right, down the hall." Emily smiled. "That's where we put Grace, if you want to join her."

Morgan's face lit up, turning a shade of red. "Wait. We can do that?"

"Ring rules are suspended for tonight in this house."

Morgan hurried out of the room and down the hall.

"But Morgan," Emily said, getting his attention before he opened the door. "Remember what I said about rest. The clock is ticking. But yeah, go be with your wife. And don't wake the neighbors."

Still smiling, Emily turned back to Xavier and gently shut the door behind her.

"So, how do you feel about this?" She squatted in front of him, hands on his knees. He clasped his hands on top of hers. "Can we do it?"

"You want the honest answer, or the hopeful one?"

"Maybe a mix of both?"

"I think we need a miracle. But then, we probably needed a miracle to find Alessandra in the first place. You remember how close we were to giving up?"

Emily lowered her head. "It's hard out there. It's not *easy* in here. Not at all. But we're surviving."

"Yeah. The thing is, nobody knows better than us what's outside those walls. We know what those walls *mean*. What they're really protecting us from. The life that awaits us if we leave here."

"We know what we stand to lose."

"That's right. We know exactly the difference between being here and not being here. And so, I don't know. Can we do it? We may need a miracle, but maybe we're motivated enough to will a miracle into being."

* * *

"So it's true." Stephanie tugged off her gloves and pulled Michael into the Anna Swafford Research Library, outside the lab where she was working with her team. She flipped on a light. "They really did use the virus against our own people."

"Well, it'd be a pretty big coincidence if they didn't, after what Leslie told me," Michael said. "But I'm not sure we can be definite without proof."

"The hell we can't. We can be completely goddamn definite, as far as I'm concerned. What we can't do is *convict.* What we can't do is convince anyone who doesn't want to be convinced. Not without something more concrete, at least."

"The big question I have is how they infected Hank. With the Brownings, they marched into the house, probably giving some excuse that sounded official. From what Leslie said, it didn't look like Tyrone or Cherie was concerned at the time. They let 'em in. And I suppose they could have done that with Hank, but he'd already seen what happened to the Brownings."

"Right." Stephanie pulled over a rolling chair and sat backward, leaning forward on its back. "Plus, Hank was in a more high-profile area. You and I both lived pretty much right across the street. If he resisted and made any noise, we might hear it and look over to see what was happening. I was still the leader at the time; I never would have authorized any bullshit like those thugs barging into someone's house."

"And if we went out there, they'd have to be sure to hide the vial of the virus, or…"

"Yeah. Who knows? But you're right, that's complicated. And they don't seem like guys who like complicated. So is there another way? How else might they have gotten the virus into Hank's house?"

They were both silent for several moments, and Stephanie's eyes wandered around the room. On the wall opposite her, over Michael's shoulder, was a picture of Anna. Stephanie didn't come in here any more than she had to. It was still too hard. Seeing that portrait brought the guilt back washing over her, the knowledge that Anna would still be alive if Stephanie hadn't dragged her into that attempt to get Audrey and Paul out of office. This library was a testament to Anna's meticulousness and dedication, taking it from a dusty storage closet to one of the best medical research libraries any of them had seen.

But that's what Anna did—she was a problem solver. Stephanie found herself wishing her old friend were there with them now, someone to bounce ideas off of, and to help lift the tension with a joke. What would Anna have thought about this? Would she have an idea that hadn't occurred to them yet? Then Stephanie suddenly thought she might have it.

"You weren't with us when we left for the warehouse after the...the, um, massacre," Stephanie said. "I don't know if I've ever really told you what happened that night. When you were dragged off, I wanted to go after you immediately, but we knew they'd kill the rest of us if we did. We needed to retreat to safer ground, and try to make another run at it. That was before the batteries for the walkie-talkies died, and we were able to get our hands on a couple. We were set up with the high ground at the warehouse, but we needed Audrey's crew to actually come there, while we were lying in wait. So Anna had a great idea, to lock onto the channel Audrey's team was on, pretend we didn't know we were on their channel, and make them think we were giving them our location."

Michael laughed. "That sounds like something Anna would come up with. And it worked?"

"Yeah. Well, we sent them two houses east of the warehouse, so they'd walk right past us, looking further down the road. We, um...You know we lost a couple of people there. Quinn and Trish were shot. Didn't make it. And that haunts me. But we'd have *all* died if Anna hadn't come up with that idea. You too, most likely. And I'm thinking about that idea right now. Misdirection. Almost Trojan Horse-like. Get them looking one way, and then hit them where they least expect it."

"Yeah. What about it?"

"I think it's what they did with Hank," she said. "And I think we might be able to prove it."

* * *

Michael knocked on a familiar door, trying to recall the last time he'd been here. Definitely before the election. He still knew it well, though, standing on the front porch, shivering as the sun started to dip below the horizon. Felt like it was going to be the first cold night of the early fall, and he hadn't brought a jacket.

So far, there was silence behind the door. Was anyone home? Where else would he be at this time? After about a minute, Michael lifted his arm to knock again when he finally heard some faint footsteps and then a lock clicking. The door opened.

"Michael."

"Hey, Nick. Do you mind if I come inside?"

Nick looked suspiciously over each of Michael's shoulders. "Is it authorized?"

"I'm authorizing it right now."

Nick nudged the door further open and walked back into the house; Michael slipped out of his ring and carried inside with him, leaning it against the wall and walking into the living room, where Nick was sitting in an armchair.

"Been a while," Nick said. "How's this bullshit with Audrey going? Or will calling it bullshit get me attacked again?"

Michael cringed, then settled into the couch. "I heard you were having bad headaches for a while after that. Have they gotten any better?"

"They come and go." Nick shrugged and touched his forehead. "It's probably something I have to live with."

"Yeah. I'm sorry about that. Hope it gets better."

Nick sat still, blinking, expressionless.

"What do you want, Michael? I've learned over the past year or so that you only stop by here when you need me to do something for you. So spit it out."

"I…I know." Michael lowered his gaze; he couldn't bring himself to make eye contact with a man who had been his best friend for more than two decades—until the past couple of years, when lots of events had conspired to drive a wedge between them. "I can't argue with you on that. We're not exactly hanging out and watching football anymore, are we? I wish we could go back to the way things were, man. I'd fucking give *anything* to go back to that world. And that's honestly what I'm trying to do. Or to get us somewhere close to it, anyway. I'm trying to be a part of the solution. And I'm really sorry if that can make our friendship seem…transactional."

"There's no friendship, Michael. I don't know what we have at this point, but I sure as hell wouldn't call it that. You interact with me when it's convenient for you, and you fucking brush me aside and avoid me when it isn't. We were 'friends' until all the shit went down with Rachel, but then I was a pariah, and you kicked me to the curb. Then you wanted to kiss and make up when you and Steph needed me to lie to the whole goddamn town to try to save her ass from getting voted out of office, but then Zac exposed us all as liars, and you forgot I existed again. Until now, that is."

"I'm sorry. I just—"

"Shut the fuck up with your goddamn sorries. I don't wanna hear it, Michael. I really don't. You're sorry. Sure. Yeah. Whatever. You think you're doing the right thing? You think you're trying to get us our world back, and then everything will be awesome and totally worth all you've sacrificed? Then stop apologizing, and tell me what it is you want this time."

"Look, you know how Andy, Benjamin, and all of them feel about you. I've *had* to avoid you to show them I'm committed to their cause. If they knew I talked to you, they'd suspect I wasn't with them. It's a tight line to walk."

"Then whatever brought you here now must be pretty fucking important."

Michael looked up and nodded. "Yeah. It is. And you're right. I do need something. I need help. Stephanie needs help. Hell, the whole damn town needs help. For the same reason I couldn't be seen interacting with you, I can't be going rogue around town. I still need to have some semblance of their trust, or things are gonna get much worse than they are now."

"You mean like them sending the Pellicos and Vicarys out into the wilderness to die a slow, agonizing death?"

"Yeah, well, I don't see any way to stop the deportation at this point. But I'm here because we found out that Audrey and her men got ahold of the virus and used it against the Brownings and Hank."

Nick's eyes grew big. "Wait. You're serious?"

"Yeah. I am. Stephanie and I know that much, but what we don't have is hard evidence. That's where you may be able to help."

"Me? How can I help? I don't know anything about what they did."

"This deportation is going to create a distraction for the next, I'd say, at least half a day. I need you to go to Hank's old house and look around, see if you find anything that could tie back to his being infected. Then try Leslie's old house, up in the attic. There's a locked trunk that belonged to Hank. You need to get inside of it. It's probably a long shot, but we need to know if there's anything in there that might give us a clue as to how they infected him. If we can demonstrate that, I think we've got 'em."

"And I assume we don't have a key to the chest?"

"There probably is one, but we don't know where," Michael said. "Quite possibly somewhere in Hank's house. But Leslie couldn't find it when she looked."

"And then what?" Nick asked. "Let's say I get into the chest. What do we think might be in there?"

"I don't know. But Leslie said it's strange for it to be locked, and it felt empty. Maybe it's a long shot, but we're thinking maybe Hank had a reason for making it tough to get into."

Nick paused, and his mouth curled. "Or it's just an empty fucking chest. But yeah, if it's our best chance, I'll do what I can."

Michael stood and extended his hand; Nick reached out and shook it.

"Also, Nick." Michael reached into his back pocket, pulling out an N95 mask and a pair of latex gloves Stephanie gave him. "Wear these when you're in the houses. Just to be safe. Thanks."

When Michael entered Audrey's office, the room was already full —George, William, Andy, Benjamin, and her three men were standing around in front of her desk where she sat shuffling papers.

"...and we'll give them a little bit of time to—nice of you to make it, Michael." Audrey looked straight at him. "Are you going to help us out with this?"

"Oh. Of course. Yes." Michael could feel himself stammering as he shut the door and squeezed in between George and Andy. "Sorry. Got hung up."

"Where *were* you?" George asked. "We were all here on time."

"Hospital. Checking on the vaccine's progress," Michael said. "That's pretty important, don't ya think?"

"Is that *all* you've been doing?" George raised his eyebrows.

"What the *fuck* does that mean?"

"Hey!" Audrey banged on the desk, and everyone turned to face her. "This isn't the time for this juvenile shit. All right? We need to go over the plan. This is the priority. If you've got something else to say to each other, save it until you're out of this office because I don't want to hear it. We can't afford to slip up here. You all with me?"

Heads nodded around the room.

"Good," she said. "Now, as I was explaining, we want all of you except my men to be at the gate at dawn. Armed. Make sure the aliens can see you're armed, but don't point the guns or threaten them. I fully expect them all to go quietly. They're not stupid enough to think they can fight us off with four people. But anything can happen, and we need to be prepared.

"So, we'll give them a little bit of time to show up on their own. Look for my flashlight from the window up here to signal when their time's up. Then, I want George and William to come get Derrick, shackle him, be sure to grab the provisions bag we put together for him, and walk him down to the gate. If the others are watching, maybe that'll show them we mean business, and stir them to turn themselves in."

"And if not?" Michael asked.

Audrey paused, staring at him. She refused to blink. Michael could feel his throat drying out.

"Do you have to interrupt me, Michael? Is that necessary?"

"I'm just wondering if this is the best way to go. *Politically*, I mean."

"Politically?" she said.

"Right." Michael looked around the room, trying to make eye contact with anyone, but they were all avoiding his gaze. "Look, I think we all agree that there's good reason to deport the aliens. In tough times, you circle the wagons and all that. I get it. But I'm hearing a lot of disagreement, even resentment, with the idea of kicking them out into the woods, essentially leaving them to die."

"You're *hearing* that?" Andy said. "From *who*, Michael? Who is it you're out there talking to?"

"I'd *prefer* not to—"

"This is bullshit!" George yelled. "You're 'hearing' it from your fucking self and that murderer of an ex of yours!"

"What? No!" Michael said. "You really don't think there are any opinions other than yours in this town, George?"

"Legitimate, unmade-up ones? No, there aren't. Everyone with eyes can see the damage these people have done."

"What about the buildings they've helped put up? The garden they've helped cultivate?"

"Oh, I don't give a fuck if they've grown some goddamn potatoes. Anyone can do that shit. They've been *out there*! They were out there when the virus struck. It's not a chance we can fucking take anymore! We need a clean slate!"

"I think Audrey's men here may object to you suggesting they're unclean, George."

Audrey slammed her first into the desk and stood.

"Cut it the *fuck* out! Both of you. We all need to be pulling in the same direction, not having petty disagreements. Jesus."

She sat back down and shook her head.

"Okay, Michael. What you're *hearing* isn't surprising. There's nothing we're going to do that everyone will agree with. It sounds like we may need to reiterate to the people that we're *absolutely not* leaving them to die. The provisions bags we've put together for them are a hell of a lot nicer than anything I had when we set out from Graysburg. We didn't have shit. All they have to do is comply with the request, and they'll have a really healthy start—blankets, enough food to last them a few weeks if they ration wisely, a couple gallons of water, a wristwatch they can use as a compass, some extra warm clothes. This isn't a difficult decision. I think we're being more than fair.

"As for those who disagree, well, I'm sorry, but they're gonna have to live with it. One of your problems, Michael, was that you never seemed to fully understand the role of the leader is to make really tough decisions that are in the best interests of the people of the town, even if the people themselves don't realize it. It's like a parent making her kid eat his vegetables. He may cry and scream and thrash about. He may even hate you for it temporarily. But you have to stand your ground because, ultimately, you know better. You can see the long game. And the long game is survival."

24

"Can we tell what they're doing?" Emily asked, standing over Xavier's shoulder as he looked through his rifle scope out their second-story window, the remnants of pink tattered curtains clinging to the rod above like shredded rags.

"Not in great detail, but yeah. I can see well enough to tell the two men who walked up toward the mansion haven't come back yet."

"Could you hit them from here?" Morgan asked.

Xavier pulled away from the scope and looked back at him. "No way. That's gotta be…what? Four hundred yards? This scope works pretty similar to a pair of binoculars at this distance. Still, it'll help to give us a heads up for when they come our way."

"What are they waiting for?" Grace asked. "They know we're at our houses."

"Giving us the chance to go quietly, I assume," Emily said. "Or, at least, wanting to give the appearance of that. I mean, I'm sure that's what they'd ultimately prefer. I don't think a gunfight in the middle of the town is the best look for them. That's what they're gonna get, though, if they try to force us out."

"Wait, guys," Xavier said, looking through his scope again. "The men who left are back, and there's a third with them."

Emily crowded in behind him. "Can you tell who it is?"

"Pretty good guess it's Derrick, since he's the only other outstanding immigrant, other than Audrey's men. Hands are secured behind his back, and he's shuffling his feet as he walks. Ankles might be shackled too. One of the men with him looks like William, so I'm thinking the other is George. Still don't see Audrey's men anywhere. Even at this distance, they'd be pretty recognizable."

Morgan stood from the bed. "What are they doing to Derrick? Is he okay?"

"I can't really say if he's *okay* exactly, but he's standing upright. Looks like they just took his wrist shackles off; his arms are hanging loose at his sides, and he's shaking them. One of the men is kneeling in front of him. Yeah, and now his legs are loose. A couple of the men are pointing guns at him. Another one just handed him something."

Emily clutched his shoulders. "What is it?"

"I'm…not *sure*." He squinted and adjusted the sight. "A duffle bag, I think. He just threw it over his head, across his shoulder. And, oh god, the gate's swinging open."

Grace gasped. "They're really gonna do it, aren't they?"

Emily was thinking the same thing. Reality was sinking in, as she heard the play by play of Derrick being kicked out of the town he'd contributed so much to, even nearly giving his life while helping Father Hayden, one of the most respected members of the community. All the goodwill he'd built up didn't matter at all to Audrey and her crew. Derrick made one mistake, and he was thrown into confinement. They decided immigrants were bad to have around, and that was all he was to them. If Audrey would do this to Derrick, nothing was going to stop them from doing the same to Emily, Xavier, or anyone else in that house with them. Their contributions didn't matter. Their humanity didn't even matter. Audrey had decided they weren't pure enough as Alessandrans, so they had to leave. And if they were going to find a way to stay, they were going to have to fight for it. She had hoped it might not come to that, but now she knew it would.

"The gate's closed." Xavier looked around the room, his eyes welling with tears. "Derrick's gone."

"And we're next," Morgan said, and everyone turned to him. "Are we sure about this? They've got what? Five armed men we can see, and at least three more men we can't, not counting

Audrey? And that's assuming no one else helps them who we aren't expecting."

"We can handle it," Xavier said. "I know it's gonna be hard, but we've got the high ground. We have the advantage of being together and knowing they're coming."

Morgan stood again and started pacing. "Okay, but what then?"

"What do you mean?" Emily asked.

"What's the goal? Do we really think there's a chance we'd shoot at them, and they'd just call this off? That we'll just get them to stand down, and we can continue to live peacefully in Alessandra? We're not talking about that, are we? This isn't a gunfight; it's a goddamn revolution."

"But we don't have any choice at this point," Grace said. "Do we?"

Morgan grabbed Grace's hand. "Sure we do. We leave our guns here, put our hands high in the air, and start walking down the street toward the gate. X said they gave Derrick a bag and didn't hurt him on the way out. That's the provision bag Audrey mentioned yesterday. They kept their word on that. It'd be a start, at least. It's better than dying up here. Or out there."

"Do you hear yourself? If you leave just the two of us here, we're sitting ducks," Emily said. "We *need* you. We can't do this alone."

Morgan walked over by the window. "You wouldn't have to be. You could come with us. Throw ourselves on their mercy. Take the provisions they'll give us and give it a run out beyond the walls. Look, it's not like we haven't done it before. We all lived on nuts and berries and gathering firewood and—"

"And the winter's almost here," Xavier said.

"I know! But come on. What chance do we really have up here? Be honest with yourselves. At least out there, we've got the four of us, working together to survive. Five, if we can catch up to Derrick. That's a good-sized group to gather supplies, forage for food, do some hunting, all that. Calculate the odds. Really *think* about it."

"It'd be hard," Emily said.

"Of course it will be. But we all found a way before. We're survivors, just by the very fact that we're standing here right now, discussing this. We can pull through if we stick together. Get a fresh start. What do you think?"

Emily looked at Xavier, who backed away from the rifle and nodded solemnly.

"If they're truly committed to this, he's probably right." Xavier stood and picked up a long black case from the corner of the room. "But we're sure as hell not leaving the guns."

He pulled his rifle apart and put it into the case, then slung it over his shoulder. The others packed up their guns into bags and prepared them for carrying out of the town.

"Are we ready?" Morgan asked, his hand on the bedroom door. "Let's do this."

Morgan turned the handle and opened the door, stepping into the hallway. As his head turned the corner toward the stairs, a blast rang out from the first floor and he quickly ducked back into the room.

"Shit!" he yelled.

"What the *fuck* was that?" Xavier asked.

"One of Audrey's men is waiting at the bottom of the stairs with a gun. Nearly took my head off. Jesus." Morgan sat on the bed, burying his face in his hands. "We've lost our chance. They know we're here, and they're never gonna let us leave."

"Why are you doing this?" Derrick said, as William removed the shackles from his legs. "Have we not done everything we could to justify our place here?"

"Alessandra comes first," George said. "Times are tough, and we need to focus on taking care of our own."

"But we've been here a while. When do we get to be one of you?"

George looked around at the group. "You don't."

Michael wanted to do something. He knew Stephanie and others did too. They couldn't let Audrey send these people away for no reason, but what could they do about it? Sure, if the whole town rose up together against this, they could make a stand. But everyone was isolated. There were no phones or email. How do you organize a war in twenty-four hours? Especially when you don't even know who's on your side?

And they really didn't. Half the town voted for Audrey. It was fair to say that at least *some* of them supported this move, buying into the idea that it could help keep the virus at bay.

Michael felt powerless. He had to go along with this.

He watched the gate swing open, and Derrick step to the other side of the wall. Michael flashed back to Derrick lying in the hospital bed, how determined he was to get better and to help them find whoever had attacked him and killed Father Hayden. And how he'd fought through the mental haze he was feeling to give them the break they needed, pointing them in the direction of Zac and the gurney they eventually found hidden in Zac's back yard. That was the evidence proving that Zac was at least involved in Derrick's attack. And if Zac hadn't been murdered the next day, they may have pieced the whole case together, and Stephanie probably would have been re-elected.

What would that world have looked like? Stephanie probably would have felt justified in sending Audrey and her men away at that point, then getting a crew together to shore up any possible weak spots in the wall so they couldn't get back inside. Maybe she would have learned some things from the problems with Audrey and Zac, and accepted that she might have to put more emphasis on safety than she had previously.

What Michael was sure of was that he wouldn't have ended up standing in this spot, watching a man who had been through so much here but still loved Alessandra, a man he greatly admired, unceremoniously kicked out of his home without so much as being able to say goodbye to anyone. Just brought down from the hill, unshackled, handed a bag, and sent away with the slamming of the gate.

"What do we do now?" William asked. "Derrick's gone, and the others are still holding out."

There was a flash of light from the mansion, and everyone's heads turned.

"You all saw that. Time to go smoke 'em out, boys!" Andy

said, a wide grin across his face. "They've made their choice. Guess we won't need these other four bags."

He threw his rifle over his shoulder and started walking.

"Should we give them another couple of minutes, at least?" Michael suggested.

Andy stopped and turned back. "Why? It's over. Audrey gave the signal. What's the point of standing here with our dicks between our legs any longer? They've had all morning to come, and they didn't. So fuck 'em."

"Sure. But you know as well as I do that Audrey's ideal situation is to have them come here on their own. Looks a lot better than us taking them by force or, worse, having a big gunfight in the middle of the neighborhood. So I think we should give them every chance to surrender."

"We've given them every chance already! We've been here since fucking *dawn*!" Andy dropped his gun and stalked up to Michael, nearly pressed against his face. They weren't wearing rings. "No. Ya know what, Michael? I'm really tired of your shit. I think you've got a hard-on for these aliens. You're a goddamn bleeding heart, aren't you? You want to keep these *viruses* here because you think it's mean to do what we have to do to protect our town."

"Five more minutes. That's all I'm saying. Then we'll go."

"George? Do you agree with this bullshit?"

"Michael, I think Andy's right," George said. "I think it's time to put an end to this. Waiting any longer isn't gonna accomplish anything, and would be defying Audrey's orders. She's expecting us to move."

"Damn right." Andy banged his shoulder into Michael's as he spun around and picked up his rifle, then started walking again. "Let's do this."

"Wait!" Benjamin yelled, and everyone stopped. "Who's that coming up the road?"

Michael squinted, and he could quickly tell it wasn't any of the immigrants coming to turn themselves in. Part of him hoped they didn't, because he didn't want this to be so easy for Audrey and this crew. On the other hand, he worried it was going to get ugly if they didn't.

But this person was too big to be one of them. No, this was clearly one of Audrey's men, jogging in their direction, a freight train barreling across the cracked and broken pavement. It was Nathan.

"We found 'em," Nathan said, with no trace of being out of breath. "They gathered together in Xavier's house; we see the four rings downstairs. And they're armed. Hoping to take us out. But we've got 'em pinned down pretty good."

"Fuckers!" Andy said. "They're asking for it now."

"Nice job, Nathan," George said. "Let's head that way, boys. But be careful. We take 'em, dead or alive. At this point, most likely dead."

25

Unlocking the gate, Audrey pulled it open and walked inside the pen in her mansion's courtyard. It looked a bit barren, but not terribly unclean. A long table with chairs and a tent overhead sat at the far end of the pen, with two small tents to its left. It was a bit exposed to the elements and probably got very hot during the summer months, but she was generally pretty pleased with how her men seemed to be treating the women who were locked up here.

She could see a shadow moving around in the tent closest to her, and she walked in its direction.

"Leslie?" Audrey said. "Come on out and sit at the table with me. We need to talk."

She heard the tent unzip behind her, and Leslie clambered out, then sat down opposite Audrey at the table.

"Good to see you, Leslie. You look well. How is my team treating you? Are you eating well?"

Leslie nodded meekly. "Yes, ma'am."

"Good. I'm glad. I'm sorry you have to be here, but I trust you understand why it's so important that we keep you quarantined while the virus is still active. Soon, we plan to have a solution to the virus problem, and perhaps we can work out different arrangements. Would you like that?"

She nodded again, but said nothing, her arms folded on the table.

"There's something important I need to know first, though," Audrey said. "Are you aware of what's going on right now, as we speak?"

Leslie shook her head, her eyes refusing to meet Audrey's.

"My team is out there, working to deport all the aliens that Stephanie invited into the town. It was an invasion, enabled by my predecessor, and I'm doing what I can to correct it. It's the only way to make sure the blood of Alessandra is clean, and we can all have a fresh start, post-virus. Don't you agree?"

Leslie paused, appearing to swallow hard, and nodded almost imperceptibly, head bowed.

"I'm glad to hear that, Leslie. Because there are some among my team—I won't say who, exactly—but there are some who question where your loyalty lies. Derrick, of course, was one of *them*. An alien, illegally breaching our walls and living amongst us. And this is the man you were caught sneaking around with. In his *house*. Willfully violating so many laws, and endangering everyone in this town with your reckless behavior. Why were you doing that?"

"I don't…I was so lonely, Ms. Reese. And it got the better of me. I'm sorry."

"So you recognize how selfish your behavior was? You admit it was a stupid mistake that you'd never do again?"

Leslie nodded.

"Because there's no place in this town for those who blatantly flout the laws that are meant to protect us all. You think we all don't crave human touch from time to time? That we don't all feel isolated in our own way? But you know what we do? We sacrifice, for the good of the *community*. Remember, we're not some sleepy little mountain town. This is the largest, best organized human colony remaining in the *entire world*. And we've only survived this long because we've been willing to make the sacrifices and tough decisions others weren't willing to make. But doing that requires every single one of us pulling in the same direction. We're only as strong as our weakest link. And I know you don't want to be our weakest link. Because if you are, you'll have to leave right alongside the aliens."

"No…I want to stay. Please." A tear dripped down Leslie's cheek. "Whatever you want from me, I'll do it. I just don't want to go out…*there*. I want to do what's best for Alessandra."

Audrey smiled. "That's what I needed to hear. Thank you, Leslie. I'm glad to know you're on the right side of this. I didn't want to have to lose you. Also, I don't know if I ever got a chance to say this, but my condolences for Hank. He was a good man. But those Browning aliens gave him the virus, and we're not gonna let that ever happen again."

Nick walked out the back door of Hank's house and removed the N95 mask Michael had given him. The house had been abandoned and locked since Hank's death, so Nick had to break a window to get inside. He didn't guess it would be noticed any time soon. Everyone was still afraid to go near the place, for fear of the virus clinging to the walls or something.

He'd gone through every room, every dresser drawer, every closet and under every bed, and he finally came across a small keychain with two small keys attached, tucked behind an antique armoire in the corner of Hank's bedroom. He was hoping one of these would get him into the chest.

Nick had no idea what they expected him to find, but he thought it was worth the effort to try. If this was something Audrey did, everyone needed to know that. They'd have to find something directly linking her to it, though. And Nick guessed this was a logical first step toward that. Maybe he'd find something. Probably, he wouldn't. He hoped Michael and Stephanie had some sort of plan after that, because he didn't.

Nick still couldn't believe this was where they'd ended up. After Andy and Benjamin had ambushed him and knocked him out, he'd had to force himself out of bed, pounding another near-handful of weak, expired aspirin to make sure his vote got in for Stephanie. But that'd been more out of principle than anything. She hadn't done the right thing by him, dragging him into that situation to lie for them about witnessing William as Hank's assailant, but there was no way hardly anyone would want Audrey back in charge after everything that had happened, right?

When Nick woke up later that morning, groggy with a pounding head, word was already out that Audrey had won. And that Michael had been the deciding vote. None of it had made any sense to him. Audrey was a tyrant who had ripped the town in two the last time she'd been in charge. Why would anyone—least of all Michael—want to put themselves through that again? Had he forgotten being kidnapped and nearly killed by Audrey's brother? About Nick and Stephanie having to risk their own damn lives to get up to that compound and save his ass? He was signing up for that *again*?

And now, predictably, Michael needed Nick's help to push back against some atrocity Audrey and her crew had committed. This was where all roads seemed to lead. They always ended up coming to him when push came to shove, after they'd exhausted all other options. And every time, he sprang into action, making up lies, running into a hornet's nest, or going on wild goose chases.

In the end, maybe I'm a sucker. A sucker who's being used.

He got to Leslie's house and walked around to the back. Michael had said no one would be paying attention this morning, but Nick still felt like using the front door was a little too conspicuous. Going in through the back meant there was little chance anyone would see him.

He put on his mask because it was easier than carrying it, stretched the gloves onto his hands, then turned the knob; it was unlocked. The door swung open, and he walked into a small hallway that led to the kitchen. He found the stairs around a wall to his left, then went up and stopped to look around when he got to the landing. Where would the attic entrance be? He peeked in a couple of rooms before finding the master bedroom and went inside, scanning the ceiling the whole time. He was starting to wonder if he'd be able to find the attic at all, and then it occurred to him to check the closet in the back corner.

Nick pulled the door open and looked inside, his eyes immediately turning upward, and there it was—a long rectangular door with a string hanging down. He carefully pulled on the string, and the door swung down. Nick reached up and braced the ladder, carefully letting it slide down to the floor. He climbed up and flipped a light switch, but nothing happened. That was a habit that was tough to break, even this many years into the apocalypse.

The attic was dark, but there were slits of sunlight coming in through small, shuttered windows. That was enough to allow him to at least look around without tripping over everything, and he could feel his eyes gradually adjusting to the darkness. Looking for the chest, he accidentally kicked something; when he looked down, he noticed it was a flashlight. It started to roll away from him, but he grabbed it, picked it up, shook it for a second, and hit the button. A beam of light illuminated the far wall, a large chest sitting in front of it.

Crossing the room, Nick dug the keys out of his pocket and knelt down in front of the chest. It looked like it had some age on it, a scuffed gray patina concealing what may have been a light brown body. The lid had a hump in the middle, with vertical brown stripes giving the effect of leather straps straining to hold it from bursting. Two more brown stripes crossed the front of the chest horizontally, with a series of dull gold stars lined up between them.

The copper lock sat in the center of the lid. He yanked on it to be sure, and it felt secure. Nick examined the keys; they looked like they might be slightly different, so maybe only one would fit the chest. He shrugged and picked one, pulling the bottom of the lock toward him so he could see the keyhole. He put it in, and it fit well enough. Nick took a deep breath and twisted it, but it caught hard. He tried to turn harder, but nothing budged. It wasn't the key.

Undeterred, he pulled it back and shuffled over to the second key. It wasn't a warm morning, but he could feel sweat starting to bead on his forehead; he wiped his sleeve across his brow and inserted the next key into the lock. Again, it slid in easily. He shut his eyes tightly and tried to turn it, but it stuck again. No sign of movement. He put more force into it, leaning his body into the key, trying to will it to turn. His face turning red and his wrist burning, he kept pushing, as if he could open a lock by sheer physical force.

Then, suddenly, it turned with such speed that his hand

smacked into the side of the trunk, and he let out a yelp in pain, pulling his hand away to clutch it to his body. Before he could be relieved that the chest was unlocked, though, he noticed there was something in his hand. It was the head of the key. The rest of the key was still embedded in the hole.

If there was a way to get into the chest, it wasn't going to be through that lock.

26

"What do we do?" Grace was frantic. "Can we tell them we're surrendering? Would they really shoot us?"

"They tried to shoot me on sight," Morgan said, his head cradled in his hands. "Just being here together is a violation. I'm not sure they're in the mood to accept a surrender. This was a mistake."

"No, it was our best chance to survive this and stay in Alessandra," Xavier said. "We were doomed if we stayed isolated like they wanted us to. Banding together and pooling our resources gives us a fighting chance."

"Does it?" Morgan said, lifting his head to look at Xavier. "I don't see us doing a lot of fighting right now."

"Maybe we should be," Emily said. "How many men did you see downstairs?"

"I didn't have much time to count as that bullet whizzed past my skull. But in that short flash, I only saw one."

"Okay. And we have four. So we may have an advantage in manpower. We also have the high ground, and we need to not give that up easily. They're gonna be wary of coming up too fast because they're at a disadvantage, and they know it. I'll stay by the door and listen for any footsteps coming up. If so, I'll send them a message that getting upstairs won't be without its risks. X, get your rifle back out. We need to figure out where the other men are. Hopefully, they're still waiting at the gate."

Xavier pulled the gun off his back and laid it on the ground, reassembling it and setting it up by the window. Getting the scope in place, he dialed in the focus and looked at the gate.

"Shit," he said. "They're gone."

"All of them?" Grace asked.

He pulled back from the scope and looked at her. "All of them."

"God damn it." Morgan flopped back on the bed. "They're coming this way. I fucking know it."

"We *don't* know that, Morgan. They may not have any way to know where we are. They could be going anywhere," Emily said. "Can you find them, X? We need to know what we're facing."

"I can try."

Xavier turned back to the scope and started scanning from the gate up toward the mansion, down to the square, over to Walt's Bar and the far wall, into the residential area with rows of single-family homes. Roughly half the town was behind him, blocked from his view. If they were headed toward Morgan's or Grace's house, he probably wouldn't know it. If they split off into smaller groups of one or two, they might be tougher to find, but he figured they'd stand out as the only people on the streets without rings on.

As he swept further from the gate, constantly adjusting the focus was getting irritating, and he realized he didn't need the scope that much anymore. He lifted his eyes and looked down at their street, then followed it straight out in the direction of the gate, looking for any sign of movement. Then he saw it. His eyes closed, and he slowly shook his head.

"They're coming this way," he said. "One of Audrey's men is out front."

Grace screamed and jumped onto the bed, lying face down with an arm around Morgan's midsection.

"That's it," Morgan said. "They're gonna fucking kill us. Right in this godforsaken room."

"If you two keep lying there crying, you're absolutely right," Xavier said. "Emily and I can't hold them all off by ourselves. Look, we were ready to surrender with you. But that looks like it isn't an option now. So there's nothing to do but stand our ground and try to be smarter than they are."

"What the hell difference does it make?" Morgan said. "We're dead either way."

"If you're gonna die either way," Emily said, "wouldn't you rather maybe take one or two of those bastards with you than die like a coward lying in bed?"

Morgan paused and looked at Grace, who looked up at him. She closed her eyes and nodded. He sighed and hoisted himself up, grabbing his gun off the floor.

"Fair enough. Let's see how many of these fuckers we can pick off before they blow our heads off."

Michael wasn't sure how he'd hoped this morning would go down, but this wasn't it—the immigrants holed up together in Xavier's house while he marched there with Audrey's well-armed crew. They didn't know how much firepower the immigrants had, but it sounded like they were all in the front upstairs bedroom. That meant approaching from the street was risky because they could be an easy target. But the only other way to get to them was by going inside the house from the back. Michael, of course, didn't want to do either.

Now, though, he was putting his own life on the line for a cause he didn't believe in, heading for a potential shootout right in the middle of town. He wondered how this was going to end. How many lives were going to end in the next few minutes? Was there still a way to end this peacefully?

Michael, George, and William split off from the group and cut through the yards to come around the back of the house, where Nathan said the other men would let them inside. Andy, Benjamin and Nathan were going to carefully inch their way along the street, using houses as cover to get as close as they could and draw attention so the others could approach from behind.

When they got to the back door, it immediately swung open; Michael was the last to step inside. Both men were still downstairs, holding rifles.

"What's the situation?" George asked.

"There are four of them upstairs, first door on the left," one of the men said. "Someone started to come out a half hour or so ago, and I took a shot, but I'm pretty sure I missed, and he ducked back inside."

"Have you tried to go up?"

"Stairs are narrow, and they creak really loudly. We'd be pretty exposed."

"Well, we can't keep sitting down here with our thumbs up our asses. We need to put an end to this bullshit as soon as possible. We've got to get up there and confront them. We've got cover from the front, and that should draw their attention away from us a bit."

"How do you suggest we do that without getting shot ourselves?"

"I've got an idea," George said, lowering his voice. "Go around this side of the house toward the front. Figure out which window they're in, but don't get yourself seen. After a few minutes, get in position to take your shot. When you do, that'll be our signal to open fire."

"What about you?"

"I'm gonna go upstairs. You guys stay right here and back us up if shit goes south. And Michael, you're coming with me."

"How close are they?" Morgan asked, pulling a chair by the window, near Xavier.

"A hundred yards, maybe. Getting closer to a range I can work with. But a few of the guys broke off and headed around back."

"Shit." Morgan started to stand up. "Should one of us try to jump across the hall and protect our back side?"

"No, we don't have enough people to split ourselves up like that," Emily said. "The only way for them to get to us from back there is up those stairs. We'll hear them if they try, and they'll have nowhere to run. We're in the best spot we can be."

Morgan looked back at Xavier, who nodded; Morgan settled back into his chair. Grace stood behind him with her rifle propped against the wall.

"Okay. So we wait, then? It's starting to feel like we're being suffocated in here," Morgan said. "They're gonna take us from both sides."

"I'm watching what we can watch. They're staying close to houses now, sort of darting between them, which tells me they know we're armed and are trying to make themselves small, moving targets. But they're still getting closer. Keep an eye out behind me, though, to make sure the others don't double back around the other side of the house and try to get us that way."

The sun continued to provide them with more light, making it easier to see clearly down to the street below. For all the tension in that room, the world outside was eerily quiet and still. No voices. No footsteps. Not even a breeze. Just the cool early-fall air and the sound of heartbeats filling up the bedroom.

No one made a sound as Morgan stared out the window, searching for any sort of movement. The waiting was unbearable. It was like standing, eyes closed and naked in the middle of a busy highway at night, bracing for an impact you knew was coming but had no idea of when. Every second brought it closer. It could come from any direction. Morgan saw no way they were escaping without shots being fired. And once the first trigger was pulled, everyone in that room was on borrowed time.

He could see Xavier slowly swiveling the rifle, no doubt following the men as they scrambled down the street. Morgan wondered how good a shot Xavier really was. He said the rifle was pretty accurate at fifty yards, but that was probably with a stationary target. Hunting men in an urban setting was quite a bit different from target practice. Xavier lifted an arm and wiped his sleeve across his forehead, then pressed his eye back against the scope.

Morgan felt Grace kiss him on the cheek, then tip-toe across the room toward Emily, who was motioning her to come. When she got there, Emily whispered something into her ear, and she nodded, then knelt on one knee beside her, lifting her rifle and pointing it at the door. Morgan wondered what they were doing. Did Emily hear something? Maybe there *had* been a noise he couldn't quite place, but he'd been so focused on outside that he hadn't paid it much attention.

Then a gunshot rang out from where Morgan should have been looking; he swung his head back in that direction and saw a tall man with a rifle pointed toward their window. Morgan started to lift his own gun, but it felt like an ice pick was jabbed into his left shoulder when he did. He saw his shirt was torn open, and he was starting to bleed. He slumped against the wall and slid down to the floor. As he landed, a cacophony of gunshots filled the air, engulfing him as the world started to go black.

"You know what a military crawl is?" George asked, his voice low.

"I think so," Michael said. "Never did a tour or anything, but I think I've heard of it."

"Good. Because that's basically what we're gonna do up those stairs. If we stay skinny, I figure there's enough space for us to go up side by side. This will keep us low to take away their height advantage, and should be a hell of a lot quieter than marching up. You ready?"

Michael nodded, but George didn't see confidence in him. That might be understandable—this was a dangerous situation. He probably hadn't been through too many of those, where his life was hanging in the balance. George had debated taking William with him since he had law enforcement experience, but he didn't trust Michael enough to turn his back to him when Michael was armed. George knew if he and William were both crawling up the stairs and Michael decided to switch teams, he could quickly take all three of them out and then get upstairs to help the aliens even the score.

Would he do that? George wanted to believe Michael was committed to Audrey's mission, but he never got the sense that Michael completely bought in like the rest of them had. He still had a foot in Stephanie's idealized world, and George wasn't convinced he could ever be fully pulled away from that mindset. If it were up to him, Michael would be on the deportation chopping block or locked away, but Audrey still felt like there was value to be pulled out of him, so here they were.

Which meant this was also a good opportunity for a test. Michael wasn't going to be able to sit back and watch events unfold. George was going to throw him right into it.

He laid on his stomach, feet on the floor at the foot of the stairs, arms bent a few stairs ahead of him, his rifle laid underneath and parallel to his right arm. Michael mimicked his position, squeezing in next to him on the stairwell. George gave a quick nod, and then started up, sliding his stomach along the steps, alternating arms and legs powering him upward as he went. It wasn't comfortable, and it was tight with Michael beside him, but they were able to stay nearly silent, absent an occasional knock of their rifles against the steps.

George didn't want to rush; they were methodical about the climb, all the better to avoid making noise and ensure there wasn't a slip. He knew if a foot slid off a step, if one of them dropped their rifle or yelled out after banging a knee, the aliens upstairs would hear them, and there was a good chance they'd be shot before they could get in position to fire back. That was the disadvantage of crawling up the stairs—they were borderline defenseless if caught by a foe with firepower and the higher ground. But it would give them the element of surprise if they could execute it well.

And George knew they'd done that as his right arm hit the landing at the top of the stairs, pulling his chest up over the top and then resting on his elbows. Michael scooted up next to him, both of their rifles pointing ahead down the hall. Now, George thought, the advantage was theirs.

They looked at each other, and George started to smile. Michael's brow furrowed.

"What now?" Michael silently mouthed the words.

George's smile widened. He lifted his left arm and put his hand against the wall, right next to the door to the bedroom where the aliens were waiting. Then he scratched, not too loudly, but enough that he thought they'd hear it and wonder what the noise would be. If they opened the door to investigate, George and Michael were in position to fire immediately. If not, hopefully he could at least get their attention away from the window for a minute or two while Audrey's man got the position he needed.

George pointed his rifle at the door and motioned for Michael to do the same. Now, all they could do was wait. The silence hung heavy in the hall as George listened for any sign of movement, something to suggest they'd heard the scratch and were reacting. But he heard nothing. What was going on in that room? There was no way to know; until they heard the gunshot from outside or the door started to open, all they could do was lie there, prone against the stairs. Michael's rifle was rattling a bit; his hands were shaking, and sweat was trickling down his cheeks. George thought again about Michael's lack of experience in these sorts of situations. This was the partner he'd chosen, though. He was going to have to ride it out with him. This would be such close range that he hoped it'd be hard for Michael to miss.

Then the shot blared, that unmistakable sound rattling inside the room. There was silence for another beat, and then George heard a woman's scream, along with footsteps running to the other side of the room. He knew they'd never have a better chance as the chaos unfolded behind the door, and pushed himself up, signaling Michael to follow him. Standing in the hall, he pointed his rifle at the door and opened fire.

27

Stretching his fingers around a rock in his right hand, Nick peered through the shed window, standing high on his toes to scan as much as he could inside and decide if it was worth breaking the window and climbing inside. He hadn't found anything in Leslie's house to help him get into the chest, but then he remembered Michael telling him about the shed he and Stephanie had found in Zac's back yard, and that they'd been about to break in when Michael discovered the gurney they were looking for hidden under some shrubbery across the yard.

Now, Nick stood looking into the same window Stephanie had been eyeing that day, thinking about squeezing through it to get inside. He was a little taller than Stephanie, and probably had a bit more upper-body strength. She was leaner, but not by a significant amount. It crossed his mind that pre-pandemic Nick would have laughed his ass off if you'd have asked him to get through this window; he'd have pictured himself dangling from the side of the shed, his love handles unforgiving against the edges of the narrow opening. But he guessed he had to be down close to 100 pounds from his highest weight; a diet of little more than fish and vegetables wasn't one that was fit for maintaining a chubby middle-aged-man body.

The inside of the shed looked cluttered and haphazard, shabby metal shelving half empty while tools littered the floor and hung from hooks on the walls. Three shovels with chunks of red clay still clinging to them, garden shears turning brown with encroaching rust, a wheelbarrow with a wheel missing so it lolled helplessly to one side. Nothing in sight that was going to cut open a padlock, but there was plenty he couldn't see. He didn't know where else to look for the right tool, so he figured this was his best shot. Nick lifted the rock, looked toward the street to make sure no one was watching, and smashed it into the window. The glass splintered immediately, nearly cutting his hand as it crashed into the bottom side of the window frame, pieces clattering onto the metal shelving and the grass at Nick's feet.

He rubbed the rock around the window frame, breaking off any excess glass that could cut him as he slid through. The last thing he needed to come away with out of this was a gash—or lots of little cuts—that could get infected. Then he took a dish towel he brought from Leslie's house and tried to sweep away as many small shards as he could, particularly on the bottom where his hands were going to be. It wasn't going to be perfectly clean — he could tell some very small pieces of glass were going to stubbornly cling to the imperfections in the surface no matter what he did — but he wanted to make it as safe as he possibly could before he threw himself up there.

Nick carefully placed his palms on the bottom of the window frame and pressed down slowly, waiting to feel little bits of glass. When he felt confident enough, he took a deep breath and pushed down, putting all his weight onto those hands, his arms straight and taut as he lifted his chest over the threshold. Slipping onto his stomach, he could reach one of the metal shelves and grabbed it, pulling the rest of his body up.

He yanked on the shelving, sliding his chest and then stomach onto the top shelf and getting his legs up into the window. As he started to ease them over to the shelf, he heard a loud creak and felt his balance shifting away from the window; before he had time to adjust, the shelving was collapsing beneath him. In the brief seconds before he hit the ground, he looked for something to grab onto, something to prevent him from falling onto whatever might await him below, but there was no lifeline. No coincidental rope hanging from the ceiling. All he could do was brace for impact.

The first thing he felt was something metallic near the small of his back and then a wooden smack against the back of his head as he hit the concrete floor with all his weight, the shelving tumbling down on top of him, a tack hammer hitting him in the side and a rubber mallet sending a bolt of pain up his leg as it collided with his right ankle.

Then, as quickly as everything fell apart underneath him, it was all still again. He shook his head and took a breath, rolling over to reveal a shovel he'd landed on. As he did, he kicked at the shelving, brittle and weak, bending at his will across to the other side of the shed. He crawled away from where he'd landed, pushing himself to his feet and stretching, trying to figure out if he was hurt. There was a light pounding in his head; he reached to the back of it and touched, wincing at a stab of pain. Twisting, he could feel some soreness in his back, but it wasn't too bad. He noticed there was a tear in the right shoulder of his shirt, then noticed the gnarly blades of a hand tiller he must have missed landing on by mere inches.

Near the tiller, poking out from underneath the mess, he saw a pair of long black grips. He paused for a second before scrambling over and grabbing them. He pulled, but they didn't budge easily. He kicked at the pile of stuff on top of them, but they were still too buried. He started moving things by hand, tossing them carelessly across the shed, metallic clanks hitting the wall. As he did, he revealed more of the tool—long, red, parallel arms reaching forward. Finally, when it looked uncovered enough, he yanked again, and it mercifully began to move, a little bit at first, then fully unearthed after one final hard pull.

He stood and looked, then began to smile. Bolt cutters. Time to head back to Leslie's place.

Nick stared down at the chest's lock, the bolt cutters in his right hand, flashlight shining from his left. He laid down the flashlight with the beam pointed at the chest, then lifted the cutters and stepped forward, opening up the blades and bringing them up to the shackle. He squeezed the handles together, and the blades closed around the shackle, taking it into a vice grip. Nick hoped for a quick slice, but that didn't come. He squeezed harder, his muscles tightening, forearms burning as he waited for the lock to snap.

After several seconds, he loosened his grip and let the bolt cutters rest on the floor as he caught his breath. He wondered how long they'd been sitting in that shed, collecting dust and whatever else. Had they been used a lot? Were they ever sharpened? He wasn't an expert, and really couldn't tell much by looking at them. If this didn't work, he didn't know what his next step would be. Surely there were other sheds in town that might have stray tools, but he couldn't think of one. And it wasn't like he could go door to door asking to borrow someone's bolt cutters. Besides, he was running out of time.

Before he could try the lock again, he heard a pop in the distance and stood up straight, listening. Then there were a few more, followed by silence. Gunshots? What else could they be? He wondered what had just happened. Emily, Xavier, and the rest didn't deserve to be banished from the town, and they certainly didn't deserve to be shot on sight. But Nick didn't have time to dwell on it at the moment. He had a job to do, and he needed to maintain the resolve to get it done.

He lifted the bolt cutters again and settled them into place. He took a deep breath, expanding his chest as far as it would go and holding the air in for a few beats of his heart.

Build up the tension. Steady yourself. Ready to put everything you have into this.

Finally exhaling, he squeezed the handles again, a deep sound slowly rising up his throat, tumbling off his tongue and building to a crescendo, all sandpaper and determination. The yell climbed the walls and echoed through Leslie's attic, Nick's arms exploding as he screamed, his head turned to the roof. Throat raw. Shoulders pierced by a thousand pins. He refused to give. He could handle finding nothing in this chest. But he couldn't bear the idea of letting this lock beat him. In the moment, he was going to be heard by the heavens themselves before he let this lock escape the morning intact.

Then, suddenly, the blades jerked together, and he heard a

thunk on the attic floor. His eyes flew open—his lids were sore from being pressed so tightly together—and he looked ahead. Lying in front of the chest and glistening in the flashlight's beam was the padlock body, snapped from the shackle that dangled from the chest.

Hurriedly, he dropped the bolt cutters and pulled the shackle out, tossing it across the room. He shook his arms and rolled his shoulders, still feeling the effects of breaking the lock, then tucked his fingers under the lid and slowly lifted.

As the inside of the chest revealed itself, he kept seeing nothing. How could it be possible, though? What reason would there be to lock an empty chest? Had Hank forgotten nothing was in it, and just locked it absent-mindedly? Surely, after all this, there was something more to it than that.

The lid opened all the way now, resting back on its hinges, Nick leaned forward to scan every inch of its insides. When he did, he finally saw it wasn't empty. At the bottom, lying alone, was a square of red cloth.

Is that…?

He reached in and touched it, then picked it up to examine it more closely, turning it to see nothing unusual on either side. He was sure. It was the voting cloth for Audrey. Hank would have hung Stephanie's green one out of his window the morning of the election—the day he died—but the red one somehow ended up locked by itself in his chest.

They only received those voting cloths the previous day, so that meant Hank, in one of the last things he did while he was still alive—likely while suffering from the debilitating effects of the virus—removed anything else from this chest to place only the cloth inside, then locked it and got rid of the key. Why?

Nick didn't know the answer, but he hoped maybe someone else would. He tucked the cloth into his pocket and left for the hospital.

28

The sound deafening, Michael cringed as he pretended to pull the trigger on his rifle, George firing round after round into the bedroom, obliterating most of the door in the process.

Michael slid to his left, pressing himself up against the wall closest to the bedroom to make himself a small target for any bullets that were flying out. He couldn't see anything inside, just George's body convulsing each time he pulled the trigger.

Poking out the door, Michael saw a rifle barrel quickly jut out into the hall and fire. Then George flinched wildly, slamming against the wall behind him, dropping his gun and reaching for his right shoulder. It fired again; George screamed as his left leg collapsed underneath him, and he clutched his thigh.

Footsteps came rapidly up the stairs behind Michael, William nearly stepping on him to get to the hall, firing his gun wildly, and Audrey's men with him barreling through what was left of the door with their guns held steady at shoulder height.

Michael's head fell to the floor as silence once again fell on the hall, replacing the chaos that probably only lasted a few seconds but felt like hours. He was suddenly exhausted, adrenaline draining from his body like water through a sieve. He knew all the immigrants—Xavier, Emily, Morgan, and Grace—were lying dead in that room. All of them. Gone. Lives snuffed out in mere moments, as if they'd never been there. They didn't deserve this. They didn't do anything wrong. They accepted an invitation to live in this little community, then did their best to contribute wherever they could. And for that, they were pinned down and violently murdered.

Then there was a woman's voice, and Michael lifted his head to hear it better.

"No! No! He's hurt!" Emily yelled. "We need to get him to the hospital. Wait! What are you doing? Stop!"

Michael heard a man's guttural scream, and then one of Audrey's men emerged in the hall, dragging Xavier down the stairs by his arms, stretched high above his head. The other large man came out with Emily flung across his shoulder like a sack of flour, yelling and beating on his back as they went down the stairs.

William scrambled out of the room and fell at George's feet.

"What's wrong? Where are you hit?" William asked, as George grimaced and moaned, then pointed at where the bullets struck him. "Okay. We need to get you to the hospital ASAP. Michael, you need to fucking run there. Tell them we need the goddamn ambulance!"

Michael was still in a daze, and his ears were ringing. He heard the words, but it sounded more like a nearly unintelligible warble than real English. His breathing was shallow and thin, feeling like he couldn't get enough oxygen. He could tell William was asking him to do something, because William was looking at him with a mix of urgency and annoyance that made Michael want to punch him in the face. But he didn't have the energy for that, and he was pretty sure that meant he didn't have the energy for whatever William was asking him to do either.

"Benjamin's dead!" Andy yelled up from the bottom of the stairs. "They fucking *killed* Benjamin! Those filthy alien bastards! If they're not already dead, I'm gonna kill the rest of them with my bare goddamn hands."

Andy stepped over Michael into the bedroom. William took off his shirt and ripped it in half, then wrapped one piece around George's thigh and another across his shoulder.

"Where the hell *are* they? I know there were four of them," Andy said, coming back out into the hall. "I only see two bodies lying in there. If any of them got away, I swear to god…"

"The men took 'em," William said as he tied the second piece of fabric. "They're gone."

"You mean they got out of here fucking *alive*? After that? Not a chance. I'm chasing those assholes down."

He started for the stairs, but William leapt up and pushed a hand to his chest, slamming him against the wall.

"There's no time for that. Okay? They're done. Don't worry about them. George needs help. He needs an ambulance. You need to run to the hospital, as fast as you can. Tell them to get the ambulance here, fucking *now*. Or we're gonna lose George."

"But I…"

"*Go*! Now!"

Andy blinked a few times, then stiffened his shoulders and sprinted down the stairs. Michael glanced up and saw William glaring at him, but he had nothing left within him to worry about that. The room started to swirl around him, and Michael could feel his stomach turning. In a full convulsion, Michael vomited on the floor next to his rifle, and William jumped out of the way. It felt like the world was shifted on its axis, nothing still, nothing firm.

Then it all went black.

29

Stephanie nudged the door open and peeked inside; Michael rolled over in bed and looked at her.

"How are you doing?" Stephanie asked as she walked toward the bed and rolled a chair over.

He sat up halfway and fluffed up his pillow, leaning back against the headboard.

"Not too bad. Headache's…not gone, but pretty dull. I think I'm mostly all right."

"Good." Stephanie smiled. "We'll be getting you out of here soon. I'll have Victor bring your regular clothes up so you can get dressed and head out whenever you want."

"How long was I out?"

"You've been asleep for the better part of thirty hours or so, I'd guess. Mostly dehydration. Since the, um, incident with the immigrants."

"Oh, shit. What happened there? Where is everyone?"

Stephanie bowed her head, and then looked up, fighting back tears. She paused and cleared her throat.

"By the time we got to Morgan and Grace, they were dead. Shot in that room." She swallowed hard, biting her lip. "Emily and Xavier were sent away. Locked out of the town. For a while, we could hear Emily screaming."

Stephanie had to stop, shutting her eyes tightly as tears streamed down her face. She shook her head and pressed her palms into her cheeks, wiping the tears away and trying to get her voice back.

"You could...hear her screams through most of the town. It was unbearable, Michael. She said Xavier had been shot, and he'd die out there. I tried to go down there, maybe convince them to at least let him get the medical attention he needed. But when I got to the front door of the building, one of Audrey's men was standing there with a rifle pointed at me. He shook his head. There was nothing I could do."

"Good god," Michael said. "So what happened?"

"I don't know." Stephanie shrugged. "Eventually, the screaming stopped. I guess she gave up, but I don't know. Maybe they can figure something out. They're pretty resourceful. And hopefully they'll find Derrick out there too."

"Or maybe Emily and Derrick both will end up scared and alone."

Stephanie nodded silently, starting to cry again.

"What about George?" Michael asked. "Did he make it? I remember him being shot."

Stephanie took a deep breath. "Yeah. You two shared the ambulance over here. He's a couple of rooms down."

"Shit. He killed them all, Stephanie. He stood outside that room and fired his gun through the door, trying to kill everyone in there. I didn't fire a single shot, I swear. I just...couldn't do it. But I'm stuck. Do you understand? If they know I'm not with them, they're gonna kill me. The only chance we have to get Alessandra back is to keep pushing forward, together."

Stephanie wrapped Michael's hand in hers and squeezed, then patted it lightly. She knew she'd probably never fully get over Michael voting against her, or wondering what this world would be like if he'd voted the other way. They had Alessandra, and he handed it over to someone else. Now, they were back in a position of having to wrestle it back from the forces threatening to tear it apart. But she'd been far from perfect herself, and she had to accept that they were flawed people who made mistakes. The question of someone's character wasn't whether or not they screwed up, but how they reacted to those missteps and took steps to correct them. Given the hand they'd been dealt, Michael was trying to play it as well as he could.

She stood up to leave, but then stopped.

"Oh, and big news," she said. "That little mission you sent Nick on? It may have paid off. Get this…the chest was empty except for one thing—a red voting cloth from the election."

Michael sat up a bit, and his eyes narrowed. "A red voting cloth? The one for Audrey? That's strange. What do you think it means?"

"That's what I'm working on now. I don't think Hank locked it in that chest for no reason. If I'm right, it could be the evidence we need. Also, one more thing…while we're hopefully pinning one crime on Audrey and her crew, want to help me nail them for one more?"

On her way back to the lab, Stephanie stopped in front of George's room. She knew she should get back to the research, but she couldn't help herself.

As she walked in, she saw George unconscious and hooked up to several tubes. In the old world, neither of the bullet wounds would have been likely to do any long-term harm. Neither hit a major organ or artery. But infection was always a threat in post-virus Alessandra, so it was important they did what they could to hold that off if they were going to keep him alive.

Was that what they wanted, though? George had murdered Morgan and Grace—and tried to do the same to Emily and Xavier. How had he gotten to that point? He'd once been a trusted member of Stephanie's own team, with the essential job of keeping watch over the town's entrance. She would have never thought he'd be capable of doing anything like this. What was it about people who worked under Audrey that they almost always got caught up in her spell? That they'd defend anything she did, and violate all their principles for her? How did someone so vile and so tyrannical inspire such loyalty among her followers? Were they actually convinced she was doing the right thing? Did they see the immense power she had, and want a piece of it for themselves? Or did they see the way she treated those who opposed her and figure it was better to be the friend of the totalitarian than to be crushed under her boot?

The psychology of it was hard for Stephanie to understand. It wasn't something she could sympathize with. The sheer selfishness of it, of being a leader who replaced the interests of Alessandra with your own. Audrey could spin these decisions in whatever way she wanted, but she knew that was exactly what she was doing. She was building a metaphorical castle around her power, and guarding it with sycophants who would cheer when she tossed breadcrumbs from the balcony.

Looking down at George now, Stephanie felt a mixture of pity and disgust. Was he still the man she'd known before, or had that George been overridden, replaced by a blind follower of beneficial tyranny? They were doing all this work to keep him alive, but for what? So he could continue to enforce Audrey's insane rules and terrorize the town? Maybe they'd all be better off if there was one fewer Audrey follower in Alessandra.

She'd never stood over a patient and been tempted to do anything other than everything she could to save them. But, standing there, she felt an overwhelming urge come over her; there was an extra pillow beside George. He was already unconscious and plausibly teetering on death. No one would be surprised to find him without a pulse. Nobody would suspect a thing.

Stephanie walked carefully around the bed, making as little noise as possible. She lifted the pillow and held it below her chin. Two, maybe three minutes. That was all it would take. He probably wouldn't thrash around or anything. Hell, he'd probably never wake up. Just continue further into the deep sleep he was already in. In a way, it'd be a kindness. George wouldn't have to feel all this hatred and anger anymore. He could fade into oblivion, leaving this cruel world behind.

She leaned across the bed, clutching the pillow tightly in her hands. She really wanted to do this. It was the right thing to do. Hold it there for a couple of minutes, and the rest would take care of itself. It would be easy.

Leaning over further, the pillow inches from George's face, Stephanie heard footsteps outside the door, and she froze as Victor walked inside.

"Oh. Hey, Doctor Sloan," he said, glancing up from his paperwork. "What are you doing in here?"

"Switching him to a fresh pillow." Stephanie pounded the pillow with her fists, slid the old pillow out from under George, and put the new one underneath his head. "Thought he'd probably been on the old one for a while."

"Oh, that's okay. You don't have to do that stuff. That's what I'm here for."

Stephanie laughed. "Yeah, I know. I was just here. Can't take the nurse out of the doctor, ya know?"

"Totally get it. Thanks for the help."

30

"I don't trust Michael, and neither did…*does* George," Andy said, Audrey looking on from behind her desk. "He's not one of us, Ms. Reese. I think we need to do something."

"It sounds like you're questioning my judgment," Audrey said. "I think you should watch yourself."

"With all due respect, Ms. Reese. I understand. I'm not trying to question you. But *we're* the ones who are out there with him from day to day, seeing how he behaves, getting a feel for his mindset. And I'm saying we don't like what we see."

Audrey stood up and walked around her desk, leaning against it. "Just because he's not as enthusiastically bloodthirsty as you might be, that doesn't mean we need to take some drastic action. He's smart. He has the respect of the people of the town. Having him as part of my team helps bring credibility to *all of us*."

"That's politics, and—"

"Politics fucking *matter*, Andrew. You've never been in charge of shit, so I understand you've never been in a position to care about that, but politics matter. Optics matter. The credibility of an administration matters. I'm able to be more aggressive in my policies because Michael is perceived as trustworthy, one of them. If he's still on board with what we're doing, they figure, there must be something to it."

"You don't need that, though. No one's questioning your authority. You can do what you want."

"Can we run roughshod over everyone, implementing whatever the hell we want? Sure. That's what I did before. But look where that got me. And I'll be *damned* if I'm letting this town turn on me again. Michael's a tool to help protect me from that. So you're gonna have to bring me something a lot stronger than you not trusting him for us to do anything to him."

"There were no spent casings," said William, standing in the corner of the room. "Underneath Michael when we picked him up outside the room where the aliens were camped out. No spent casings from his rifle."

Audrey turned her head toward William. Silence hung over the room for a moment.

"No casings?" she asked.

"Not a one."

"And next to George?"

"A bunch of them lying around everywhere."

"So what are you suggesting?"

William looked at Andy, then back to Audrey. "We don't think he fired."

Audrey turned to Andy. "Is that right?"

Andy shrugged.

"Were they both using the same gun?" she asked.

William nodded. "Yeah. The Ruger. We all were. We've got that stash of them in the basement."

"How do you know the casings underneath George weren't also some of Michael's? The Ruger's semiautomatic. Casings can fly several feet, and he didn't have a wall behind him to knock them down like George did, from how I understand it. Isn't that right?"

"Well…sure," William said. "But you think *all* of them ended up next to George?"

"Did you guys also find some on the stairs?"

"I don't think—" William started.

"There were a couple." Andy shook his head. "I had to step over one when I ran up."

Audrey smiled and glared at William, who sank back against the wall.

"If you're going to accuse men I've appointed of being traitors, you need to come stronger than this, guys. I refuse to be made a fool. And I'm not going to jeopardize what we're doing here because you all can't fucking get along. This isn't high school. This is an unforgiving world that we're living in, and petty in-fighting isn't gonna get us anywhere. So Michael is not to be touched. You understand? He's one of us, unless he shows he isn't. Got it?"

They both nodded.

"But I will do one thing," Audrey said. "I think I have a way to…keep an eye on him, let's say. Stephanie too. I think he'll prove me right. We're gonna have to see."

Walking in the back door of Stephanie's old house, Michael was flooded with memories. Mornings curled up on the couch together. Making meals in the kitchen. The aroma of oregano and basil simmering in a pot, filling the house. That time he banged his shin on the coffee table and they spent ten minutes laughing through the pain. They'd had their share of fights and disagreements here, but this had largely been a place of happiness for them. And he'd been a big part of putting an end to that.

He needed to focus, though. He was here for a reason, and he couldn't afford to waste time. Audrey and her crew still thought he was in the hospital, so they wouldn't be keeping an eye out for him, which meant he had a better chance to slip away undetected now than at any other time.

It seemed Michael and Stephanie were back on the same side again, but he felt very much stuck in between, having to maintain his ties to Audrey while trying to secretly undermine her when he had the chance. It wasn't where he wanted to be. He knew this was a line he wouldn't be able to continue walking for too long.

Right now, he and Stephanie were gathering evidence and building a case. Michael agreed it was the right move, but he also knew it could get them killed at any time. He felt like they were both in the gallows, noose around their necks, bags over their heads, hoping for someone to shoot the rope at the last minute. But wishing for that magic bullet was pretty long odds, and the floor was going to open up underneath them in seconds.

He walked down the hall, past pictures of Stephanie, her

family and friends. One of her and Michael in better times. Back when they were a real couple, one of millions throughout the world, imperfect, evolving, but trying hard to make it work. It felt like a lifetime ago. He'd never wished more that he could go back and tell that younger Michael to hang on to those moments as they trickle away. They're gone so fast, and if you don't look around and appreciate them as they happen, you'll regret it later. He wanted to tell his younger self that was as good as life would get, and he should try harder not to let it walk away. Not to let *her* walk away.

Michael entered Stephanie's old bedroom and turned to his right, toward the closet. That was where she told him to look. He hoped she was right, because he didn't think he could risk taking the time to turn the house upside down searching. He opened the accordion door and peered inside; it was dark, and he forgot to bring a flashlight with him. He walked across the room and thought about throwing open the curtains, but the only windows in the room overlooked the front yard and street; he couldn't risk someone passing by to see him inside, so he decided to open one of them only enough to get a sliver of sunlight to cut across the room, straight into the closet.

He went back to the closet. The thin slice of light wasn't perfect, but it was enough to allow him to see some of what was inside. Stephanie told him to find a shoebox on the left upper shelf, tucked into the corner behind two large grocery bags. When he reached up, he could feel the grocery bags where she said they'd be. Michael grabbed them and pulled them down, tossing them on the floor. He couldn't see what was behind them; not only was it too dark, but the shelf was too high for him to reach easily.

Michael jumped and stretched his arm as far as it could go toward the back of the shelf, and it did feel like there was a shoebox back there. He was six-foot-two and couldn't reach it, so how had Stephanie gotten it back there? He figured there had to be a small ladder somewhere, but he didn't know where. He took a step back and leaped forward with more force, slapping the side of the shoebox but not getting any real grip on it.

Looking to his right, he noticed the light hitting a large plastic storage container underneath a pile of clothes and shoes. He swept everything aside, sliding the box out and climbing on top. It wasn't the sturdiest object—he felt like he might fall straight through the lid at any moment—but it was tall enough that he could get his hands on the shoebox.

He pulled it toward him, and took it down from the shelf, stumbling and nearly falling as he hopped off the box. Michael laid the shoebox on top of the container and pulled off the lid. There was one thing inside, and it was exactly what Stephanie had told him would be there—the knife, sealed inside a plastic zip-top bag. The knife he'd found in her house after Zac's murder, that made him think she did it. Turned out, she hadn't gotten rid of it. She kept it. And now Stephanie said she believed it could help them prove the murderer was Audrey and not her.

Michael put the lid back on the shoebox and started to step around the container when he heard a creak from the front of the house, and his heart stopped. A click as a door closed and then light footsteps. Suddenly, he wasn't alone.

31

"Hey, Nick." Stephanie pulled off her rubber gloves as she walked from the lab into the hospital's lobby. "What brings you by?"

"Wanted to check in on Michael. Heard he ended up here. Also curious if you've learned anything yet about the cloth I dropped off."

Stephanie shook her head. "Afraid you're gonna strike out on both for now. Nothing on the cloth, but we're making progress. Give us another day, and I think we'll have a result. As for Michael…" Stephanie looked around and leaned in closer to Nick. "Don't say anything, but he's not here. He's fine. He was dehydrated and probably in some sort of shock. But I sent him to my old place to get the knife I think killed Zac. Once he brings it back, I think we can show Audrey did it."

"Damn. And he's doing that now?"

"As we speak. Should be back any minute, in fact. Always hard to tell how much time has passed, but it feels like it's been a little bit."

"Enough to be worried?"

Stephanie looked away, tapping her toes on the floor.

"No. No, I think it's probably fine. But he should be back soon if you want to hang around."

Nick shrugged. "What else am I gonna do?"

Stephanie reached out and gave Nick a quick hug, then turned to go back to the lab when she heard someone come through the hospital's front door. She swung around to see Leslie, hands tied in front of her, with William close behind. Stephanie forced a smile and walked toward them.

"Good to see you, Leslie," she said. "What can I do for you two?"

"She's sick," William said. "Her stomach has been hurting. Been throwing up and stuff. Maybe food poisoning. We're not sure."

Stephanie looked sideways at William, trying to keep her focus on Leslie. "Okay. Does that all sound right, Leslie?"

Head down, she nodded silently.

This seemed strange to Stephanie. Leslie didn't present like most food poisoning victims she'd seen. Especially once vomiting and stomach pain began, most people were pretty much confined to bed for a bit. They certainly weren't walking a half mile across town. Yet here Leslie was, agreeing with whatever William said.

And this was the worst possible time for William to show up. If Michael walked in now, wielding a large knife wrapped in a plastic bag, there was no telling how bad this was going to get.

"All right, then. So you're dropping her off, William?"

"Yeah. And I'd like to see George and Michael before I go. Report back to Audrey on how they're doing."

Stephanie turned to the reception desk and tapped a red button that triggered two beeps through the hospital's intercom.

"That'll get one of our nurses down here quickly to take Leslie to a room and get her set up. As for George and Michael, I can provide you with an update right here if that's all you need."

"It'd really be better if I could see them myself."

Victor came bounding down the stairs.

"Victor, take Leslie up to Room 4A and get her started on some fluids," Stephanie said. "We think she may have food poisoning."

He nodded and took her by the arm, leading her upstairs.

"So…" Stephanie turned to William and smiled. "Both of them have had a fairly recent round of emazepam, and they're sleeping. It'd be dangerous for you to disturb them at the moment. But we could gradually wake them if needed. It's the only way to be safe if you really have to see them. It'll take roughly half an hour."

"Fine. I can wait."

"Okay, then. I'll have Victor administer that after he gets Leslie set up. We'll do George first. I'll let you know when he's ready for you. You can wait here in the lobby."

William eyed Nick as he pulled a chair out and sat down.

"Nick," Stephanie said. "I have a couple of minutes free to show you what we were talking about up in my office. You want to come with me?"

Nick looked confused, but then perked up. "Oh. Yes. Wasn't expecting you to have time that quickly. Thanks. Let's go on up."

When they got to her office, Stephanie shut the door behind him.

"Shit," she said. "Okay, so I bought us about a half hour, assuming William doesn't try to go rogue in the meantime. I'll try to keep an eye on him. Or have *someone* keep an eye on him. I don't know. But you need to find Michael and get him the *fuck* back here, okay? And bring him in the back way. We can't have him strolling in the front door with William sitting right there."

"What's the back way?"

"It's through the loading dock. Michael's spent enough time here visiting me. He'll know what you mean. Just get to my house, fast. Hopefully, you'll run into him on the way. But get him back here and in his bed as goddamn fast as you can."

32

Michael stood stock-still, trying to control his breathing, the box lying in front of him. Who was inside the house? Did they know Michael was there too, or was this a random intruder with particularly bad timing? Michael's chest thumped so loud that he could swear the other person would be able to hear it; he wanted to smother it with his arms to muffle the sound, a full-body drumbeat.

Was his best bet to stay in the closet and wait? Or was there a better place to hide? Even if there was a better spot, it was probably too risky to get there. The house was so quiet that the sounds of any footsteps on these wood floors would surely carry down the hall, giving him away.

But the closet door was still open. Closing it would provide him with a bit more time and security. Maybe this other person wouldn't even bother looking inside a shut closet. If he didn't know Michael was there, why would he? And if this person did push open the closet door, Michael could have the element of surprise.

Now, there was a question, though—did the door creak when he opened it the first time? He wished he remembered. It had all been so quick. This was supposed to be a fast stop. Get in, grab the knife, get out. It hadn't occurred to him to note if the door had a squeaky hinge.

He decided the hinges were all too old, too poorly maintained over the past few years. It wasn't worth taking the chance, as much as he wanted the door closed. In case this person meant him harm, he couldn't afford to give himself away that easily.

Instead, he quietly lifted the box with the knife in it and slowly lowered himself, squatting behind the large storage container he'd climbed on top of to reach the shelf. He found that if he got low enough, it had enough height to conceal him. Carefully, he slid it back further into the closet, pinning himself between it and the pile of stuff against the back wall.

Footsteps were coming down the hall, methodically covering the same distance he had a few minutes earlier. The person didn't seem to be checking any other rooms. As far as Michael could tell, the person was coming straight back to Stephanie's bedroom, as if they knew he was there.

Or because they wanted the knife too, and knew where it was.

The intruder stepped into the room and stopped. Michael swore he could hear the person breathing, heavy and rough like sandpaper on skin. Michael instinctually held his breath, wanting not to make the slightest noise. Footsteps began again, then stopped for a few seconds. A couple more steps, and another pause. Then a jarring screech as the bed tore across the floor, slamming into a wall. Whoever this was had flung a king-sized bed across the room like it was a pillowcase.

The footsteps came closer, marching over and stopping at the threshold of the closet. Michael didn't dare look, rolled tight into a ball, as close to the floor as possible, tucked tightly behind the box. He was confident the person couldn't see him. Not without making a real effort to look back there, anyway. And if they did, Michael was going to be ready.

For the moment, though, all he could do was wait, listening to their breathing as they stood there. Michael closed his eyes and prayed they'd leave. Decide the house was empty and walk out.

Then it happened; the footsteps began again, headed away from the closet and back across the bedroom. Michael almost felt like he could breathe again, but remained still, listening closely. Was he going to get out of this? His heart continued to beat fast, echoing in his chest. It was almost over. He waited to hear the footsteps leave the room, go down the hall, and then out the front door, clicking shut behind him.

But suddenly there was silence again. The steps didn't seem to be moving now. Nothing. Just stillness. What was happening? Why weren't they continuing to go? *Please go.*

Four big stomps tore across the floor and into the closet. Michael barely had time to register what was happening before the container box was jerked violently away and he was exposed, looking up at a mountain of a man hunched over him and snarling. Michael shook.

Nick figured it took him less than ten minutes to get to Stephanie's old house, as he approached the back door. As long as Michael was inside, they'd have plenty of time to get him back in place at the hospital before William went to check on him. Maybe he was having trouble finding the knife? If so, another set of eyes couldn't hurt.

If Michael wasn't there, though—whether he'd been spotted and taken away or took an unusual route back to the hospital—Nick didn't want to think about what would happen next. Nothing good. He knew that much.

His feelings toward Michael and Stephanie were complicated. He sort of lamented the fact that they were still his best friends, through everything, and that said more about his own isolation than it did about their closeness. He'd gotten to know Hank a little bit, but then he died from the virus. He had such a history with Michael and Stephanie, and he knew they trusted him more than anyone else. That was why they always eventually came to him when times got difficult. And that was why, despite sometimes feeling used, he always put aside his pride and helped where he could. They were the only people who *did* trust him. And something deep down made him want to hold on to that.

That was on his mind as he turned the knob and pushed open the back door, stepping inside. He was ready to walk in normally and shout Michael's name, but he noticed the front door was cracked open, a sliver of light slashing across the living room couch. Nick stopped.

Surely, Michael wouldn't have used the front door. Seemed too risky. And if he had, it'd make no sense at all to leave the door open and signal that someone was inside. That was inviting people to come investigate, and that was the last thing he'd want. Nick couldn't imagine Michael would be that sloppy. And if Michael didn't leave the front door open, that meant someone else had.

Just then, Nick heard a loud crash from the back bedroom, and Michael yelled. Feet scrambled across the wood floor, and something large slammed into a wall. Nick's heartbeat picked up its pace, and he was frozen for a moment. Michael was here. And he wasn't alone.

Nick sprinted down the hall and entered the bedroom to see one of Audrey's men, his back hunched, stalking toward Michael curled up in the far corner of the room, blood starting to trickle down his forehead. The mountainous man hadn't taken notice of Nick yet, as he stood still in the doorway, trying to assess the situation. Nick leaned over to look around the man and make eye contact with Michael, who shook his head and seemed to quickly see Nick before looking away.

Nick wasn't sure what to do. The man didn't appear to have a weapon, beyond those massive limbs. They could try to take him two on one, but Nick didn't see any chance they'd win that fight without some other advantage. Had Michael found the knife? If so, it didn't look like he had it. And if he didn't have a knife, Michael was about to be either beaten into dust or taken away to be killed later.

So Nick stomped his foot three times loudly; the man stopped walking toward Michael and turned around, a menacing sneer on his face. The man began coming after Nick, and he was quicker than he looked like he would be. Even with all that bulk, those powerful legs churned forward when they wanted to, and the man was nearly on top of Nick before he had time to react. Quickly, Nick slid across the floor to his left, his feet nudging against the wall underneath the front windows as the man lunged for him and missed.

Stumbling onto an elbow and falling onto his back, Nick began crab-walking backward, toward the corner where Michael had been. Before he could get there, though, Michael leapt up and began running. Was he leaving Nick there to deal with this monster? Then Michael ducked into the closet, rummaging quickly before emerging with what looked like something wrapped in a plastic bag. Looking more closely, Nick realized it was a large knife.

Nick felt himself being lifted in the air, his feet dangling, kicking wildly as they begged for solid ground. Mammoth hands wrapped around his throat and he gasped, looking for air he couldn't find. He pounded the man's arms, but it was like beating on a tree trunk. They didn't budge, as if he hadn't felt it at all. Nick could feel the life draining out of him, the desperation of not knowing if you'd ever taste oxygen again. His feet kicked, arms flailed, but he didn't have much energy left. Nick's eyes began to close.

Then, he felt the grip loosen, and he crashed to the floor, crumpled into a ball in the corner. Nick rubbed his sore neck and opened his eyes, looking up to see the man swinging his arms at Michael, whose knife and plastic bag were now covered in blood. Nick still felt weak, but a surge of adrenaline got him on his feet; he ran over and kicked at the man, trying to sweep his legs out from underneath him. The man's knees didn't buckle, but that did get his attention, prompting him to swing wildly toward Nick, connecting with his shoulder and sending him stumbling across the room.

The man then screamed, clutching at his right side as Michael yanked the knife away and thrust it deep into the man's left side. The man tried to swing again, but there was less energy in it, and he missed Michael while throwing himself off balance. He tried to catch himself against the wall, but he hit it hard, his head banging into it first, then his back, and he slid down to the floor with a hollow thud, arms limp at his sides.

Michael immediately ran over to him and didn't hesitate, burying the knife in the man's throat and slashing across it, a plume of blood spraying across the room, covering Michael's shirt and much of the floor around him. The man's head slumped forward, lifeless. Dead.

33

"So, tell me what's been bothering you," Victor said, as he untied the rope that was securing Leslie wrists while she sat on the edge of a hospital bed in the middle of a stark white room.

She'd been rehearsing the answer to that question on the walk over to St. Francis. It was all a lie. She certainly had stress, and she wouldn't mind having a psychologist to talk to after everything that had happened, though she hadn't had any issues with her stomach. But they wanted her to have some ailment that would be vague enough to be difficult to detect, and would give her an excuse to stay in the hospital for at least a few days. It was better than sitting alone in that pen. She realized she was effectively trading one prison for another temporarily, but some basic human interaction and a relatively soft bed might do her some good.

The real reason she was here was that Audrey needed eyes and ears in this place, and Leslie was her best shot to have someone who was alert and on her side bringing her intel from St. Francis. She was supposed to pay particular attention to Michael and Stephanie. Anything she could see or hear, file it away and pass it on to one of Audrey's men. Even if it seemed like nothing, Audrey said to err on the side of telling them too much rather than not enough.

And something about the way she was told about this made Leslie suspect saying she hadn't heard anything wasn't going to be an option. She needed to dig something up. Whatever she could. She knew her life and her place in Alessandra was hanging in the balance. After her affair with Derrick, there were probably people who thought she should be banished along with the immigrants. Whatever misconceptions they had about the nature of those from outside the town, maybe he'd passed it along to her. Or, at the very least, she'd been willing to overlook that in favor of illicit lust, and that probably made her a slut on top of everything else. Even in a post-apocalyptic world, some corrosive misogynistic double standards died hard.

Leslie wasn't proud of caring about any of this. She tried to convince herself Audrey might have some legitimate purpose to all this, but she knew deep down that she was helping the enemy. And she wished she was strong enough to refuse, to risk everything on a matter of principle.

Because she'd always considered herself a strong person. In her old life, she had been a proud entrepreneur, being frugal for years to save up enough money to buy a franchise of a regional fast-casual restaurant, and rolling the resulting fortune into five more locations across Georgia. She employed hundreds of people, running her restaurants tightly to the books, hiring the right people, and pushing them to give their best every day. It was a role she felt like she'd been well suited for, and she'd been wildly successful as a leader.

Then the world collapsed underneath her, and no one needed franchisees anymore. Leslie's skills and business degree didn't have much of a place in the new Alessandra, and now the only goal she felt like was worthwhile was to live to see tomorrow. One day, the pendulum had to swing back toward normalcy. She'd find her place in this world again. Surely. Reality couldn't be this cruel. She just had to live long enough to see it. She had to survive today, every single day.

If that meant compromising her integrity from time to time, so be it. If that meant acting meek so her captors would go easier on her, that was what she'd do. This wasn't a world anymore where you could afford to think about everyone else's well-being. This was the immutable laws of nature writ large, underscoring every decision people made. She could lament the morally bankrupt decisions Audrey was making, but wasn't she trying to get to tomorrow as well? Wasn't everyone?

And so, Leslie settled into her bed, Victor fluffing a pillow underneath her as she laid back, more comfortable than she'd been in days. She looked up and saw the black brackets on the wall that used to hold a TV. She had a small glass of water on a tray next to her. This wasn't so bad. He'd get her an IV and some light food to try to absorb whatever might be going on in her gut. Meanwhile, she was going to do what she could to figure out what Michael and Stephanie were up to. It might not be the principled thing to do, but it would give her the best chance to see another tomorrow.

34

I don't like this.

Stephanie's mind raced as she paced the hospital's second-floor hallway, hoping to hear Nick and Michael coming up the back stairs and keeping an eye on the front in case William decided he couldn't wait any longer. She knew his patience had to be getting shorter. She could see the hospital's solar-operated clock, hanging high above the front door, so she knew it had been thirty-four minutes since she sent Nick to retrieve Michael. And if William craned his neck a little bit, he could see it too.

It shouldn't have been taking this long. She thought that maybe she hadn't left the knife where she told Michael she did, but she was ninety-five percent sure it was in that spot in the closet. Even if not, though, Nick knew how urgent it was for them to get back to the hospital quickly. If they couldn't find it right away, they had to forget about it for now and come back. Surely, Nick could convince him of that.

If there was no way they were frantically searching for the knife, that left only two possibilities: either Michael wasn't at the house and Nick was still trying to find him, or they'd run into some sort of trouble once they got there. Both were major issues, with the clock ticking incessantly. Stephanie felt so incredibly helpless. All she could do now was stall as long as possible, and hope Nick and Michael came up those stairs in time.

"Stephanie!" She heard William's voice echo from the lobby and knew it wasn't the time to register her irritation at not being called Doctor Sloan. She took a deep breath and walked toward it.

"Yes, Officer Greene?" She said, in her friendliest voice, plastering on a wide smile as she came down the stairs. "How can I help you?"

"You said it would be thirty minutes."

She maintained her smile, trying to walk him back to the seating area. "Well, that was an estimate. You have to understand nothing in medicine is exact. Different people react to drugs in different ways."

"And you're saying neither one of them is ready to be seen yet?"

"I'm sorry, officer. You'll be the first one to know when they are, though."

"I think I'm done waiting. I've got work to do, Stephanie. Important work for Audrey. I can't spend all day sitting here not doing shit. All right?"

"I understand you're a very important and busy man, and we appreciate your patience. I have to look out for the patient's best interest, though."

"Well, that's a risk we're gonna have to take. I'm going up. You can help, or you can stand in my way, and things are gonna get ugly pretty quickly."

This was what she'd been afraid of. She'd bought as much time as she could. She tried to reason with him, but that had mostly been killing time too. She kept going in her head how long it should be taking. How many times had she walked between that house and the hospital? Hundreds, at least. It was eight minutes at her normal walking speed. It had been close to forty now.

She could keep fighting him. Run up and lock the doors to both rooms. Try to stand behind the idea that she was protecting the patients, and see if that would save her in the end. But at some point, it was going to look suspicious, in addition to pissing William off. And she had to keep in mind that she was still their prisoner, and they could revoke her permission to be at the hospital at any time, tossing her back in that pen instead. Or kill her if she was causing too much trouble to be worth keeping around. She didn't have a lot of leeway here. She might have to throw a Hail Mary and hope for the best.

"Okay, officer." Still smiling, she stepped aside and began walking toward the stairs. "Follow me. We'll check in on George first. He seems to be the closest to being ready for you at the moment."

"Are we…" Michael said between pants as he sprinted across town with Nick, "…gonna make it?"

"We better…goddamn…hope so."

They knew running could draw more attention, but that was a chance they were going to have to take. Neither of them had any idea how much time had passed, but it was almost certainly more than they could afford. The fact that more of Audrey's men hadn't burst in the door at Stephanie's old house and hauled them away right then had been a good sign—maybe they hadn't quite been found out, or Stephanie hadn't told them where to look yet—but taking a leisurely stroll back to the hospital wasn't an option.

Chest burning, legs turning to mush, Michael pushed through it and charged ahead, clutching the knife in blood-smeared plastic wrap, still running through his head the events of that morning. How had that really happened? What was supposed to be a simple task of retrieving an old knife had resulted in one of Audrey's men being killed. Audrey was very protective of them, and there was no telling how severe her reaction would be once she found out.

Michael and Nick had agreed there wasn't much they could do with the body. They couldn't bury the guy. Even if the two of them could carry him outside—and, at almost certainly over 300 pounds, he would have been a load—they didn't have either the time or tools necessary to dig a grave big enough.

So what could they do other than drag him into the closet and shut the door? They did what they could to wipe up the most obvious blood, but they figured someone looking in there would still spot enough burgundy specks to investigate further. And once the man started decomposing, it would only be a matter of time before someone noticed the stench.

If they could make it back before William found out he wasn't still in his hospital room, though, Michael thought they might be okay. After all, he'd have the alibi of being laid up at St. Francis, with even William able to vouch for him. And no one would have any reason to think Nick was involved at all.

But if they didn't get there, it might not take Audrey and her team long to connect the dots.

"Stephanie said…you'd know how to get us in from here," Nick said, hopping up a couple of stairs onto the hospital's loading dock.

Michael nodded. "I know my way around the hospital pretty well. Even pulled a few shifts on the dock when they needed it back in the day."

Nick let Michael get in front, and he led them to a stairwell against the far wall, where they climbed up to the second level. They passed by rows of shelves that, prior to the virus, would have been constantly full of hospital supplies delivered to the dock. Now, though, they were dusty and nearly empty. They only saw a few stray syringes, wrapped tightly in plastic, and a box of surgical masks as they jogged down one of the aisles. Michael wondered if they even remembered those were still down here. No new deliveries were coming any time soon.

In the back corner, they went through a door and then hit the steps up to the main part of the hospital. The next two floors up were for the old parking garage, with the third being the ground floor, followed by the second floor where Michael's room was. Michael took the steps two at a time, with Nick following close behind. One flight. Two. Michael could barely believe he had the endurance for this, but adrenaline was an amazing thing.

His legs were slowing down as he turned onto the fourth flight, but he knew he had to power through. Dig deep and find the energy to get to the top. He was almost there. Just a few more steps.

Grinding hard, Michael reached the second-floor door, Nick coming up a few steps behind.

"Thanks…for coming…with me," Michael said, hands on his

knees. "You've gotta stay here, though. You're not…supposed… to be here."

Nick nodded and slammed his back against the wall, sliding down to the floor.

Michael put his hand on the door handle, pushed it down, and stopped, turning back to Nick. "Listen, though, man. If it sounds like I get caught…run. Get the fuck out. You weren't here."

Michael nudged the door open a crack, enough to see into the hall, his room twenty paces to his left.

Stephanie's heart was pounding as she escorted William up the stairs. She pushed open the door and stepped aside so William could walk through toward George, who was awake but fairly groggy and full of pain medication.

"I'll step outside and give you two a few minutes to chat," she said. "Tap on the door when you're ready to go, and I'll put him back under."

As William pulled a chair over next to the bed, Stephanie stepped back into the hall, carefully shutting the door behind her.

How much time did she have now? Five minutes? Ten? She wasn't sure George was going to be much of a conversationalist in his current state, but she hoped he could be lucid enough to keep William talking for a bit. She was beginning to lose hope, though. She had this sinking feeling that something terrible had happened to Michael and Nick. And, if so, none of this charade really mattered. They'd come for her soon enough. Audrey's men would burst through the doors of St. Francis, march upstairs and carry her kicking and screaming back to that dirty, stinking pen to meet whatever fate they had in store. Firing squad? Torture? Starvation? The one solace came in that maybe they could all three face it together. Maybe she wouldn't have to die alone, shivering uncontrollably in a one-person tent.

Then she heard it—a latch down the hallway turning. Her head rose, turning in the direction of the sound. Had she imagined that? She was sure it sounded like the door being opened, but she didn't see anything. She was almost quivering, waiting, hoping the sound really had been what she thought it was. If so, though, why wasn't she seeing anyone emerging from the door?

Beginning to doubt herself, she finally saw the door push open a little bit, and someone peeked through the opening. Even from this distance, she knew those were Michael's big brown eyes. Frantically, she started motioning for him to come through into the hall.

His room would be the second door on his left. He'd have to pass Leslie's room, and Stephanie was a little ways further down, almost to the front stairs. She didn't want to stray too far from George's door, and she sure as hell couldn't yell, but she needed to get his attention. Flailing her arms wildly, she finally made eye contact.

He shoved the door open and stepped into the hall, shrugging as if to ask, "What should I do?" Amid the nerves, she wanted to smile when she saw he was holding the knife, but whose blood was that? He was harried and perhaps scraped up, and he was missing his shirt, but he looked mostly fine. Something terrible had happened, but she'd have to find out more later.

She waved her arms toward her body several times, then pointed to his room. Quick motions. Convey urgency. He was frozen there, one foot still holding the door open in case he needed to make a fast escape. She needed to unfreeze him.

From behind her came the tap on the door. William was done.

Shit.

This was the moment she had to make a decision. William would be expecting her back in the room within seconds. She was supposed to be right by the door. Michael's foot still held the door to the stairs open. She could abort, signal for him to go back through that door, run, escape, hide. Save himself, and she'd take whatever heat came her way when William found out Michael wasn't there. Maybe he could slip out the side gate and hole up at that old cabin nearby for a bit. Maybe he'd have a chance.

But then the decision was made for her, as Michael let the door close and took off down the hall. She heard another impatient tap, but she ignored it, transfixed by Michael sprinting past Leslie's room. She heard George's doorknob start to rattle, but Michael was still in the hallway. William couldn't barge out now. Not when they were this close. She took a deep breath and grabbed the doorknob on her side, stopping it from turning. She felt him trying harder to get the door open, and she had to grip it tighter, holding it stiff to her body to keep it closed.

Michael ducked around the corner and into his room, leading Stephanie to breathe out for what must have been the first time in several minutes, and she turned to the side, letting go of the doorknob. It swung open, and William nearly stumbled backward.

"What the hell was that?" he said, catching himself against the wall.

"What was what, Officer Greene?" Stephanie plastered that same smile on her face again.

"I tapped and you didn't answer, and then I couldn't get the door open."

"Oh. I was down checking on Michael to make sure he was okay for a quick visit. And yes, sometimes these doors do stick a bit. Unfortunately, handymen are a little scarce these days."

William frowned and stepped back to let her get to George. She was trying to tell if he suspected anything, but she wanted to act normally, administering the sleep drugs she'd given him earlier.

"Sorry about the trouble, Officer Greene. I hope you and George had a good talk. If you're ready, we'll go see Michael now."

Lying in her bed, barely awake, Leslie heard a noise outside her room. Were those footsteps? They were moving quickly, like someone was running. Why would someone be sprinting down the hall? It was odd enough that she sat up and watched to see what was going on.

She sat up straight and moved into a crawling position, shifting toward the foot of the bed, where she could see through the open door into the hall. As she did, a shirtless man went streaking past, and then quickly the footsteps stopped.

She pressed her eyes tightly shut and laid back in her bed. There was no question who that was. And he looked pretty spry for a man who was supposed to be recovering in the next room.

35

"So, bottom line—is George gonna make it?" Audrey asked, sitting at her desk.

William grimaced. "Everybody I talked to seemed to think so. But bullet wounds can go sideways pretty quickly. They're doing their best to prevent infection. If they can get him healing before bacteria takes over, they feel pretty good about it."

"I understand." Audrey threaded her fingers together and leaned forward. "But Michael seems okay?"

"He didn't get shot or anything. Stephanie said it was dehydration or some bullshit like that. He was breaking out in sweats and seemed to be struggling to get comfortable in his bed, but there's nothing wrong with him that won't get better in another day or two. He needs some rest and fluids, apparently."

"Well, hopefully everyone will be back on their feet soon enough. We already lost Benjamin. We don't need to be down any more men if we want to keep control of the town."

"Is control really all you can think of?" Andy said, standing in the corner of Audrey's office, his voice strained. "You talk about Benjamin as if he was a robot you built to help execute your plan. He was a human being. He was *my friend.* Can we acknowledge his contribution and recognize he *gave his life* for this vision you have?"

"We all know who Benjamin was, Andy. And we all mourn his death. But the reality is, the world keeps spinning. The work doesn't stop because we're sad. The people trust me to keep my focus on their well-being, and what steps need to be taken to ensure we don't skip a beat. That's why I'm in this chair. Do you disagree with what we're doing here?"

"I don't…no, I don't disagree," Andy said. "It was necessary. And Benjamin was on board with it too. I…"

"What is it you *want*, Andy?" she asked.

"I don't know. It's hard. I can't believe he's gone, and I want someone to pay for his death. I want someone to take responsibility. Those fucking aliens shot him, and they got to continue living. He's gonna be buried under layers of dirt, and they're gonna be walking around as if nothing happened."

"We kicked them out of the town," Audrey said. "They're not gonna live long out there."

"Sure. But I was ready to strangle the life out of them myself. Right then and there. And if your men hadn't already carried them off, I swear to fucking god I would have. But here we are. They're alive, and he's not. And I have to live with that. It hurts. It fucking *hurts*. That's what I want us all to feel. Don't act like it's not there."

"Fair enough. It's acknowledged. And the aliens aren't the only ones who deserve to pay. They wouldn't ever have been here if it weren't for Stephanie. And once we get this vaccine done, you'll get your chance to make her pay."

"Holy shit, Michael," Stephanie said, after he told her about what happened that morning. "I'm sorry for sending you there. It never occurred to me—"

"Me neither. I know. It's not your fault. There was no way to see that coming. I honestly wonder if he happened to be walking down the street when I adjusted the bedroom curtain. I needed more light."

"Ah. So maybe he saw the curtain move and decided to check it out."

"Exactly. Seemed like he pretty much made a beeline to the bedroom," Michael said, sitting up in his hospital bed. "Almost like he knew I was there."

"Wow. I'm so glad you two made it out okay. I'll send someone to check on Nick. Hopefully, he's at home. And since you're all right, the question is, where's the knife?"

Michael smiled and reached under his pillow, sliding it out from underneath.

"Open the drawer on that table over there, and you'll find the plastic bag it was in," Michael said. "It stayed on the whole time, so I think *most* of his blood ended up on there. Some made it onto the knife, though. You think that'll contaminate it too much?

Stephanie held the knife and looked closely at it, turning it to let the light hit it from several angles.

"It's probably okay. The thing about bloody knives is that blood has a tendency to gather in nooks and crannies where you'd never expect it if you don't put a hell of a lot of effort into cleaning it. And even if you do, it's easy to miss any grooves in the blade or the tiny bit of space between the handle and the blade. We don't need much to make a DNA match, and we've got everyone in town's blood from H6N1 tests over the past couple of years."

"How long is that gonna take?"

"Couple days."

"And what do you *think* you'll find?"

"I think Audrey planted that knife behind my couch after she walked me back to my house that day, hoping you would find it and think I killed Zac," Stephanie said. "So the smoking gun to me would be Audrey's blood on that knife. That would prove it must have been in Audrey's possession at some point, and that would show us she was the one who left it there. I made the mistake of trusting her for a brief moment. I'll never do that again."

36

"What do you mean you *can't find* Conrad?" Audrey paced in the hall of the mansion, her eyes narrowing.

"We don't know where he is," Nathan said. "Didn't see him most of the day yesterday, but we didn't think too much of it. Then he didn't come back to his room last night."

"How do you know?"

Nathan looked at the third man, then back at Audrey. "Neither of us ever heard him. Checked his room this morning, hoping he'd be sleeping in there, like usual. But nothing. Bed looked like it hadn't been touched."

"There are a lot of rooms in this place. Could he have slept somewhere else?"

Nathan shrugged. "He never has before."

Audrey closed her eyes and breathed in deeply. "Where did you see him last?"

"Here. Early yesterday morning. We were all going out on patrols, keeping an eye on things."

"Did he have a particular area of town he was supposed to watch?" she asked.

"Not *really*."

"What the hell does *that* mean?"

"We...didn't do it organized or anything like that. We all sort of..."

"Wandered aimlessly?" Audrey's eyebrows rose.

"It was never a big deal! It was mostly a show of force. Let people know we were out there, keeping watch. An intimidation thing. So we walked the streets. People are a little on edge since the shootout the other morning, so most of them were staying in. It was really quiet."

"So, you're telling me something happened on Conrad's patrol." Audrey folded her arms across her chest. "And now he could be fucking *anywhere*?"

Nathan shut his eyes and reluctantly nodded.

"God damn it! Okay, both of you, get the hell out of here and start looking for him. Bang on doors. Ask people if they saw Conrad at any point yesterday. Maybe you can start by figuring out where he was patrolling. Check with Andy too. I'll go to the hospital and see if he happened to find his way there. I should probably check in on George, Michael, and Leslie anyway. Go now. I want Conrad found *today*."

Leslie had only been awake a few minutes when she heard a light tapping on her door. It swung open, and Audrey peeked her head inside.

"How's everything going over here?" Audrey asked, closing the door behind her.

"Nice having a real bed."

Audrey walked deeper into the room, stopping right next to the bed, her shadow blotting out the light over Leslie's head as she leaned over her.

"You like it? Get me what I want, and we can arrange something where you get these kinds of accommodations more often. But we both know you're not here to appreciate a pillow-top mattress. Do you have anything for me yet on Stephanie and Michael? Anything I should know?"

Leslie had anticipated the question, but she hadn't known how soon it would come. She wondered what might have triggered Audrey being impatient and desperate enough to prod her for information after barely twenty-four hours at the hospital.

Could it have something to do with Michael sprinting down the hall while clutching to something that was covered in blood?

Surely, Audrey didn't already know about that, or she wouldn't have any need for Leslie to confirm it. Unless this was some sort of loyalty test. But there was no way to be certain Leslie had even *seen* Michael, much less put together what was going on.

No, Leslie suspected Audrey had no idea what she'd seen, and was looking to learn what Leslie could tell her. Judging by Michael's hallway sprint when he was supposed to be recovering in a hospital bed, Audrey was right that he and Stephanie were up to *something*. And judging by the blood-covered object in Michael's hand, that *something* was pretty violent.

Perhaps it looked a lot worse than it really was. But lying in this hospital bed, Audrey looming large over top of her, Leslie had to decide if she wanted to share what she saw.

It would be worth something to Audrey. Maybe it would earn Leslie some major points with her, and that could be valuable down the line.

On the other hand, Leslie still wasn't sure she should help Audrey at all. What side of the fence did she need to be on? If Audrey was going to be in power for another ten years, it'd be worth being on her good side. But Stephanie and Michael had taken her out before. If they had some plan for doing it again, that might be worth knowing before Leslie decided how forthcoming to be.

Leslie couldn't say Audrey wasn't intimidating, though. She had these eyes that seemed to burrow into you and make a nest. You wanted to do anything to get her to pull them back, to set you free again. She didn't like feeling so *seen*. It made her uncomfortable. Part of her wanted to tell Audrey everything. Get it over with. Save yourself. Make a friend in a high place.

The longer she waited, the more that was what she thought she'd end up doing. Time was going to make this harder. The deeper those eyes bore into her skin, the more she'd squirm to get them out. Whatever answer she was going to give, it needed to come now. She couldn't let this linger any longer.

Leslie swallowed. "Haven't seen a thing yet, Ms. Reese. I'm gonna need more time."

"Doctor Sloan," Victor said, and Stephanie shook her head, then removed her goggles and looked up from the microscope. "Ms.

Reese is here. She said she needs to speak with you."

She sighed and took off her rubber gloves, walking past Victor out the door of the lab, her white coat flapping behind her. When she reached the hall, Audrey was standing a few feet away.

"Good to see you, Ms. Reese. Is this important? I know you're aware how busy we are."

"I wouldn't interrupt you if it wasn't. How is Michael doing?"

"Um, pretty good. We thought we'd be able to release him yesterday, but then he broke out in sweats as we brought him out from under some medication, so I decided to keep him for further evaluation to be safe."

"Hmm…that's what he said too."

"That's what *he* said? You talked to him?"

"A few minutes ago, yes. Visited him and Leslie. Wanted to get an idea of how everything was going."

Stephanie wanted to stare daggers through Audrey, but what could she do? They both knew Audrey held all the power in this situation. Stephanie didn't like anyone bothering her patients without authorization—particularly Audrey, who could boost their stress levels—but she couldn't stop it. And Michael was more of a show patient at this point anyway. Since he had been so sweaty when William visited, Stephanie had to keep him longer.

Now, though, she wondered what Audrey had talked to Michael about. Very few people knew what had happened, but Stephanie was concerned that could change at any moment.

"Did everything seem to be meeting your standards?" Stephanie asked.

"It appeared so. Stephanie, when do you think Michael will be ready to get back to work?"

"He's close. Barring a setback, we can let him leave by tomorrow. He should probably take it easy for a day or two, but I don't see any reason he can't be back to normal within a couple more days."

"I was hoping it could be sooner than that."

"Sooner? Why, if you don't mind me asking?"

"Well, you know we lost Benjamin," Audrey said. "And George's injuries are fairly serious, so he won't likely be back to normal any time soon. It's hard being down three men."

"My professional recommendation would be to work him back into full capacity gradually, or you'll risk a relapse. A couple of days shouldn't be that big of a deal, should it?"

Audrey paused, looking away and appearing to ponder something. Then she raised her head and looked directly at Stephanie.

"Would you tell me if one of my men had been brought here?"

There was something in Audrey's tone that Stephanie didn't like. It made the question feel more like an accusation. Her throat suddenly turned dry, but she tried not to show any outward sign of being nervous.

"Of course I would. Without even a second thought. Do you think one of them was brought here without you knowing?"

"Be sure to get word to me *immediately* if any of them comes through those doors. You understand?"

"Absolutely."

Does she know? Stephanie wanted to press her for more information, but she needed to play dumb. Buy time. Stretch this out as long as she could.

"Okay," Audrey said. "And I'm going to take Michael with me. I think he'll be happy resting in his own bed at the mansion. That'll help us to get him to work as soon as we can. Thanks for helping him, Stephanie. I'll take it from here."

37

"How is it fucking *possible* you haven't found him yet?" Audrey screamed, her voice strained. "You've been looking for an entire goddamn day! Where could he possibly be?"

Standing in the town square, William looked at Andy, who shook his head.

"I really don't know," William said. "Unless you want us to search every square inch of every house, I don't know where else we can look."

Audrey knew what everyone was trying desperately not to say to her face. She wasn't stupid. She knew that every hour that passed, the chances of them finding him alive dwindled closer to zero. They all knew that. The situation was bad.

At this point, there were only two possibilities she could think of—either he'd wandered away outside of the wall for some reason and then gotten lost or hurt, or he was lying somewhere dead. The town wasn't all that big. If he were alive within the walls, they'd have found him by now. He had no incentive to intentionally hide, and no one would be stupid enough to harbor him for this long either.

What bothered Audrey the most was the idea that she might never know what happened to Conrad. He'd been loyal, staying beside her through so many hardships, and was one of the main reasons she was still alive today. Not only had she been unable to protect him from some awful fate, but now she might not be able to give him the honored burial he deserved.

Could he have fallen into the lake and drowned? She had no

idea if he was a strong swimmer. If he had gotten in over his head in the water, would he have been able to make it back to shore? Would the water at this time of year be cold enough to send him into shock? If so, his body should float to the surface, assuming nothing was holding him down. The thought was too hard to face, though. Did she have it in her to order them to go check the lake? Everyone would know what that meant.

She wanted to project confidence that Conrad was still out there, never to show any signs that she was giving up, but how long was that sustainable? And who would have the balls to tell her when that time had passed?

No one. She was going to need to know that answer herself. And she wasn't there yet.

"Well, then, maybe that's what we have to do," she said. "But first, I say we give the people a chance to be deputies for us on this. If he's in the town, we're gonna find him, god damn it. Go knock on doors and tell everyone to meet in the square as soon as they can get there. It's time for another speech."

Waking up in his room at the mansion, something close to terror immediately gripped Michael again. The whole walk back from the hospital with Audrey—slowed so he could pretend to be struggling with each step, hoping she'd relent and send him back—he'd worried that she somehow knew. That she'd figured out what he did, and was taking him to be executed or sent away from Alessandra. The uncertainty and lack of control were maddening.

She didn't say much, only that they needed him back on the front lines as soon as possible, and she felt that would be easier if he was at the mansion rather than sitting isolated at the hospital. Was that all this was, though? Was she biding time, torturing him and waiting for the right moment to extract her pound of flesh?

And if she didn't know yet, she surely was a few steps away. They had to be aware the man was missing. From there, they'd find his body, figure out he was murdered, and then start trying to determine who might have done it. How long would it take those roads to lead to him? He wasn't sure, but the answer wasn't forever. And it wasn't like she needed to convince a jury of his peers that he was guilty. Her own suspicion was really all that was necessary.

Michael didn't want to work for Audrey anymore. Mentally, he was checked out. The immigrant raid was the final indignity, but this had been building for a while. He didn't want to do it. He didn't want to be part of the society she was trying to build. Again, though, he didn't see any way around it. There was only so much resisting he could do. Maybe there was a place where he'd draw a line and refuse to help, damn the consequences. Maybe a more principled man would have already done that.

But he still believed their best chance to save the town from Audrey was by him staying upright and embedded with her team. He couldn't be of any help outside those walls or dead. Sometimes, a desperate man can't afford to have principles.

The door to his room began to creak and slide open, light seeping through the crack and slowly sweeping across his bed. Michael shut his eyes tightly, and his body went stiff.

"Michael…" Audrey said, her voice barely above a whisper. "Are you awake?"

He didn't move. Didn't want to face her. He summoned every bit of will in his body to try to keep from making even the slightest movement.

Michael could feel her getting closer, her presence approaching the side of the bed. He was praying she'd turn around and leave.

I'm sleeping. Let me be. Go. Please don't come closer.

Then he felt her hand on his shoulder, jostling lightly at first, then with more force as he continued to remain still. Whatever she wanted, he was going to have to deal with it.

Michael let his eyes open, blinking slowly, then reaching up and rubbing them with the palm of his hands, trying to mimic someone abruptly pulled out of a deep sleep.

"Hi, Michael. Glad to see you're awake. How are you feeling?"

He shook his head and rolled over on his back. "Tired. Was hoping to sleep a little more, to be honest."

"Ah, yes. Sorry. Don't see that happening right now." She smiled and sat on the edge of the bed, then patted his foot through the blanket. "There's work to be done, Michael. I need you down at the square as soon as you can get dressed. I'll grab you some clothes and walk you down there. Gonna have a big announcement."

38

"You wanted to see me?" Stephanie said, softly closing the door behind her as she stepped into Leslie's hospital room.

Leslie propped a pillow up against the headboard and sat with her hands folded in her lap.

"Yeah. Pull over a chair."

"You look and sound a lot better than you did when you got here." Stephanie sat down, holding a notepad, using her feet to roll the chair toward Leslie's bed. "Maybe we can get you out of here soon."

Leslie gave Stephanie a sideways glance. "That's not gonna happen."

Stephanie felt her chest tighten, but she picked up the notepad and raised her pencil. "What do you mean? Are you feeling worse? If so, you should talk to Victor about—"

"Just shut up. Okay? Shut up. I need to tell you something, and you need to listen."

Stephanie silently lowered the notepad and nodded, her heart beating faster.

"I'm fine," Leslie said. "I'm not sick. Never was. I was brought here to keep an eye on the hospital, particularly you and Michael. See if I could learn anything about what you guys might be up to, or *something*. I don't know exactly what they were expecting."

"You're a spy." Stephanie felt like the words burst out of her.

"I guess so."

"Why are you telling me this?"

"Because I saw Michael. When he was running down the hall past my room a couple of days ago. And he was carrying *something* with blood on it. I don't know exactly what he was up to, but I know he wasn't sick and resting in bed."

Stephanie tried to swallow, but only came up with sandpaper. She shut her eyes and buried her head in her hands, rubbing her temple and trying to control her breathing.

"Audrey," Stephanie said. "She spoke to you yesterday. What did you—"

"It's fine. I didn't tell her anything. I just said I needed more time. So don't worry. At least…not *yet*."

Stephanie sat up straight. "Not *yet*? What does *that* mean?"

"Look…I'm gonna be honest. I don't want to help them. If I had a choice in the matter, I wouldn't be here. But you know as well as anyone the power they have over my life. You know what they're capable of. They've already taken Derrick from me. All that's left is to hurt or kill *me*. Audrey expects information. That's why I'm here. So far, I've been able to hold her off. But, at some point, I'm gonna have to give her *something*. And if Michael is all I've got, I'll have to give him up."

"You can't tell her," Stephanie pleaded. "If you give up Michael, you're sentencing him to death. Me too, Leslie. Audrey will kill us both. You have to understand that."

"But it might mean I get released from that awful pen. Get a nice, soft bed. Better than this one. Could earn me some favor from Audrey later on."

"You'd send us to death just for a softer fucking bed?"

"I already told you I don't *want* to. Okay? I'm not blind. I can see she's not the leader we need. You had *my* vote. But what do you want me to do? She's not gonna wait forever. It's just been a couple of days, so I've probably got a bit more time before she gets insistent. When that time comes, though, I need to have something to give her. Preferably something *good*."

"What are you saying?"

"Well…if you were to give me something *else* to share with Audrey, maybe I could forget about the Michael situation altogether. That could just be our little secret. I won't even ask what you two were up to. But think about it. What can you give me that'll make me forget about that? This can be beneficial to both of us, if you play it right."

"Yeah. I just need time to think. How long do you think you have?"

"A day. Maybe two? I don't know. Not long."

"Okay. I'll get back to you."

Stephanie stood and pushed the chair back against the wall. As she opened the door, she turned back to Leslie.

"Oh. And Leslie…thanks for telling me. You did the right thing."

Leslie nodded. "We'll see. But this conversation never happened. Just get back to me before Audrey does."

"Hello, everyone. Thanks for taking the time to join us this morning." Audrey held the bullhorn on stage, with Andy, William, Michael, and her two men standing behind her, arms crossed at the wrists in front of their bodies. They all looked ahead, their stares unyielding.

"I had been hoping not to bring you all back here until we could announce that we had the long-sought vaccine, and I'm sure what many of you were anticipating today. Unfortunately, despite plenty of progress, we're not *quite* ready for that. Something else important has happened that requires all of our attention. In short: we need your help."

By this point, standing motionless on stage, Michael knew what was coming. On the walk down, Audrey told him what she knew—Conrad was missing, and she was going to enlist the whole town to help find him. Michael was glad they were walking when she told him because it was harder for her to give that intense stare, the one that made you feel like she was hammering a nail into your soul, making you want to confess anything to wrench free from her grip. He had tried to react with surprise and sympathy, but he worried he'd provided some signal to her that he'd already known, maybe that he'd even been involved.

That was silly, though, he knew. He had the perfect alibi. As far as Audrey was concerned, he had been in a hospital bed the entire time. As long as she believed that, he'd be in the clear. He still had to hope no one saw them running through the streets that morning. He'd have no defense if they did. Once someone could place him anywhere *other* than in that hospital bed, his story would unravel. Maybe that wouldn't happen. But he couldn't help but feel like he was a dead man walking unless they could find a way to turn the tables on Audrey soon.

"I'm sorry to report to you all that one of our own is missing." Audrey paced the stage as she spoke. "One of my wonderful men—Conrad—who has done so much to help this town, given so much of himself to Alessandra, has been missing for more than a day now. We've searched throughout the town, but there's only so much ground we can cover with our small group. George is still in the hospital, and Michael is just getting back on his feet. There are a couple hundred homes in Alessandra, many unoccupied. There are other buildings like the old furniture factory, the hospital, old city hall, and businesses like Walt's Bar and the nearby convenience store.

"Sweeping all of those on our own would take the kind of time my team simply can't afford. If Conrad is hurt, maybe even dying, we need to find him *yesterday*. At the absolute first possible moment. Time is of the essence here. That's why I'm bringing you all together to request your assistance. Please join us. Knock on doors. Enter abandoned homes and buildings. If you need to go ring-less for this work, I understand. But be very careful. Keep your distance from others, and move quickly.

"Those who are willing to help, see Andy after we're done to get your assignments on what part of town to check. I can't tell you how much we all appreciate it. And if you have *any* information whatsoever, no matter how innocuous it may seem, please pass it along to one of us immediately. Conrad was last seen as he was heading out two mornings ago for a patrol around the town. If you saw or heard anything remotely unusual since then, let us know. It could be the tip that points us in the right direction. It *could* save Conrad's life. And I would be forever in debt to you if you helped in that way.

"Thank you all again. I won't keep you any longer. Let's get out there and find Conrad today."

"Hey, Andy," Michael yelled as he scrambled down the stairs from the stage. "I'll take him with me, if that's cool."

Andy looked Nick up and down, then shrugged and motioned toward Michael.

"Good to see ya, Nick," Michael said, stopping with their rings almost touching. "Glad you wanted to help with this."

"It's the least I could do. Conrad has been a valued member of the community. It's important that we find him."

Michael bit his lip and nodded slightly. "Yeah. I'm taking Kimsey Street since I used to live there and am familiar with the homes and such. You wanna come with me?"

"Lead the way."

39

"Well, we're here," Nick said, as the front door of Stephanie's house clicked shut behind him. "What can we do?"

Michael could feel his breath getting shorter. "I…don't know."

"You don't know? Why are we *here*, Michael?"

"Because somebody fucking *had* to come, Nick! Okay? It's not like we could convince Audrey that Stephanie's house was the one that wasn't worth checking. So, I figured it's better we do it than anyone else."

Michael's head was pounding. He curled his hands into fists, trying to dig his fingernails into his skin to distract himself from his tightening forehead.

"Fine. Sure," Nick said. "We need to go back there and see what the damage looks like now. We didn't have time to do much cleanup before, and I doubt two days of sitting improved things any."

Nick started walking through the living room toward the hall. Michael stood still at first, trying to get his legs underneath him. He felt wobbly, like he might collapse. He needed to move, though. He almost wanted to slap himself, to feel something other than this dread and fear that had gripped him from the moment he approached this house. It wouldn't let him go.

As he saw Nick turn the corner into the hall, Michael slowly lifted his right foot, then quickly put it back down, the room spinning around him. He looked down at the floor, wanting to see it sitting solidly beneath him. It wasn't swaying. The world was still. He took a large breath and closed his eyes. Breathe in. Out. Sucking it deep into his lungs. Starting to feel human again.

I can do this. I have a job to do. If there's a way out of this, we'll find it.

"You comin'?" Nick said, peeking back around the wall to look at Michael still standing where he'd been before.

Michael opened his eyes and looked up, pausing for a moment before nodding and heading in that direction.

When he got into the hall, he saw the bedroom door shut and remembered they'd pulled it closed before they left. Nick grasped the handle.

"You ready?" he asked.

"Yeah," Michael lied. "Do it."

Suddenly, Michael could see it all, revealing itself in a panorama before him. The closed blinds were allowing only a few slats of light to pepper the ceiling, and the rest of the room was blanketed with shade, but the room was bright enough to see blood splattered on the walls and floor, darkening almost to black as it dried. It was a grisly scene.

"My god." Nick was the first one to speak. "I knew it wasn't good, but I didn't remember there being *so much* blood."

"Yeah. Me neither. Nobody with a working set of eyes could miss this."

"Could we pretend we didn't come in here? Say we took a quick glance inside the front part of the house but didn't think it was worth looking through every room?"

"I don't see how. The instructions have been to search everywhere thoroughly."

Both of them looked at the shut closet door, and a trickle of dried blood that had seeped underneath.

"What about cleaning it up?" Nick asked.

"With what? It's dried. We can't go grab some soap and flip on the tap in the kitchen."

"Hell, Stephanie's gotta have cleaning stuff here," Nick said. "Nobody throws that shit out. Does she have a little broom closet or linen closet somewhere?"

Michael walked back down the hall to a narrow door off the

kitchen and pulled it open. Nick was right. There were several bottles of household cleaner in spray bottles, along with a large bottle of bleach. Nick nudged him out of the way and grabbed two cleaner bottles and the bleach, then smiled, handing one batch of cleaner and a rag to Michael.

"Will this still work?" Michael asked. "What's the shelf life on bleach?"

"Hell if I know." Nick unscrewed the cap on the bleach and sniffed. "Eh. Smells more like salty water than bleach. But unless you've got a better idea…"

"No, I guess we can try it. Can't see how it could make us *more* fucked than we are."

"That's the spirit. Let's do this."

"It didn't work." Michael threw his rag across the room and it hit the wall, flopping down to the floor. "It's still there. We're screwed."

Nick stood up and stepped back to get a full view of the room. "No, I think it'll work."

"What do you mean? I still see *everything*. We didn't get rid of any of the blood stains."

"Well, yeah. They're not *gone*. This bleach is probably past its prime, and there's honestly gotta be some ideal bleach-plus-water-plus-club-soda solution or some shit like that, but we don't have that stuff, and neither of our stupid asses knows what it is anyway. But look at it. It's lighter than when we started. That's more of a light red than a blackened maroon."

"So what? Somebody who looks for more than two seconds is still gonna see it."

"Yeah, but you're not thinking in terms of plausible deniability," Nick said, putting his hand on Michael's shoulder. "We don't need this room to be perfectly spotless. Will someone who comes in here and takes the time to really look at it notice there's something up, and maybe those are blood stains? Sure. But when is that gonna happen?"

"We're already checking it, though. How can we say *we* didn't see this?"

Nick shook his head. "Come with me."

He walked toward the door, and Michael followed him. They stopped in the hall outside the room, turning to look inside.

"Okay," Nick said. "Would you say we've got pretty decent light right now? Sun's out. It's early afternoon sometime in the early fall. Shades are closed, but we're gonna leave them that way."

"Sure. This is about as much light as you're gonna get unless you open those."

"Right. Now, pretend you don't know where the blood is, or that there's any there *at all*. Don't stand here and study the room. Put yourself in the shoes of someone who has no reason to think there's anything in here, who's probably been dispatched to check here even though it's already been checked, and may very well be annoyed by the fact that he's even here. He wants to give a cursory look and check a box that says he didn't find the decomposing body of a giant anywhere inside. What does that guy see?"

"You want me to pretend not to know there are blood stains when I was there to see it happen?"

Nick rolled his eyes. "Take a quick glance into the room, look away, and tell me what you see."

Michael looked at Nick for a few seconds, then turned to the room, looked around quickly, then spun back to Nick.

"So?" Nick raised his eyebrows.

"I don't know. I see them."

"But look…here's the point. Let's even say someone else could see them later. We're talking days or weeks. That buys us time. The real question isn't necessarily whether or not this person might see the stains. The real question is whether, *if* that person saw them, *we* could be justified in saying we either didn't see them or didn't think much of them if we did. Because that's really all we need: plausible deniability."

Michael looked back into the room, shaking his head.

"Maybe." He sighed. "But, even if so, you're forgetting one *huge* problem."

"What's that?"

"The rotting body of a giant *is* still here. In the closet. And I'm no expert on human body decomposition, but I'm pretty sure the stench is gonna be way more noticeable than whatever stains might be back here. Within a few days, it'll hit you in the face like a wrecking ball the moment you open the front door, if not sooner."

Nick looked away and nodded slowly. "We're gonna have to do something about that, aren't we?"

40

"She's waiting for you in her office," Victor said, walking ahead of Michael and Nick into St. Francis. "Go on up."

"And Doctor Sloan didn't say what this was about?" Michael asked.

"Nope. Just that she had an update for you, and that I should find you. If you think it's okay to bring Nick along, that's fine by me. I'm sure she'll kick him out if it's something he shouldn't hear."

Michael nodded and started jogging up the stairs, Nick beside him.

They still had unfinished business with Conrad's body, but that was going to have to wait until after dark anyway. They passed their all-clear assessment of Kimsey Street along to William and started heading further toward the lake when Victor approached, telling them Stephanie needed to see Michael immediately.

A million thoughts were running through Michael's mind as he neared her office upstairs. What was this about? Whatever it was, he knew it had to be important. There was risk in sending Victor out into the open to take him away. If one of Audrey's men had been around when Victor found them, would Victor have been discreet enough to wait until Michael was alone? Did he know Nick was trusted enough that it wasn't a problem?

He opened the door and walked into the office, where Stephanie was sitting at the desk. Two large plastic bags containing paper with handwritten notes were lying in front of her.

"Michael, glad you could—oh, Nick's here too," she said.

"Is that…" Michael looked back at Nick, then to Stephanie. "…all right? He can wait outside if you want."

"Yeah, it's fine," Nick said. "I didn't want to be seen wandering alone when I was supposed to be with Michael."

"No. Stay." Stephanie waved a hand. "You're part of this, Nick. You've been a huge help, and I'm sure we're gonna need you to take this to the next step."

Nick nodded and closed the door behind him, sitting in a chair next to Michael.

"Okay," Stephanie said, passing the plastic bags on her desk. "You're both probably curious why you're here. Nick, on the right are the test results from the red voting cloth you brought back from the chest in Leslie's attic. And Michael, on the left are the test results from the knife you recovered from my house. I know we all risked a lot to get these, so let me first thank you both for doing what you could to get these materials for testing. We need every bit of evidence we can get if we're gonna have any chance of taking Audrey down."

"So, don't leave us in suspense," Michael said. "What do the tests say? Have you read them?"

"Right. Yes, I've read them. I *wrote* them, in fact. But let's have a look together, okay?"

She reached into the plastic bag on her right and pulled out the paper. Underneath it was the red cloth, which she was careful not to touch.

"For the cloth, the material was a combination of cotton and linen, and it absorbed information from the environment pretty well. We found skin cells from George, Hank, Nathan, and Conrad, so several people handled it. But, most interestingly, we actually found trace amounts of dead H6N1 virus cells within the fabric. We can't think of any reason that'd be on the fabric unless it was purposefully placed there."

"Wow. So do we think he wanted someone to find that?" Nick said. "I'm just trying to wrap my head around this. Do we think *Audrey's men* used the red voting cloth as a delivery device to infect Hank with the virus? Or could they say the virus got there because Hank handled the cloth after he was sick?"

"Sure. I mean, they could *say* anything. But that's not really how the virus works. It needs a host. It's happy to move from one host to another if there's an easy means to do so. But going from a viable host to a piece of cloth wouldn't make any sense. My guess would be that Hank locked it in the chest so that no one else got infected, figuring correctly that, by the time anyone broke into the chest, the virus wouldn't be active anymore."

"Nailed it on the first one," Michael said. "How about the knife?"

Stephanie reached for the other bag and pulled it open, sliding the paper out from on top of the knife.

"So, there was a bit going on here. There are lots of fingerprints on the knife, but they're a bit of a non-starter since we don't keep any sort of fingerprint database. All we can say there is we saw prints from three different people. What was more interesting to us, though, was the blood. The way blood works is we have to match the DNA to what we have on file. And, luckily, with everyone testing for the virus, we have plenty of DNA samples to match against in our lab. Now, normally you'd say that DNA can't tell us with a hundred percent certainty that it came from a single individual, but we more or less can here, given that the population of even *possible* people it could be is so small.

"What we found was that there is some amount of Zac's blood on the knife, embedded in some of the smaller crevices. But the vast majority of the blood on that knife isn't Zac's. It's Audrey's."

"Holy shit," Michael said. "And where do we think Audrey's blood came from?"

"My suspicion pretty much from the beginning was that Audrey left that knife in my house, hoping someone would find it and think it was the weapon that I killed Zac with. She wanted it to have blood on it, so I'd guess she cut *herself* before leaving it. But either way, there's no logic to me owning a knife with Audrey's blood all over it. That shows the knife belonged to her, not me."

"This is incredible," Nick said. "What do we do now?"

"First, tell me where you two stand with the situation at my house," Stephanie said. "If we can get through that, it'll take a bit of work, but I think the three of us can use this evidence to take Audrey's legs out from under her."

Darkness settling in through her window, Leslie heard footsteps outside her room, and saw the door swing open. She sat up, expecting to see Stephanie come inside, hopefully with a plan for what they were going to do about Audrey. Then her stomach turned into a knot when she saw who it was.

"Hi, Leslie," Audrey said, shutting the door and pulling over a chair. "I hope they're treating you well."

Leslie's throat felt dry. She tried to swallow, but there was nothing there. Leslie hated the way she felt around this woman. With Stephanie, she could behave confidently, assertively, like the person she knew she was. But there was something about Audrey that turned her into mush, and it made her hate herself.

"Yes," Leslie said. "Everything's fine."

"Good. That's good. You know why I'm here. But before we get to that, I wanted to level with you so that maybe you fully understand what's at stake here."

Leslie nodded. She wasn't sure whether to be intrigued or scared. Maybe both.

"Conrad, one of the men who came with me when I returned to Alessandra, is missing. We've known he was missing for closing in on two days now, but whatever happened to him could have occurred up to twenty-four hours prior to that. So that's almost three days of him being maybe badly hurt, likely without food or water. Alone. Cold. Scared. And that's if he's not…"

Audrey's voice cracked, and Leslie for the first time thought she saw this woman as a human being. Like she could relate to her in some way. Conrad obviously meant a lot to her. It was eating her up not to know what had happened to him, and not being able to help him. Leslie reached up and wiped a tear trickling from the corner of her eye.

"Anyway," Audrey continued, after a few seconds. "This is why I'm so desperate to find out if there's *anything* you can tell me that might help me find my friend. He's a good man. All I ultimately want is to know what happened to him. His brothers are beside themselves, and it's tough to see them this way. So think back to two days ago. I couldn't really tell you what time. Could be any time that day. Did you see or hear anything that might help us? Maybe Conrad was here briefly. Maybe someone said something referring to him. Anything at all out of the ordinary could give us some direction."

And then it struck Leslie, right in that moment—this timeline fit perfectly for when she saw Michael. She was in a corner. She had no interest in helping Audrey, and she said she'd give Stephanie a chance to come up with something else to tell her. But she hadn't counted on Audrey coming back so soon, or a man's life hanging in the balance.

It seemed wrong to help a bad person if you could possibly help it, Leslie thought. She liked the idea of joining with Stephanie and trying to take back the town. Audrey was the one who had ordered the banishment of Derrick, a man Leslie loved. Surely, there was no way to justify being a part of whatever scheme she might be trying to pull off.

But maybe there was a way to straddle the fence.

"I think I did see something, Audrey," Leslie said. "Michael wasn't in bed the whole time he was here. Two days ago, I saw him running down the hall, right outside my room. And whatever he had in his hand was covered in blood."

41

"We don't see him anywhere," Andy said. "If he's in the mansion, he's hiding."

Audrey slapped her hand against the wall. "I want Michael found *right fucking now*! Not tomorrow goddamn morning. I want him brought to me, right here. I want to look him in the eyes and snuff the fucking life out of him. Find him for me!"

"In the dark, with no idea where to look?" William said. "We've been walking and searching and working *all day*. We're tired. Can we get some sleep and get out there in the morning?"

"*Now!*" Audrey screamed, the sound reverberating up and down the mansion's marble hall. "He doesn't deserve even *one more second* of freedom, and I'll be damned if we're gonna let him hang out for another night, doing whatever he wants. If he's not here, he's either up to something, or he somehow knows we're on to him. And that means we *must* go get him before he does more damage. Start on Kimsey, at his old house. Do it. That's not a request."

"Shit," Nick said, sitting against the back wall of Stephanie's house, his legs pulled tight against his chest. "What took you so long? I've been sitting here twiddling my thumbs in the dark since sundown, and it's not exactly warm out. I was starting to think you might not make it."

"I was getting *this*." Michael moved to the side, and Nick stood up. "It's the gurney Zac used to roll bodies up to the hospital when he was going on that rampage. Had to make a detour over to Zac's place to check, and it was still hidden in his back yard where we left it. Thought it might be useful."

"Oh, hell yes. Okay, getting this behemoth down to the lake's gonna be *way* easier now."

"Yeah. No doubt. You got the weights and stuff?"

"Couple nice-sized boulders and some bricks, waiting for us down by the lake. Few lengths of rope I scavenged too. I think we'll have enough to weigh him down."

"All right," Michael said, grimacing. "Guess there's only one thing left."

"The fun part, yeah."

They went in through the back door and headed to the bedroom, making their way back to the shut closet and stopping outside the door.

"I'm starting to smell him," Michael said. "What's he gonna look like?"

"I don't really want to think about it. Picturing it in my head is probably worse than anything we could actually see. Have you ever handled a dead body before?"

"Yeah." Michael looked at Nick. "The one in the closet."

"All right. Fuck you. Let's do this."

Nick closed his eyes and turned the handle on the closet door, slowly pulling it open, but a crack was enough to let the stench flood out into the room; Nick let go of the door and stumbled away, coughing and covering his mouth and nose with his shirt. It only took another second or two for it to hit Michael as well.

Trying to cover his face as well as he could, Michael bent over, starting to gag and wondering if he was going to be able to stop himself from throwing up. It had only been maybe sixty hours, and the odor of death was already overwhelming. It was a smell he didn't think he could describe in words, crawling into his head and permeating every surface of his body. It seemed like it had to be more than a mere odor. It was a full-blown entity, a villain determined to guard Conrad from these grave robbers.

"Jesus," Michael said, in between dry coughs. "I didn't realize it was gonna be *that* bad."

Nick was on his knees, head cradled in his hands. "I'm fucking *crying* over here, man. Good lord. I can't wait to get that thing in the water."

"But how…" Michael coughed a few more times, the stench still hanging heavy in the air. "How are we gonna get him all the way to the damn water? We can't even get the door open without collapsing into convulsions."

"Damn it. Okay." Nick stood up straight and turned toward the closet. "We don't have an option here. We've got to figure out how to do this."

He looked at the ceiling, pausing for a few seconds. Then lowered his head and grabbed his shirt by the back of the collar, yanking it up over his head. He wrapped it around his face, covering his nose and mouth, then knotted it in back.

"What do you think?" Nick asked.

"I think we're gonna freeze to death."

"You got a better idea?"

Michael closed his eyes and sighed, then copied Nick. The smell was still there, but it was muted a bit, like it had gone through a filter before hitting their nose.

"Better?" Nick asked.

"Well, it's no bed of roses, but it's surprisingly tolerable compared to the vomit-inducing stench that was hitting us before."

"I'll take it. Ready?"

Nick grasped the door handle again and continued slowly pulling it open, gradually revealing the massive body lying behind it. As the door moved further, the body started sliding, then tumbled out into the room.

Michael cringed at the sight of the corpse on the floor in front of him. "He's still mostly intact, at least from the outside. I'm glad we didn't wait much longer."

"The cool fall air probably didn't hurt us. I'd hate to see what he would have looked like by this time in the middle of July. Grab his arms. Let's get him out of here."

Turning the body over and looking closer, Michael noticed the skin had a greenish tint to it, something he'd never seen before. He had expected the limbs to be really stiff, but they were relatively pliable. He grabbed the arms around the wrist and pulled up. With Nick lifting from the legs, they had enough strength to get him an inch or so off the ground.

Mustering up all the energy they had, they stiffened their backs and shuffled out of the room into the hall, working their way toward the back door.

Nick stepped through the door and out into the yard. Michael didn't immediately see the gurney where he thought he'd left it. He squinted in the dark, but there was nothing there. They both dropped the body.

"Where's the gurney?" Nick asked.

"Was it not right here? I could have sworn—"

"Well, I'll be god damned." The voice came from the side of the house, behind Michael. He knew immediately it was Andy. When he turned to look, a gun glinted in the moonlight. "I think you two are looking for this."

42

Stephanie pushed the door open and walked into Leslie's room, looking around the corner to see her awake in bed.

"Hey, Leslie. How'd you sleep?" Stephanie thought she looked upset or maybe tired.

"Not great." Leslie rubbed her eyes. "Not sure why. Just one of those things, ya know?"

"Yeah. Sure. We've all been there. So, I wanted to—"

"How's the vaccine research going?" Leslie interrupted.

"Oh. Been doing lots of testing on mice, which aren't hard to come by around here. We *are* under the gun, but I'm honestly hoping we can do something about Audrey before she does something about us."

"You think you can take her down?"

Stephanie paused, uncertain of how much to tell Leslie. "Let's say our position seems promising. But listen, I didn't come up here to talk about all this. You asked me to get back with you within a day or so with something to tell Audrey to basically replace Michael's sprint down the hall. I think I've got it."

"Okay, great. Let's hear it."

"All right," Stephanie began. "So, I think you can safely tell her that the wall behind you there is thin enough that you can hear a lot of what's said in Michael's old room. The room's empty now, and I can keep it that way. In fact, I can lock it up and put up a "Hazardous Materials" sign or something, and nobody will want to go *near* it. Then she won't be able to test you on that."

"That seems smart."

"Yeah. And you tell her that you overheard me and Michael talking about what to do about George and William. That when William was here, he and George were talking about a coup attempt. You tell her you overheard that it seems like George is bitter over getting shot in a raid Audrey ordered, and they think George would be a more level-headed leader. She probably already knows that William is a follower, and suspects that he's more loyal to George than to her. If George fills his head with stuff like that, he'll probably believe it. You see what I'm saying?"

Leslie nodded. "I do. It's an interesting story."

"Well, I think it's plausible. Ultimately, it could end up being a good thing that Audrey brought you here. Assuming she trusts you, this gives us a chance to really create a misdirection that could provide the opening we need to execute our plan. Because not only would it put a dent in her trust for George and William, but it would make the three of us all look like we favored her over them."

"I like it. I could really see how it would help."

"So you'll do it? You'll pass that story along?"

"Yeah. This seems like a good plan. I promise I won't let you down."

Watching Stephanie leaving her room, Leslie's heart broke a little. As soon as the door clicked shut, the emotion burst from her, and she had to stuff the bedsheet in her mouth to stifle a scream as she cried.

That had been one of the hardest things she'd ever done. As soon as Stephanie walked through the door, Leslie knew what she wanted. She delayed it at first, but then realized there was no way to hold back that dam. She was going to have to figure out how to face it.

One option was to level with Stephanie, tell her that Audrey had come by the previous night, and that she knew about Michael. Leslie had protected Stephanie, though. She told Audrey that she knew Stephanie wasn't involved because she was in Leslie's room at the time, with her back turned to Michael. Stephanie never saw a thing.

"What was that noise?" Stephanie had said after Michael bolted down the hall, according to Leslie's story.

"Nothing. Victor walked by with Michael. Must have been getting him some air," Leslie supposedly replied, and Stephanie went back to preparing Leslie's lunch.

Leslie thought Audrey believed her. After all, if she would tell her about Michael, why would she protect Stephanie? And what difference did it make? If Michael was the one who killed Conrad, he was the person Audrey wanted in the end.

So, that was one option—tell Stephanie all that. She'd be upset, but at least it wouldn't interrupt her work. And she'd have to understand, right? Michael killed a man. That couldn't be ignored because Stephanie was still in love with him or something. He had to be held accountable.

The other option was to go along with whatever Stephanie suggested. Or, well, pretend to. Nod as she talked. Let Stephanie believe everything was fine. Allow her to feel that relief.

Stephanie was surely going to find out at some point, but maybe Leslie wouldn't have to be the one to tell her. It wasn't the honorable option, maybe not even the most logical one. But, ultimately, Leslie couldn't bring herself to tell Stephanie to her face that she'd told Audrey about Michael. She wanted to put that off a little while longer. Stephanie had work to do. Let her do it without worrying about Michael.

Let Leslie lie in bed, wondering if she'd done the right thing.

43

"What are we waiting for?" Andy asked, his arms flailing as he paced in Audrey's office. "They deserve to die! Both of them! Why would we use resources to keep those traitorous murderers alive for even another second?"

"It's going to be *minimal* resources, Andrew. William, I want you to prepare for them no more than the bare minimum we can feed them to keep them alive for up to two days. Give them some water. What else do we have?"

"I know we have some sweet potatoes and turnip greens."

"Turnip greens are perfect. Gives them nutrients but tastes bitter if we don't prep them, which we won't."

"We're giving them our fucking *food*? Why?" Andy stomped his feet.

"It's stuff nobody wants to eat anyway, Andrew. Look, I'm as angry as anyone at what happened. Michael blatantly lied to us, conspired against us, and then murdered one of my most loyal followers. Trust me when I say that's not going to go unpunished. Not by a *long* fucking shot. They're both going to die, and they're going to hate the hell out of life until they do. Hopefully, by the time the moment comes, they'll be *begging* us to finish them off."

"But why wait? Why not just do it?"

"They're not going anywhere. They're locked in the pen. There's no way out. And I'm waiting for two reasons. One is they still refused to tell us *why* they were at Stephanie's house in the first place. It wasn't a fucking house call. Michael left his hospital bed, snuck out of the hospital, and then had to get back there before anyone noticed he was gone. That was risky. He must have had a good reason to take such a risk. What was he looking for? Did he find it? And, if he did, where is it now?"

"But what fucking *difference* does it make?" Andy asked, leaning on Audrey's desk, then spinning away. "Maybe it was some memento from his wedding with Stephanie. Or some medicine he thought she had stashed away there. Who the hell knows? What could it possibly be that we'd give a shit about?"

"Let me worry about what we'd give a shit about," Audrey snapped. "You concentrate on executing my orders. Understood?"

Andy stood stiff, then jammed his arms across his chest emphatically, his lips pressed tightly together. He said nothing.

"The *second* reason I want to wait a short time is that I want this to be public. I want the people to *know* what Michael and Nick did, and *see* what their punishment is. I want this to send a message to everyone that insubordination, lying, and law-breaking are *not* going to be tolerated while I'm leading this town. When Stephanie was the leader, you all saw what happened—nobody respected the rule of law, and everything began spiraling out of control. A mad man was loose, and she was powerless to stop it because she basically refused to punish anyone. By the time she tried to grow a fucking *spine*, it was too late.

"And that's why I'm sitting in this seat now. The people saw that, and voted for change. They voted to put me here to make Alessandra great, not to allow aliens to take over the town and infect their families or to allow murderers to get off with a slap on the wrist. I want them to have the imprint on their brains of witnessing Michael and Nick receive the quick kick of justice. That's gonna confirm to them they put the right person in place to do this job. And if I can follow that up by introducing the vaccine and the end of the virus's threat, what more could the people of Alessandra ask for?"

"When do you want to do this?" William asked.

"We're two days from the deadline I set for Stephanie and her team. Go check on their progress. I fully expect to have something to present to the people."

"And what are we gonna do about Stephanie?"

Audrey paused, looking down. Then she raised her head.

"Once we get the vaccine, we can start the countdown on her too."

Nick crawled out of his tent and saw Michael sitting at the long tent-covered table, sipping out of a small bowl of water.

"Morning," Michael said, setting his cup down. "Does this place bring back memories?"

"No good ones." Nick walked over and sat down across from Michael. "It's pretty much what I remember. Not that I expected a lot of upgrades."

"Maybe we can speak to the concierge about the lack of amenities."

"My understanding is the concierge will sooner bash your head in with a club than give you directions to the closest five-star restaurant."

"I'm gonna give this place an awful online review."

Nick picked up the water pitcher and noticed it was almost empty.

"Did you drink all the damn water?"

"Hey, I did my best to take no more than half. They didn't give us much of anything."

"Food?"

"Nothing. I don't think we're gonna be getting luxurious treatment while we're here."

Nick looked around behind him, and could see the mansion looming over the fence, closer than he'd been to it in a long time. He could feel bile starting to rise in his throat, but he swallowed hard, trying to force himself to stay in the moment. Forget about the past. Be here now.

"Why are we alive?" he asked.

Michael took another sip of water. "You mean, why haven't they already killed us?"

"Yeah. I don't know about you, but that's what I was thinking about when Andy spotted us there with Conrad's body. I swear, my heart almost stopped. I thought that was it. He'd shoot us both on the spot and figure out the rest later."

"Then, when he didn't, I thought maybe Audrey wanted to do it herself."

"Or toss us into a fucking cage with those other two goons to let them snap us like twigs."

"Right. Without that knife, Conrad himself would have done that to both of us."

"Yeah," Nick said. "So, what gives? Why are we still above ground? There has to be a reason."

"Audrey's not getting more lenient and empathetic."

"That's for damn sure. Michael, I've been in this pen when all I had done was sleep in a bed with Rachel. We didn't hurt anyone. We didn't personally wrong Audrey. We violated a rule. And I'll tell you, the things I saw and experienced were horrific. It's giving me shivers being back in here now. I can't help but think…"

"If that was what it was like *then*, what are they going to do to us after what *we* did?"

"Exactly. And she trusted you. That makes this feel like even more of a betrayal. I don't like this."

"No," Michael said. "There's nothing to like. You could argue we'd have been better off if we *had* gotten those bullets in the head as we left Stephanie's house."

"There are definitely fates worse than death. Let's hope this isn't one of them."

Nick heard a rattling from behind—someone was opening the gate. He could see two large shadows cast on the ground from the other side of the fence.

Stomping down the hall, Stephanie shoved the door open, letting it slam against the wall. She grabbed a pillow out of a nearby chair and hurled it at Leslie's head.

"Hey!" Leslie woke up, swatting the pillow off her bed.

"What the *fuck* have you done?" Stephanie yelled. "Do you even understand the shit you've caused here? What were you *thinking*? I thought we had a deal."

"Audrey beat you here. What did you *want* me to tell her?"

"Anything. Fucking…*anything*. Pretend you're asleep and

confused. Tell her nothing has happened yet. But *not that.* Jesus, Leslie. How could you be so stupid?"

"Me? Stupid? You're the one who had Michael sprint down the hall with a bloody knife in his hand, right past my door. If you're so smart, maybe you should close my damn door next time!"

"Well, I'm sorry," Stephanie said. "I guess I didn't realize you were a fucking *spy* for the enemy when we were trying to save the whole goddamn town! My bad, right? This is unbelievable."

"Look, Michael *killed a man*, Stephanie. You're asking me to help cover that up? Really? You think *that's* reasonable? You think I'm some terrible person because I wanted Michael to be held accountable for murder?"

Stephanie slammed her hand against the wall and looked at the ceiling. "It wasn't…You don't understand what happened. You weren't *there*."

"Neither were you! Right? Neither were you. So how do *you* know?"

Stephanie stared at Leslie, her eyes narrow. "He's not a killer, Leslie. It was self-defense. That's all there is to it."

"You don't know that. Maybe he saw him out there, had a knife, and figured he could take out one of Audrey's men. Figured no one would suspect him, so he could get away with it."

"That's ridiculous."

"Maybe. Maybe not," Leslie sat up in bed, crossing her legs and leaning forward with her arms in her lap. "But what we *know* is that a man is dead, and Michael was probably holding the knife that killed him when he got back to the hospital that day. If it was merely self-defense, I hope the facts on that come out, and he's —"

"Oh, that's such *bullshit*. You know no such 'facts' are going to come out. He's gonna be guilty until proven innocent in the court of Audrey, and there *is* no innocent in her court unless she decides you are. And you have to know there's no way someone isn't paying for Conrad's death. He was one of her little pets. I don't care if he tried to run Michael over with a goddamn tank, Michael's gonna pay with his life."

"You don't know that either!"

"The only thing keeping me alive is this virus research! That's the goddamn truth! You think Audrey doesn't want me dead? Fortunately, I have a skill she's in need of, but not for much longer. We had a plan that was about to be set in motion. We were ready. One more step, and you had to tear the whole thing down because you couldn't keep your mouth shut for five minutes."

"So what happens now? There has to be something you can do. Can I help?"

Stephanie laughed. "Oh, you've helped plenty. I'm discharging you tomorrow, Audrey be damned. Maybe she'll give you a comfy bedroom for being such a good spy. It looks like I'm pretty much on my own. And there's not a lot of time left. Whatever is gonna happen, I know this much—I'm not telling you a goddamn thing."

44

Michael woke up and tried to roll over, but a sharp pain shot through his side and he nearly screamed, the ground like uneven concrete beneath his thin tent. He reached up to touch his forehead and winced; he could feel a welt starting to form.

The sun was up, and he could hear someone moving around outside the tent. If it was those goons again, he didn't want them to know he was awake. Though they might drag him out of there to finish the job they started the previous day.

"Michael, it's me. You can come out," Nick said. "There's food. Or something *resembling* food, anyway."

Relieved, Michael unzipped his tent and crawled out, the pain in his side nearly knocking the breath out of him as he did. He nearly collapsed but caught himself on his elbows, sucking in a deep breath, then pushing himself to his feet. Standing up straight was too painful, so he stayed hunched over, hobbling over to the table, a bowl of cold turnip greens sitting between the two of them.

"Shit," Michael said, almost out of breath from the ten-foot walk. "How you holding up?"

"Hard to say. Head's throbbing, but that could also be hunger and dehydration. There's a bad bruise across my midsection, and it hurts like hell pretty much whatever position I'm in. Another bruise on my right thigh, and I can't see my back, but it feels like shit. You?"

"Gotta be broken ribs. Reminds me of that time I broke two ribs in that playoff game sophomore year. You remember that?"

"God damn. Yeah. You got blindsided by that big number twenty-four. Can't remember his name. He laid you the fuck out, though. I swear, we thought you were dead."

"Got up, though," Michael said.

"Eventually."

"Still. I got through that. We'll get through this. We've been injured before."

"Yeah, but we had doctors. Treatment. Fucking pain meds. Oh, god, what I'd do for some pain meds right about now."

"Speaking of doctors…" Michael said, looking around and lowering his voice. "You think she knows yet?"

"Stephanie?"

"Yeah. You think she knows what happened? That we're here?"

"Probably. And if she doesn't know *exactly*, she can probably put two and two together since we never came back."

"Yeah," Michael said. "It kills whatever plan she had, though. We were *so* damn close. Getting rid of Conrad's body would have taken care of the evidence we did anything. We had the goods on Audrey. It was right there in front of us. How'd they find us? How'd they know we were there?"

"That's been bugging me too. We weren't in there all *that* long. And Andy's standing there when we come out? At night? It's like they were ready for us."

"Like they knew what we were doing."

"Yeah. I don't know," Nick said. "But what does Stephanie do now? Is there anyone else who can help her besides us?"

"Nobody she trusts on that level. For good reason. She's been burned a lot. With us in here, I don't know what she'll do. When she came back to rescue me out of the mansion, at least she had your help. Now, it's just her. She's resourceful, but I wouldn't say I'm optimistic."

"We're gonna die in here, aren't we?"

Michael fished a handful of turnip greens out of the bowl and set it down on a small plate.

"Yeah." He nodded and took a bite. "Yeah, we are."

* * *

Stephanie spotted Victor in the upstairs hallway and made eye contact, nodding her head in the direction of her office door. He nodded and followed her inside.

"Close the door behind you if you don't mind." Stephanie sat down behind her desk. "I'm not sure how well we've kept you updated on the virus research we've been doing, Do you know where we are with that?"

"Not really," he said as he settled into a chair. "I know you all have been working basically around the clock since Audrey said it had to be done, and I *think* the deadline is tomorrow, but it's easy to lose track. That's about it."

"Yeah, that's right. Tomorrow would be seven days. And *someone* has been working on this pretty much every minute for the past week. But they had made a heck of a lot of progress before that too, a good bit of it without me. When Audrey started that timer, we were closer to already having this solved than even *we* knew."

"That's great news! So how close are you now?"

"On the vaccine, we're getting closer, but there's still work to do there. At least a few weeks, maybe months," Stephanie said. "But we've stumbled into another answer, almost but not totally accidentally."

"What's that?"

"We believe we have what amounts to a *cure*. We'd still rather have a vaccine so we can prevent the spread of the virus to begin with, but a cure would be a massive breakthrough. It would mean no one ever has to die from it as long as we get to them quickly enough."

"That's amazing!" Victor said. "How quickly would you need to administer it to them?"

"We haven't done human trials, only rodents, so it's tough to say for sure. Probably six to eight hours after onset of symptoms. It's doable."

"I mean, this is *incredible*, Doctor Sloan. If there were still Nobel prizes, you and the team would get one for this."

"Well, it hasn't been *proven* yet. But we're sort of out of time. I can ask Audrey for more, but she doesn't seem like the type to tell the town she was wrong. So our backs are against the wall."

"That's probably true. What does that have to do with me, though?"

"Did you hear about Michael and Nick being taken into custody?" she asked.

"Yeah. Sorry about Michael," Victor looked at the floor, fiddling with his scrubs. "Didn't I hear they killed somebody?"

"You probably did. But it's not what it seems like."

Victor nodded and curled his mouth. "Okay."

"Anyway, this isn't about them, exactly. It's about me." Stephanie stood and walked around her desk, sitting in the chair next to Victor. She reached into her pocket and pulled out a vial of liquid alongside a syringe. "I need you to take this."

"What is it?" His eyes were big as he reached for the items.

"It's the H6N1 cure. Or what we very much *hope* and *think* is the cure. We have a lot more."

"All right. What do you want me to do with it?"

Stephanie sighed. "I'm about to do something very stupid. And you're the only free person I trust enough to do this job. If I'm not back here by the time the sun begins to go down, I'm going to need your help."

"What are you doing here?" Andy asked, standing in the doorway and seeing Stephanie on the mansion's wraparound porch, her ring propped against the wall next to her.

Stephanie smiled and held up a vial that was two-thirds full of liquid.

"Is that it? The vaccine?"

"The very one."

"Didn't think you were gonna be able to pull it off."

"There were some tense moments, and I basically haven't slept in a week, but we got there," Stephanie said. "Can I come in?"

Andy stood aside and motioned for her to come in. He closed the door behind her and led her down the hall toward Audrey's office.

Memories of the last time she was here flooded Stephanie's

mind, the dread of what awaited her at the end of this hall, with its impossibly bright lighting, marble flooring, ten-foot-high columns and floor-to-ceiling windows. It was ridiculously opulent for Alessandra, something that belonged in Ancient Greece or something. The last time she walked this hall, her footsteps echoing around her, she knew she might be on her way to her own death as she tried to save Michael. This time wasn't much different.

The hall fed into the large front room with a bay window looking down on the town from high above. It was the same room where she last saw Michael tied to a chair and wept when William murdered Anna. Andy stopped and turned toward her; she swallowed hard and held her chin up.

"Stay here. Have a seat if you want," he said. "I'll go get Audrey. She may want some others to be here as well."

Stephanie nodded and settled into a burgundy leather recliner that hugged her body as if it were built with her specifically in mind. After the week she'd had, she was going to have to fight sleep while sitting there.

She started going over her plan in her head, making sure she hadn't missed a step. She needed to be convincing and confident. That was the only way she had a shot at making this work. It was far from a sure thing, but she felt like she had a chance of getting through this. Michael and Nick were going to die if she didn't try *something*, and she probably would too.

Stephanie didn't like being in the mansion. Besides dredging up memories she'd rather keep buried, it felt dirty to her. She didn't know how Michael had tolerated the awful place for several months after joining Audrey's team. Stephanie turned to the bay window next to her. She could see most of Alessandra—the square, St. Francis off to the left, and streets with rows of houses leading almost to Lake Chatuga, blue and glistening in the midday sun. People down there were doing their best to survive from day to day, and here was Audrey, living in luxury, wasting solar electricity that could be shared with the town, taking up residence in a home far bigger than she could possibly need even with a team of fifty. Stephanie couldn't help but think she should have had the mansion burned down when she had the chance. That, or taken apart piece by piece, the wood used for fires, the solar panels brought down to the square. She'd considered it, but she'd never quite found the time to put the plan into action. Everything ended so abruptly. It was one of many regrets she had.

"Welcome, Stephanie," Audrey said as she approached with her two remaining men flanking her; Andy trailed behind. Stephanie reluctantly pushed herself up from the chair's embrace and walked toward her, extending her hand. They shook. "If you have the vaccine, we can start bringing back this little custom."

Stephanie smiled. "I think people would like that."

"I guess this means I was right, huh? If I hadn't pushed you to get this done in a week, who knows how long it would have taken?"

"We're all very thankful for your leadership on this." Stephanie gritted her teeth. "It's been invaluable for getting us to the finish line."

Audrey gave a wry smile and placed a hand on Stephanie's shoulder. "This is a good leadership lesson for you: sometimes, you have to really push people hard, beyond what they think their limits are, in order to get big, important things done."

It was almost physically painful for Stephanie to listen to Audrey twisting the metaphorical knife deeper, but she knew she needed to let it roll off her back. She had to keep her cool if there was any chance of her plan working.

"Thank you." Stephanie tried to force a smile. "I won't forget that."

"Good. So, what's the next step? Is it ready to use now?"

"Trials have gone as well as could be expected. I'd be honored if you and your team would be the first official recipients of the vaccine outside of hospital personnel."

Audrey rubbed her chin, a finger tracing her jawline along to her neck.

"That's a wonderful idea. It's only right that we're the first to be immune. Then we can line the rest of the town up tomorrow morning after we execute Michael and Nick. That was awful, wasn't it? What they did?"

"Um, yes. Of course," Stephanie could feel her muscles tightening. "Very unfortunate. That's not something we can tolerate."

"Even beyond the killing, it was a betrayal. I trusted Michael, and he was deceptive, manipulative, and then he killed someone I cared deeply about. Why would he do that?"

Stephanie licked her lips. "I don't know. It's…hard to understand, Ms. Reese."

"As a leader, the first time that happens to you, you have an obligation to punish it severely to ensure no one tries to do it again. But the second time it happens to you, you're a fool. You saw your trust violated, and then you gave it up again anyway. Do you think I'm a fool, Stephanie?"

"I…no, of course not. You're as smart as anyone I know."

Audrey stared for a moment, and Stephanie felt pinned to the floor.

"Yes," Audrey finally said. "So, I hope it won't be a problem if I have you give *yourself* the vaccine first. As a precaution. I trust you understand."

Stephanie never wavered from eye contact. "I completely understand, Ms. Reese. You're too important to the town; you can't afford to take chances with your health."

Stephanie pulled the vial and syringe from her pocket, yanking the cover off the needle and turning the vial upside down. She inserted the needle into the vial, then flicked the syringe a couple of times and pulled the flange back, the open part of the barrel filling with the liquid.

She pulled a small bottle of rubbing alcohol out of her pocket, flipped it over quickly onto a cotton swab and dabbed it onto her arm, where she planned to put the needle in. Audrey and her team were watching closely but keeping their distance. Stephanie's arm wanted to shake, but she had to be steady.

Taking a strip of cloth out of her pocket, Stephanie wrapped it around her bicep and pulled it tight, clenching her fist a few times. She didn't believe in god but, in this moment, she didn't know what else to do but say a small, silent prayer. She felt powerless to do anything else. She was prepared for this, but it was still hard to do.

Stephanie stuck the needle into her arm and slowly pushed the flange down, injecting the liquid into her body. When the syringe was empty, she pulled it back out and set it on the table.

She forced a smile. "And that's it. Simple. There's still plenty more left for all four of you."

Audrey stood up straight and crossed her arms. Then she looked at Andy.

"Go confiscate what's on the table. And check her for anything else she has on her."

"Wait. What are you doing?" Stephanie asked, as Andy patted her down, pulling another vial of liquid and a couple more syringes out of her back pocket. "Do you not want to take the vaccine?"

"Like I said, Stephanie, I have to be careful. What's the incubation period for H6N1? Somewhere around six hours? We're gonna keep you in quarantine for a little bit to make sure you don't show any symptoms. If you're okay by nightfall, everything's good to move forward. And if you're not, well, I guess the execution will take care of itself, won't it?"

45

Nudged forward with a five-foot pole, Stephanie was led down the back stairway and across a strip of courtyard to the gate for the quarantine pen. Andy—wearing a mask—pushed her aside so he could unlock the pen and force her inside, locking the gate behind her. She quickly noticed there were still only two tents to sleep in.

Slowly, she walked toward them, hearing the zipper come down on the one furthest from her. A head tentatively peeked out.

"Stephanie?" Michael said, scrambling out from inside the tent, concern in his voice. "What the hell are you doing here? What's going on?"

Nick's tent opened then, and he watched Michael start to jog past before stopping and doubling over, pressing an arm to his midsection.

"Stay away from me," Stephanie said, then made eye contact with Nick. "Both of you. Keep your distance."

Wincing and out of breath, Michael raised his head.

"Why? What's wrong?"

"I had a plan. I thought it had a good chance of working, and it's still got a shot. But this isn't where I was hoping to end up."

"What do you mean?" Nick asked, standing outside his tent now. "Why do we need to stay away from you?"

Stephanie sighed. "We don't have a vaccine for the virus, but we have a cure that we feel confident about. I brought vials containing both the virus and the cure. The plan was to get

Audrey to let me inject her and her men with what they thought was the vaccine, but it would actually be the virus itself."

"And then *you'd* hold the cure," Michael said.

"That's right. But I anticipated her not falling for that, and wanting to see me take it first to show it was safe. And I figured I'd still have the cure, so I could give it to myself later. It takes a few hours for the symptoms to show up. In the meantime, hopefully that would get them to trust me enough to inject them too."

"And instead..." Nick said, walking over to Michael and patting him on the back. "You're here."

"Yeah. And they took everything I had on me. She wants to wait it out and see if I'm fine later this evening. If so, they'll believe me. If not..."

"You'll be dead anyway," Michael said, then looked at Nick. "And maybe all three of us will be."

"So what do we do?" Nick asked. "You said it's still got a shot of working. It seems like we're fucked."

"Well..." Stephanie said, scratching her temple. "There is an emergency backup plan."

Victor stepped outside the hospital and looked up at the sky, studying the sun. Had it peaked? Was it on its way down? On one hand, he didn't want to wait too long. Doctor Sloan had said this was a life-or-death situation. He needed to move quickly and decisively. On the other hand, this was going to be dangerous, and he wanted to believe Doctor Sloan wouldn't get herself in such a position. He'd seen her accomplish so much, and always seem to know what to do. Was she really putting her life in his hands now?

He decided to err on the side of action rather than inaction. He reached into the pockets of his scrubs to be sure he had everything she'd given him before she left—three doses of the H6N1 cure and three clean syringes. He didn't know why she needed three, but she said he was better off not knowing everything. All he needed to know was the instructions she'd given him.

Victor took off jogging, down into the street, across the square and finally hitting the hill leading up to Audrey's mansion. Stephanie had told him he needed to be careful not to be seen anywhere near the mansion. If he saw anyone around, he should back off, wait, and return when they were gone.

He knew he had the disadvantage of having the low ground, meaning it would be a lot easier for them to spot him than for him to notice anyone watching from the top of the hill. He scanned the mansion's windows, looking for any sign of movement, maybe a curtain being nudged open or a head flashing out behind the glass—anything that might indicate he was being observed.

Heart beating rapidly, he continued on, each step methodical, trying to stay low and use the hill as a sort of shield. He was supposed to go to the quarantine pen in the courtyard behind the mansion. Victor had never been up here, but Stephanie said it wouldn't be hard if he could avoid being spotted. Keep going around the north side of the mansion until you saw two large white columns, walk around the corner between those, and the pen would be up ahead, in the center of the large compound.

Almost crawling, trying to stay as low as he could, Victor made his way deeper into the compound, his shadow lengthening beneath him. With each step, he hoped to see an opening and the two columns, but there was nothing yet. Just a hill with long, mangy grass and Audrey's mansion looming ominously above him.

Then the hill started to flatten a bit, and he could finally see land to his left opening up to reveal exactly what Stephanie had promised—two large marble columns marking the entrance to the courtyard, with other out buildings in the back part of the compound. Victor stood to walk, his eyes darting every which way, looking for anyone who might stand between him and the pen.

He could see it up ahead, a tall, rusty metal fence in what looked like a fairly large rectangular pen. That had to be what she was talking about. What had she told him to do once he got there? Don't say her name. Make as little noise as possible. Rattle the gate's lock slightly, and toss the medicine and syringes over the fence. Then get the hell out of there the same way he got in.

Cautiously, he walked to the pen, moving as fast as he felt safe. He saw the gate, a padlock hanging from it. He grabbed it and took one more look around behind him. This was an angle from the mansion he'd never seen, with it towering directly over top of him, mere feet away, steps leading up to the back of the building. It was quiet.

Taking a deep breath, Victor shook the lock for a couple of seconds, then reached into his pocket and grasped everything Stephanie had given him, reared back and tossed it all over the fence. All he could do from there was hope, as he turned to run back out and down the hill to safety.

"Did you hear that?" Stephanie asked, her head swinging toward the gate.

"I'm not sure. Maybe," Nick said. "What did you think you heard?"

Dusk was moving in, and it was getting harder to see much on the other side of the pen, but Stephanie was confident she'd heard the lock move. She'd easily spent enough time in this horrible place to recognize that sound, often signaling some man coming to beat or rape her, this time potentially representing her salvation.

She didn't hear anything else but, when the gate didn't open after several more seconds, Stephanie sprinted toward it. As she got closer, she could see them—syringes and glass vials scattered on the ground. Victor had pulled it off. He'd actually done it. She wanted to kiss him. Waves of relief washed over her as she looked for each piece, hunched over the dirt, trying to make sure she didn't miss anything. She was starting to feel a headache and a little flush, but nothing was going to dull her elation right then.

This changed everything. As long as the cure worked as expected, she'd be able to stop the virus in its tracks, and Audrey would have no idea she'd done it. That was going to earn her Audrey's trust, and that was the most valuable commodity she could ask for at this point.

"Holy shit, he came through," Michael said, as Stephanie slid onto one of the benches, he and Nick both still staying several feet away. "Victor actually did it."

Smiling wide, Stephanie nodded. "Yeah. Victor came through in a *big* fucking way. Let me do this first, and I'll go ahead and give it to both of you too in case you caught it from me."

Stephanie didn't have a strip of cloth, so she pulled her shirt off over her head, the cool autumn air hitting her bare skin like pin pricks, but she didn't care. She wrapped one sleeve around her bicep, tied a quick knot and pulled it taut. She quickly found a vein on her forearm and prepared the syringe. Stephanie gave one quick look at Michael and Nick, then plunged the needle into her arm, pressing the flange down and letting the medicine flow into her body.

They heard the lock rattle again, this time followed by the gate being pulled and swinging open. Stephanie yanked the needle out of her arm and laid it on the table, trying to use her body to block it from view.

Coming in first was Victor, his head hanging limp; Andy kicked him from behind, and he fell into the dirt.

"I found something that belongs to you," Andy said, stepping over Victor as he walked toward the back of the pen. "Now I'm gonna need what's ours. Everything he brought you, hand it over."

Stephanie untied her shirt from her arm and pulled it around her front, pressing it tightly to her chest to cover up as Andy got closer. She suddenly felt unbearably cold, and started to shiver. She didn't even think it was all *that* cold outside, but her shoulders were blocks of ice; her back was covered in goosebumps. Had she gotten enough of the cure into her veins before she had to pull it out?

Andy stopped and looked her up and down.

"Only been here a few hours, and already putting on a show for these boys?" Andy laughed. "Enjoy it, guys. These are the last tits you'll ever see."

He roughly pushed Stephanie away from the table and rounded up the syringes and vials.

"What is all this shit?" Andy asked. "Must have been pretty important if he was willing to risk his life to get it to you."

"More vaccines we had," Stephanie said. "Wanted to make sure Michael and Nick got vaccinated now, just in case."

"And yourself too? Didn't you already take it?"

"I didn't take much back there. Needed to make sure I got a full dose."

Andy stared at her for a few seconds, as if waiting for her to waver, but she held his gaze. She knew she couldn't back off or show weakness. After a few seconds, Andy reached out and lightly touched her bare shoulder, running his hand down toward her breasts; she closed her eyes and pursed her lips, then slapped at his hand. Michael started to charge toward him, but Andy stepped back and pulled a pistol out of his pocket.

"Hey, now. No harm, no foul," Andy said, shoving the medicine into his pockets as Michael stared, seething. "You all didn't think I wandered in here unarmed, did you? You all stick it out here together. I'm sure you can figure out the sleeping arrangements. We'll see ya in the morning."

46

Stephanie woke up in a dark tent, crickets chirping nearby, and her headache dulled to a mild throb. She lifted a hand to her forehead, and there were no sweats, no apparent fever. She felt human. If the virus had progressed in the manner they'd typically seen, she knew she'd be deteriorating at a rapid rate by now. The thought occurred to her that she may be the first person in the world to knowingly contract H6N1 and survive. They'd done it. They'd found a way to beat the virus. They still had to produce a good bit more of the cure, but this was a major breakthrough. Even from her prison, she was going to let herself be happy about that for a moment.

She rolled over and adjusted her body on the thin bottom of the tent, the dry, lumpy ground beneath her making it hard to get comfortable for long. They'd given her a tent by herself for the night, in case she was still sick or contagious. She fought with them on that, saying she'd sleep out in the open, but they all refused.

What were they going to do from here? She didn't know. Her plan had almost worked, but it ultimately blew up in her face. This time, she even dragged Victor into it. Looking back on how everything unfolded the past year or two, the guilt was hard to push away.

How many people have my plans gotten killed? Anna, Trish, Doctor Giles, Quinn, arguably the Brownings and Vicarys. Probably Michael and Nick. And now Victor's trapped here and likely to die because of me. Was it unfair to even put him in the position of risking his life to help me?

Stephanie knew the answer, or at least she was pretty sure she did. Victor was the one person she could ask to be her emergency plan. She'd known he would do his best to follow through, wouldn't even question it. Would do as he was told, because she was the one who asked.

And now, here he was, stuck with them when all he'd done was follow Stephanie's instructions. He didn't kill or attempt to hurt anyone. He'd wanted to help. But Audrey was going to see it as a betrayal.

Audrey had accused Stephanie of being a murderer, of killing Zac in a fit of jealousy and panic at losing her power. She never laid a hand on Zac, but sometimes she felt like a murderer, as people around her kept falling because of the decisions she made. She kept walking away, but the people who tried to help her continued to pay the price for her actions.

Suddenly, there was a groan, deep and guttural. She recognized it as Nick, and she sat up, her heart nearly stopping.

"Stay away, god damn it!" he yelled from inside his tent, the shadow of his hand scraping down the side of it. "We both have it. Victor and I both have the virus. Stay back!"

Stephanie felt lightheaded, and all her muscles tightened at once. She shut her eyes tight, shaking her head violently back and forth, wanting to wake up from the nightmare. This couldn't be real. Surely not. Then nausea rose up from her stomach, and she vomited in the back part of the tent.

She unzipped the flap and crawled out, stomach in knots and muscles cramping. Michael was a few feet away, standing stiff and staring at her, eyes wide. She forced herself to stand and looked at him, shaking her head. Almost breathless, she said, "I'm okay."

Stephanie ran to the front of the pen, slamming into the gate. She banged on it, trying to make as much noise as she could.

"Someone needs to come out here!" she shouted. "We need help! Two of our people are infected! Come down here, damn it!"

"What are you doing?" Michael asked, running up from behind her. "What do you expect them to do? If you tell them about your plan, that you had the cure, they'll *kill* you."

"What do you want me to do? Let the two of them die in

agony so I survive this?"

"We don't even know if they're capable of being saved! If they've started exhibiting symptoms, it may be too late."

"We don't know that! God damn it, Michael. We have to try!"

A light flipped on in the room at the top of the staircase, and a figure started walking slowly down to the courtyard, each step methodical. Stephanie couldn't tell yet who it was.

She and Michael were silent, hearts pounding, waiting for whoever it was to get to them.

"What the *fuck* is all this racket about?" Andy said, from the other side of the fence. "You better have a damn good reason for this shit."

"Nick and Victor…they have the virus," Stephanie said, her voice strained, breath coming in gasps. "They need help. You have to do something."

"How'd they get the virus?"

"They…I don't know."

"Maybe Victor had it when he got here, and he's only now showing symptoms," Michael said. "They're sharing a tent."

"That'd be quite a coincidence," Andy said. "He happened to be infected when he showed up here, but nobody knew it?"

"What the hell *difference* does it make *now*?" Stephanie asked. "The point is they're infected, and they need help."

"What do you want *me* to do about it?" Andy asked. "You said you have a vaccine, not a cure. That's not gonna do them much good now. Unless you have something else to share with me."

So many thoughts were swirling around Stephanie's mind. If they still believed she had the vaccine instead of the cure, she could still execute her plan. By the morning, if she was okay, they'd think she had actually given herself the vaccine and not something that would harm them. She might be able to wipe out Audrey and her entire crew in one day.

To have a chance at that, though, she'd have to sacrifice Nick and Victor. Was it worth letting two men die to save an entire town?

* * *

She can't do it. There's no way.

For Michael, the scene was playing out in slow motion in front of him. Stephanie had come here to save him, but now there was nothing he could do for her. All he could do was watch.

He wanted to yell out, or to pull her aside and talk her down from where he was afraid she was headed. What would telling Andy what she'd done accomplish? At best, Andy would agree to bring the cure down for Nick and Victor, but everyone in that pen was going to die soon anyway, and Audrey would be hailed by the town as a hero for bringing them the cure to the virus.

Michael didn't want Nick to die either—especially by the brutal hand of H6N1—but there was no way to ultimately save him. Audrey and her crew held all the cards. One way or the other, they were going to kill Nick for his part in Conrad's murder. The only question was whether the virus killed him, or they did.

Victor didn't deserve this fate at all, but he had to know there was risk in coming up here, and he decided the risk was worth it to help Stephanie. Michael felt bad for him, but he was going down with them.

The one thing confessing could gain them would be time. If Stephanie could convince Andy to bring the cure so that this deadly contagion wasn't live right by their mansion the rest of the night, she'd have more time to try to figure a way out of this. She always believed there was a way, always wanted to be an optimist. It was part of what had drawn Michael to her. He wanted to believe things would work out in the same way she seemed to, that a little more time to think and plan was all you needed to defeat the forces of evil. That the battle was never lost until you were lying bloody on the battlefield.

But Michael didn't believe anymore that was the way the world worked. He thought back to when he first approached Stephanie about Audrey's lying and manipulation, the determination he'd felt then to make Audrey pay, to see her run out of town. He convinced Stephanie to join him on that mission. And, while they lost a lot along the way, they succeeded. Had he believed through everything that they'd eventually get there? Had he believed they'd find a way to win the war, if not the battle, when he was tied to a chair and nearly passing out in the mansion?

Maybe so. He could barely remember anymore. But standing there in the pen, watching Stephanie plead with Andy to help Nick and Victor, Michael didn't feel like everything would work out this time. He knew they weren't all going to make it out of this alive.

Stephanie standing silently, seemingly unable to find the words she needed, Andy gave them both a dismissive wave of the hand and turned to go back up to the mansion.

"If you wake me the fuck up again tonight, you will *seriously* regret it," Andy said as he approached the stairs. "Go to bed. There's nothing that can be done for your friends."

Suddenly, Stephanie raised her head, her back straightening, face stoic.

"You have the cure up there," she said, and Michael lowered his head, cursing under his breath. "It's in a few of the vials you took from me."

Andy stopped and looked back at them, his eyes narrowed. He started to walk back toward the gate.

"Did you say there's a *cure* up there?" he asked, his voice incredulous. "A cure to H6N1? In the stuff you brought?"

"That's right. We developed a cure. I brought it up here, so you have it now. There *is* something you can do for Nick and Victor. We can save them right now."

"But wait a second…You said you had a vaccine, not a cure."

"It wasn't something I was prepared to reveal yet," Stephanie said. "It's still…a little experimental. But it should work."

"What's in those other vials?"

"What other vials?"

"The ones that don't have the cure in it. It doesn't make any sense that you were going to give us all a cure to a virus we didn't have. What's in the other vials?"

"The vaccine. Like I said before."

Andy cocked his head and looked back and forth between her and Michael.

"Or it's the virus. Right? Yeah. Yeah, that makes sense. You were gonna infect us all. You gave it to yourself first, and then your errand boy there brought you some more of that cure so you could appear to be fine. You lying bitch."

"That's not...No. It's the vaccine. I promise! You need to help Nick and Victor!"

Andy laughed. "The hell I am. You can watch them die and think about how it's your fault that it's happening. Ya know, in a way, I respect the effort. That was pretty cold-blooded. Might have even worked if you hadn't met an even more cold-blooded bitch in Audrey. Sweet dreams, guys."

47

"I still can't believe you did that," Michael said, his arms clasped to the side of his head, trying to block out the wails coming from Nick and Victor's tent as they writhed in pain. "I can't believe you confessed."

"We've been over this. Jesus, Michael," Stephanie said, pounding her fist on the table in the pen. "What did you *want* me to do? Let them die? They're in indescribable pain because of me. And there isn't a damn thing I can do about it, except sit here and listen to them. Do you know what that guilt is like?"

"They're in there because of *us*, Steph. Us. You think I didn't play a part in all this? We've both done plenty to get us here. But I wasn't about to let that tempt me to throw it all away at the last minute."

"I didn't throw anything away. My plan wasn't gonna work anyway. Audrey wasn't gonna fall for it. The whole thing was doomed from the beginning. I couldn't sit here and listen to them die in agony for the sake of throwing my damn Hail Mary this morning. That would have been stupid."

"No, I really think it was brilliant," Michael said, sliding over to the bench in front of Stephanie and putting his hand on hers. "It absolutely *could* have worked. You're amazing at rolling with the punches, seeing one plan isn't gonna work, and then finding a new route to where you were trying to go. I honestly think that could have solved everything. It's excruciating to lose Nick, for me especially, but we were gonna lose him either way. This was our chance. What's our plan now?"

Stephanie's gaze fell, and she shook her head.

"Nothing?" Michael dipped his head, trying to make eye contact. "Any ideas at all? Are you giving up?"

Stephanie rested her head in her hands. "I don't know. I feel like it's the end. Nothing has worked out like I expected. Every time I think I see a light at the end of the tunnel, it gets extinguished. If these are the results of my plans, maybe I don't need to be the one coming up with plans anymore. I'm tired, Michael. I really am. Tired of seeing my friends die. Tired of feeling sad and guilty all the time. Maybe it's time to face it: if someone's gonna lead a revolution in Alessandra, it's not gonna be me."

The first sunlight was beginning to creep over the horizon, as Stephanie collapsed onto the table, her head falling into her folded arms, Michael looking on in stunned silence. She'd always been the one he came to for a sense of calm and direction. She'd always had the answers. But now, there was nothing there. She was empty. Finally empty. And Michael didn't know what to do. If she thought it was over, maybe it really was. Maybe they'd taken their shot, and that was it. He couldn't imagine how any one of the four of them was going to see another sunrise without doing something to change the situation they were in. And he had no plan for how to do that.

The lock rattled on the pen's gate, and it swung open. Andy and William walked through it holding pistols and two sets of chains.

"It's time to go, people. Everyone's gathering in the square for a little show," Andy said. "We'll leave Nick and Victor here. You two are the stars this time."

Stephanie could barely take full steps, the shackles digging into her ankles as she walked, the eyes of a crowd turning in her direction as she approached the town square. She looked at Michael, but he hung his head, seemingly trying to avoid seeing what was coming.

Every few steps, Andy would jab her in the back with the barrel of his pistol, maybe to remind her it was there, or perhaps to give her a few bruises of his own before Audrey got in the final shots.

As they took their first steps onto the deteriorating tile of the square, Stephanie could see that the crowd was still filling in, but it looked like most of the town was already here. They must have either announced the gathering last night or banged on doors *really* early. This was clearly a big morning for Alessandra.

Andy prodded her in the direction of the stage steps, and she stepped up onto them, Michael beside her, silent, head still hanging. Stephanie wondered what he was feeling—dread, sadness, shame, some combination of those? She could relate. She wished she could say or do something to reassure him that everything was going to be okay. That there was still a path, still hope. But she was resigned to what was coming. She figured maybe she even deserved it. She was tired of fighting.

They turned Stephanie and Michael to face the crowd, with Audrey standing in between, holding the bullhorn at the front of the stage. There was a low-volume chatter emanating from the crowd, the sound of anticipation, that something memorable was going to happen.

"Welcome, everyone!" Audrey said, a smile beamed across her face. She seemed as ebullient as Stephanie had ever seen her. "So happy you all could join us on this momentous morning for Alessandra. I've promised a major announcement that will change everything here and pave the path for a new, exciting future, and I will absolutely deliver on that promise. But first, it's important that we deal with a bit more cleansing so we're ready to take those steps with a fresh start, as a people *together*, all pulling in the same direction."

She took a few steps back and gestured dramatically to Stephanie and Michael, as if presenting them as prizes, generating a murmur from the crowd.

"You all know Stephanie and Michael," Audrey said, prompting a smattering of boos. "Long-time Alessandrans. And no one hates more than me to have to punish our native, true-blood Alessandrans. Nothing hurts my heart more than that. But, you see, sometimes even your flesh and blood can turn against you, and it's *essential* to take action when that happens. If you don't, that's how you can lose an entire community. If you see Stephanie and Michael getting away with unacceptable behavior, it's easy to justify that same behavior in yourselves. And you can't build community that way.

"To whom much responsibility is given, much is expected. And, sadly, my fellow Alessandrans, Stephanie and Michael here have repeatedly not lived up to that standard. I've given them chance after chance. Probably too many. I accept the blame for that. I *wanted* to see the good in them. I *wanted* to believe they could be productive, well-behaved members of our community. But they've violated my trust—*our* trust—for the last time, my friends. We're going to cut out the cancer so that the rest of us can live on as a healthy host."

Andy and William prodded them again, prompting the prisoners to step to the front of the stage, with Audrey circling behind them. Arms and legs shackled tight, Stephanie and Michael could barely move as pistols were pressed to their temples, and many in the crowd gasped.

"Because not all of you are aware of everything that's happened, I'm going to read off a list of their transgressions, so you can fully understand the depth of their betrayal," Audrey said. "I'll start with Michael. Helped to lead a violent coup of me, in which dozens were killed. Made ugly pornography and showed it to everyone right here in the square, encouraging others to do the same. Member of Stephanie's criminal administration. Helped to cover up Stephanie's murder of Zachary Latham. Committed espionage in plotting with Stephanie for yet another government overthrow. Failed to defend his position and allowed George Yates to be shot and nearly killed. Murdered Conrad Bloom in cold blood."

Audrey's voice cracked just a bit, and she paused, looking down at the stage. She swallowed hard, rose her eyes back to the crowd, and continued.

"Helped to plot the H6N1 infection of four members of my administration, leading to the infection of Nick Dyerson and Victor Davis, both of whom are very near death as we speak."

The members of the crowd seemed to cry out in unison, hands covering open mouths, many people beginning to cry. Michael still said nothing. He looked defeated.

Stephanie thought he deserved a better fate than this—shackled and perp-marched onto stage as his supposed crimes were read out loud to his friends and neighbors. His biggest mistake—voting for Audrey—wasn't even on the list. But even with that, did it make as much of a difference as they'd believed at first? Would Audrey really have taken a vote for Stephanie as the final word and slinked off without causing more problems? In the world where Michael voted for Stephanie, would they both be dead already, victims of Audrey's own overthrow, led by her goons and a minority of determined Alessandrans who somehow believed in her vision for the town?

Maybe Audrey ending up in that mansion was inevitable. Maybe Stephanie's decision on whether or not to let them inside hadn't really mattered. None of it had. It was all leading here. Fate was like a freight train heading down the track, set in its destination and too heavy to stop.

As the crowd noise calmed, Audrey continued: "These transgressions, committed over multiple *years*, constitute more than mere violations of law. No, these are deep breaches of community trust. This is a man who we all granted authority as a leader. And when leaders commit such violations, it's far worse than when normal, everyday citizens stray. And it must be dealt with harshly. William."

At the sound of his name, William spaced his feet wide and stiffened his right arm, holding the pistol against the back of Michael's head. Michael seemed to be sobbing, his shoulders convulsing as he stood before the crowd.

Stephanie held her breath. She didn't want to see this. If they were going to die on this stage, she'd assumed it would be at the same time. Surely they weren't going to make her watch Michael take a bullet to the head. After all this, everything they'd been through, this couldn't be the way it ended. It was too sudden, too much.

Then the sound of a gunshot reverberated through the air,

shaking the foundation of the stage beneath Stephanie's feet. Before she had a chance to close her eyes, she caught a nauseating glimpse of Michael's head exploding, and fell to her knees, an impotent scream on her lips.

He's gone. He's really and truly gone. It's not possible.

They'd had their ups and downs, but she had to face that he was her best friend, and there wasn't anyone close. Hadn't been for a while. There was no one who knew her like he did, who could make her laugh, and make her feel loved like he did.

On the edge of the stage, Stephanie started to vomit, but it had been so long since she'd eaten that there was nothing to come up, her stomach convulsing dryly, nothing coming from her mouth but a trickle of saliva and water. It felt like her body was trying to expel anything within it that had witnessed the moment of Michael's death, to cleanse herself of that memory completely. How could she live otherwise?

Stephanie felt a yank on her chains, and they dug into her ankles, sending sharp pain shooting up her shins and causing her knees to want to buckle. She lurched forward and nearly fell off the front of the stage, but Andy pulled hard again, holding her up while cutting the chain across her right arm and midsection. Stephanie cried out, then rolled over to her side.

Blood beginning to run down her shirt, Stephanie felt another hard tug, and she pushed herself back to her knees, then slowly stood up. Her legs were throbbing angrily; she felt stinging pains across her arms and stomach. She welcomed the pain, tried to let it wash over her completely. It was all she wanted to think about. To feel pain was to be alive, and to succumb to it was to block everything else out. Pain was her reality.

"Ladies and gentlemen, I'm sorry you had to witness that," Audrey said, the crowd beginning to calm down after several minutes of loud chatter and people looking away. "But *had to*, you did. It's important that there's no mistake about the consequences for what these two have done. That you *all* know what happens to traitors to the cause we should all be fighting for. The future is very bright for Alessandra, but each one of you has to make a conscious decision to walk into that light with me. We have to do this together, or you won't do it at all. There's no room on this train for rebels or freeloaders. We're one team. One mind. One Alessandra!"

Audrey held a fist high in the air, and people in the crowd began mimicking the gesture, first a few, and then gradually everyone. Silently, they stood like that for what seemed like minutes, fists thrust toward the sky, a symbol of solidarity that Audrey surely hoped would unite them as they went forward.

"Good. Then you're all with me. And, before we get to the major announcement, there's one more piece of housekeeping to complete." Audrey turned toward Stephanie. "This woman, you all know well. And if Michael's list of transgressions seemed long and tawdry, Stephanie's makes his pale by comparison. I'll have you know, everything Michael did, he did at her behest. Every bit of chaos and violence and worry you've experienced over the past two years has been at her hand. Stephanie has set out to sow discord and seize unchecked power at every possible turn, at the full expense of your own well-being. She's shown she cares about nothing but herself, and so she must meet her end today as well."

Andy lifted his pistol and pressed it to the back of Stephanie's head. Unconsciously, she began to hold her breath, continuing to concentrate on the pain.

"So you fully understand, I want to read off her list of crimes against Alessandra before we issue the punishment, and then I want to hear you all call for it. I want to hear my people, full-throated in favor of doing this. Stephanie's crimes began when she questioned the impeccable work of Doctor Richard Giles, her *superior*, hounding him and eventually prompting his death. This was a sign of her lack of loyalty and respect for any authority that wasn't her own. The pornographic film she did with Michael was all her plan, trying to convince everyone to turn against me. She organized an ambush of several of the best members of my team, not only leading to their death, but to the death of Trisha Curtis and Quinn Peterson, upstanding citizens who we've all mourned. From there, she invaded my mansion, leading to the death of Anna Swafford and my brother, Paul—"

Audrey suddenly stopped talking, her head turning to her left, looking over the crowd. Many of the people followed her gaze in that direction. Stephanie was still in a daze and barely paying attention.

"Is that smoke?" Andy asked, his arm holding the gun going limp. "It looks like it's coming from near where the gate is."

"That's not just smoke," Audrey said, the bullhorn hanging at her side. "I see flames. The goddamn gate is on fire. How is the fucking *gate* on fire?"

The crowd was beginning to get restless, with everyone now turning to look at the smoke.

"I don't know!" Andy said. "Should we go check it out?"

"Um, yes. I mean…Wait a minute. Let me think about this."

"I could go ahead and take out Stephanie first," Andy said. "Let's not leave unfinished business here."

There was a crash and then a whistle from where the fire was raging, and everyone could hear the unmistakable sound of horse hooves pounding the ground.

"No!" Audrey said. "We're going to need as much manpower as we can get. Make sure everyone gets themselves armed."

"What's going on?" William asked.

"The marauders. They found me. And if we don't stop them, they'll burn Alessandra to the ground."

48

"How are you with a gun?" Audrey asked as Andy unlocked Stephanie's shackles, the crowd madly scrambling for their homes to gather whatever weapons they could.

"I'm from North Georgia," Stephanie replied. "I can hold my own."

"Look, we're gonna need every hand we can get," Audrey said. "I know these people. They're brutal and ruthless. And, from what I can see, it looks like their numbers have swelled since they invaded Graysburg. Remember, we'll have our eye on you all the time. Turn on us, and I swear to god we'll take you down right then and there. But help us defeat them, and maybe we'll find our way to forgiving some of what you've done. Deal?"

For the second time in a couple of days, Stephanie shook Audrey's hand, this time as shackles fell from her body.

She didn't think for a second that she could trust Audrey. But, at this point, they wanted the same thing: to see Alessandra remain standing through this onslaught. And if she took a shot at Audrey or one of her men, it was only going to reduce the amount of manpower Alessandra had to fight back. For now, at least, Stephanie figured her best bet was to go along with them and see what help she could be.

"Can we make it to the mansion?" Andy asked Audrey, as he handed Stephanie a rifle they'd stashed on the back of the stage. "We have a lot more firepower up there."

"We should definitely try," Audrey said. "Let's do it."

She started running, Stephanie, Andy, William, and her two

men close behind. As they reached the bottom of the hill, though, a man on horseback raced past them—maybe thirty feet away—and climbed the hill with ease without even a glance at them. They all stopped and fell to the ground, trying to stay out of sight.

When he got to the top, he stopped next to the mansion, turning to look around, his horse calm. Without dismounting, he reached into a satchel slung across his shoulder and pulled out what looked like a flask. He took a swig of it, then splashed some on the side of the building before reaching over with his torch and setting the wall ablaze. William gasped and started to stand, but Audrey pushed him back onto his stomach as they watched the flames catch, then begin to spread across the east side of the mansion. The man fled on horseback down the hill and behind them into the town.

"Are those gunshots?" Andy asked, straining to try to see what was going on in the town as the heat of the flame began to radiate down to them.

Stephanie pushed herself up and jogged a few steps up the hill, the mansion now engulfed in a raging blaze that would surely turn it to mostly rubble in a few hours. She looked back over Alessandra, and the scene was one of chaos—at least a dozen men on horseback criss-crossing through the town, firing on residents who were fleeing in panic. One after another, the people fell face first on the cracked and broken streets of Alessandra, horses indiscriminately stomping on them as they sprinted past. And the flames were raging down there too, houses set on fire, chasing some people out the front door directly into the path of bullets.

Stephanie didn't know why the marauders were doing this, what the men had to gain from leaving a path of pure destruction, but here they were. It was hard to watch and think they had much hope of stopping the carnage from continuing. They had no horses, no way of attacking with the same level of speed and precision. And most of Audrey's men had small handguns that wouldn't do much good at anything other than relatively short range.

The rifle she'd been handed, though, was a .338 Lapua, scavenged from the home of someone who fled the town and never returned when the virus struck. Stephanie wasn't an expert on guns, but she figured she had far more effective range than the others. From her perch halfway up the hill, heat from the mansion's blaze radiating off her back, Stephanie could see a good bit of the town. It was a little less than a mile from here to the lake, so she guessed almost everything in the town could be technically in range for this gun. Of course, it was one thing for targets to be technically in range, and it was quite another for her to be able to hit them, especially when many of them were moving quickly on horseback. But it was worth a try.

Stephanie set the butt of the gun against her right shoulder and steadied it, looking straight down the barrel. Men on horseback streaked across her field of vision, firing on people who came near. She scanned slowly across the town, looking for an opportunity. Then she spotted three of the men huddled on foot behind a house, their horses standing idly by. She closed her eyes and took a deep breath, her finger resting against the trigger. The gun was heavy, more than she was used to from years before, when her dad would take her hunting or to the range as a young teenager.

She couldn't be nervous or hesitate; they could jump back on their horses at any moment. So, with the gun pressed hard beneath her shoulder, she pulled the trigger, and the rifle recoiled hard against her. She winced, but then straightened back up, aimed, and fired again into the group of men as Audrey and her crew covered their ears and scrambled away.

When she lowered the gun, Stephanie could see one of the men writhing on the ground, and it looked like he was clutching at his leg; the other two were looking around frantically, trying to figure out where the shot had come from. Stephanie quickly fell back down to her stomach, trying to make herself small against the side of the hill.

"Step away from the rifle." She heard the commanding voice and felt cold steel against the side of her head. She looked up at the sky and slowly pushed up to her knees, then rose to her feet.

One man had his gun on Stephanie, and there was another with a gun pointed at her companions.

The man next to Stephanie gestured behind him, and someone started to climb off the horse.

"Hey," Derrick said. "Good to see you again, Stephanie. Sorry it had to be like this."

"What are you…" Stephanie could barely find the words.

"What am I doing here? Emily is here too, down in the town somewhere. Xavier didn't make it this far, unfortunately. But we all did find each other. Or, rather, these men found *us*. Wandering. Searching for food. They knew we had to be *from* somewhere. We were in too good of shape to have been surviving on our own for all this time. They said they'd give us food and protection if we led them back here. It took a few days, but we found our way back. I'm sorry. But we were gonna die out there. It was gonna happen. Soon. They'll take what they can and ransack the rest of Alessandra. Ultimately, we'll all be able to survive a while longer. This is what they do."

"How could you do this?" Audrey asked, starting to walk toward Derrick until one of the men pointed his gun at her and pulled the hammer back. "These aren't good people. They destroy. They're going to leave us with nothing."

"Like you left me, Emily, and Xavier with nothing?"

"You know that's different," Audrey said. "That wasn't personal. I only did what was best for the people of this town. We were trying to build up our own. I hate you got caught in the middle of that."

"You don't hate that. If you did, it never would have happened."

"We can give you the cure!" Audrey blurted out, and Stephanie's eyes grew wide. "Let us live, call off the destruction of our town. In exchange, we'll give you the cure to the virus."

"You're saying you have a *cure* for the World Killer?" one of the marauders asked. "That's impossible."

"It's not. Stephanie had the virus about twenty-four hours ago, she took the cure, and look at her now—as healthy as she's ever been. Ask the researchers at our hospital, and they'll tell you the same thing. It's real."

Like that, Audrey was throwing away all the research, all the nights of fitful sleep, working in shifts, trying to get across the finish line with this cure. It had been Doctor Lawry's main focus since the moment the virus was first reported, and Stephanie helped lay the foundational work in the first year or so. By the time Audrey gave them the one-week deadline, they were already very close, but they knew so much could go wrong that promising any particular day was foolish. They'd done it, though, through a mixture of expertise, tireless effort, and sheer desire. Then, in a few short moments, Audrey gave it all away.

Maybe it was the gamble she had to make in order to save the town. Perhaps she had to bargain away something to give them a chance, and this was their biggest chip to play. It would have been the last play for Stephanie, though, not the first.

The men on horseback looked at each other.

"Go check it out. See if it's bullshit," the man near Audrey said. "If not, it's ours. Take it all."

49

Leslie rolled over in bed and heard a faint, rapid popping sound coming from nearby. The window in her room looked out the back side of the hospital, over the wall and out into the woods, so she couldn't tell much from there.

She climbed out of bed and opened her door, walking into the hallway and leaning against the railing that overlooked the first floor. From there, she could see through the large windows, facing the square, the main part of the town to her left. Initially, she noticed a good deal of black smoke off to the right, near the town's gate. Had there been a fire? Then she caught a glimpse of something moving fast—horses, with men riding. And it appeared the men were firing on townspeople.

Alessandra was under attack, and St. Francis was quiet as a church.

Leslie sprinted back into her room and threw open the closet, grabbing her clothes. She stripped off her hospital gown and flung it into the far corner of the room. She shimmied out of her jeans, fumbling with the zipper and button with trembling hands. Pulling her sweatshirt on, she spun around to retrieve her old tennis shoes, diving back into the closet to fumble around for them in the dark.

Leslie went back into the hall, pushing her hair back out of her face as she tried to figure out what to do. On one hand, whoever these people were, they hadn't entered the hospital yet. Maybe they wouldn't. Perhaps they were after something that had nothing to do with St. Francis. On the other hand, this was the most prominent structure in town besides the mansion—and Leslie's jaw fell open as her eyes turned toward the hill where that mansion had stood for so many years, only to see angry flames rising high into the air.

What in the world did I miss?

Technically, she was supposed to have gone with everyone else to the square that morning to hear Audrey's speech, but she brushed it off, wanting to sleep in. And with the information she'd given Audrey, she knew she'd earned the ability to take a few liberties. She'd hear about anything important anyway, so why bother dragging herself out of bed?

She never expected this. The brick and marble hospital wasn't going to be as easy to burn down as a large, wood-paneled house, but Leslie had to assume these intruders had more in mind than a little bit of mischief if they'd wreak such destruction.

She didn't know her way around the hospital building all that well. She figured there was a back way out, but she wasn't sure where it was, or where it would let her out. There were a few doors down the hall to her right, but was it worth the risk to start trying doors when she was uncertain where they led? If she ended up in a locked garage or something, she might be trapped and cornered when the killers arrived.

The front door was her surest bet when it came to getting out of there quickly. She started to head that way but stopped. There were a few other rooms on this floor. The only people who would have stayed behind instead of going to Audrey's speech would have been patients and a few essential hospital personnel. Did they know yet what was happening? Could she leave them here to be massacred?

She knew Michael wasn't in his room, so she moved to the next door, peeked in and saw it was empty. The next one was closed, and she wasn't sure who might be in there. Leslie turned the knob and pushed, but the door only budged a few inches before striking something heavy and coming to a stop. She pushed hard a few times, and whatever was blocking the door didn't move easily. Had the patient blocked the door, or had someone else done it and then slipped out? Either way, she wanted to know what they were hiding.

Leslie leaned all her weight into the door and felt it budge a little bit, the heavy object inside the room screeching against the floor. After moving it a few more inches, she could squeeze through the opening, even though it was still fairly tight. Sideways, she slid between the door and the frame, holding her breath and standing up straight to make herself as thin as possible, arms pressed tightly to her sides.

As she did, though, she noticed a smell coming from inside the room. She couldn't quite put her finger on it. Was it musty, perhaps? Mold? Whatever it was, it was putrid, almost prompting her to turn back. But she had come this far, and the smell only made her more interested in what she was going to find.

Turning the corner around the end of the door, she saw what was blocking it—the hospital bed. There were all sorts of items on top of the bed. A desk, lamp, two chairs, even a metal storage cabinet. Just adding more weight to make it tougher to move. Then her eyes moved to the head of the bed, and she nearly gagged.

There was George, his ghostly white face covered in boils, eyes wide open, the blankets covering most of his body. Leslie had never seen someone who had died from the virus, but this was what she'd been told they looked like. It was horrifying, more so than she had imagined. She scrambled back out the door as fast as she could, breathing heavily, on the verge of hyperventilation.

Shit. If he had the virus, what the hell does that mean? Is it loose in the hospital? Who blocked his door? It's hard to imagine he'd have had the strength to do it himself.

The questions swirled in her mind, but she didn't have time to get answers. If she could find Stephanie alive, maybe she could ask before Alessandra was burned to rubble. She started sprinting to the stairs, hitting the first few before a man leapt off a horse outside the front door and charged inside. Behind him, she saw maybe a dozen more on their way. She was too late. They were here.

50

"This can't be what you want," Stephanie said, sitting on the hill next to Derrick, watching a large group of marauders charge toward the hospital while a few others continued terrorizing the town, firing on people and setting homes ablaze. "This place was good to you. We took you in. Now, look at—"

"You kicked me out too," Derrick said. "Essentially left me for dead. Don't forget that part."

She was silent for a moment.

"You can't put that on us. That was Audrey's doing."

"I *can* put that on you. All of you. The people here voted for her, knowing full well who she really was. I knew what was coming. If you didn't, you were a fool. And why was she even here to begin with? Because you allowed her to be. You walk the Trojan Horse right through the town gates, and this is what you get."

"So, what now, then? We sit here with a gun pointed at us, watching Alessandra burn? They're not gonna make any sort of deal with us, are they? This isn't an exchange for the cure."

Derrick shrugged. "You're still alive for now, so who knows? But I wouldn't count on getting anything out of this. Unless you want to join us."

"Us?"

"Sure. I can think of worse fates."

"Oh, Derrick…this can't be the life for you. You're a good man. These men kill and rape and burn. That's not who you are. You're a builder, not a destroyer. How can you want to be a part of…*this*?"

Stephanie gestured at the chaotic scene in front of them. A cool breeze cut across them as the mansion's fire began to die toward embers.

"They don't care who you are. Where you're from. What color your skin is," Derrick said, drawing a circle in the dirt with his finger. "It's not the life I would have chosen for myself. It's not a life I'd be proud of, where I could hold my head up while kissing my wife and daughters goodnight. But they're not here anymore. Haven't been for years. I don't have any family. No one to be good for, to share a life with. That's all been taken away from me."

"You can't give up, though. This is throwing it all away. This is turning to the dark side."

"Where am I supposed to turn? The world doesn't give a damn about me. I've got to help myself. And the marauders will give me the structure I need to make it. They're disciplined and driven. They command authority, and do what they want. And, god damn it, they eat well at night. I want that. I'm tired of the struggle."

"You're tired of the struggle, are you?" Stephanie said. "What about Emily? I don't see a lot of female marauders around here."

"Oh." Derrick lowered his head. "You noticed? Yeah. Well, it's not that women don't have a place on our crew. They're useful. She's here because she was helpful for navigating. But the other women are back at camp, cooking, keeping the fires going, doing some light hunting, making sure the tents are set up, all that. I haven't been with them long, so I don't know exactly how all that works."

"Men like this take what they want, Derrick. I guarantee you the women back there are living a life they wish they weren't."

"Yeah, well, who isn't, right? What do *you* want? You want running water back? A full fridge? Bubble baths? Everybody's living a shitty life here, Stephanie. You have to decide if living a shitty life is a better choice than not living at all. Those women are fed and clothed and sheltered. Today, that's a hell of a lot more than most people have."

Out of the corner of her eye, Stephanie saw men streaming out of the hospital's front doors, covering their faces and appearing to be coughing. Horses were running in the opposite direction as the men tried to mount them, tossing them off and galloping away in panic, leaving the men sprawled on the ground.

"Is that smoke?" Derrick asked.

Stephanie looked through the large windows peering into the hospital's front lobby, and thought she saw a black cloud coming into view.

Leslie figured her only chance was to find a back way out before they spotted her and came upstairs. There was no telling what their intentions were in bombarding St. Francis, but she had no intention of waiting around to find out.

Her mind said to run, but she didn't want them to hear her footsteps against the hard vinyl floor, so she tried to keep each step light, staying up on the balls of her feet and lifting her heels in the air.

Almost halfway back down the hall, she heard a sound like a bell ringing from up ahead and froze. She was pretty sure that was the elevator, and it was stopping on her floor. They had her trapped. Could she climb out a window? She wasn't sure how bad the fall would be from the back of the building. Even two floors could be enough to sprain or even break an ankle, though. And it was possible hospital windows didn't open at all. She'd never thought to try before.

Before the elevator door opened, her heart pounding, she thought she smelled something. It was faint, but she thought it was smoke. And it was close. Could it be from the fires raging outside in the town? Maybe the wind shifted and carried the smell down to the hospital? Perhaps. But if so, it smelled different from what she'd expect.

When a head popped out from the elevator, Leslie finally exhaled when she recognized a masked Doctor Lawry, who motioned for her to come over to him.

"What are you doing out of your room?" he asked. "We need to get away from here. Keep the elevator *right here*. I'm gonna go get George."

She touched his arm as he started to run past her, and he turned around. She shook her head.

"What?" he asked.

"I already checked on him. He's…dead. We need to leave him."

He looked at her for a moment, hesitating.

"I swear," she said. "Please. Let's go."

Doctor Lawry shook his head and sighed, then stepped back into the elevator. His two assistants were also masked in there with them, along with five rifles. He handed Leslie a surgical mask, and she slipped it on. One of the assistants punched the "R" button, the doors closed, and they climbed up.

When they reached the top, the doors opened, and everyone stepped out onto the roof of the hospital. Doctor Lawry held the doors open and reached back into the elevator, inserting a key and pressing a series of buttons. The elevator remained where it was, doors ajar.

He handed a rifle to Leslie and to the two assistants, and she followed them over to the corner of the building, overlooking the front of the hospital, with a panoramic view of the burning town. So many houses were collapsing into rubble, bodies strewn across the streets, men on horseback hunting for more victims. The flames stretched from the square almost all the way to the lake, casting an eerie orange glow onto the water as the midday sun shone down on a cloudless fall day.

Leslie glanced back and saw Doctor Lawry jamming the extra rifle through the handles on the stairwell door, blocking the path to get up here from inside the building. Then he came over to where they were and kneeled down against the wall.

"What's the plan here?" Leslie asked. "Wait for them to get tired of vandalizing everything and wander back out the front door, then we get into a gunfight with them?"

"We should be able to do better than that," Doctor Lawry said. "We used isopropyl alcohol and old newspaper to start a pretty good fire back there. We also broke several vials of H6N1, so it's airborne in there. If it's as contagious through the air as we think it is, at least some of them are gonna be infected."

"And if they're not?"

"That's what the rifles are for."

51

Shots rained down on the marauders as they streamed out of the hospital, coughing and falling to their knees. Stephanie and the others looked on in astonishment from their perch on the hill.

"I've gotta go help," said the man on horseback. "Derrick, take this gun. Keep an eye on them. If anyone tries to go anywhere, shoot them. I'll be back."

He galloped down through the square, stopping a decent ways from the hospital. Stephanie cringed, thinking he was going to use the same rifle she used in order to pick them off at long range.

"What are you doing?" Audrey asked, and Stephanie turned toward her, realizing she was talking to Derrick.

"What someone's needed to do for a long time." Derrick held the gun out ahead of him as he walked slowly toward Audrey and her crew—Andy, William, and the two huge men. "You don't deserve to live to see what happens next. None of you do."

"But we…made a deal, Derrick. I made it with the other man. What will they do to you if you violate that? You're not in charge here, and you know that."

"Oh, screw that. You honestly think they give a damn about any sort of 'deals'? There are no contract lawyers in this world, Audrey. No fucking small-claims court. You take what you can take, when you can take it. They don't give a damn about you. You were helpful for as long as you could tell them where that cure was. But it doesn't look like that's working out."

Stephanie heard the marauder fire, but she couldn't tell if he'd hit anyone.

"No. No, it's fine," Audrey said. "Unlike your men, I honor my word. The hospital workers are violating it. So I'm willing to help you and your men take them down if that's what it takes to reach an agreement. Arm me and my men, and we're with you. We can fight back."

"You have to be out your goddamn mind if—"

"Derrick!" Stephanie yelled, and he turned tentatively, still keeping most of his attention on Audrey. "Ask yourself if you *really* want to do this, just take a life in cold blood. I understand, but is this who you are?"

He stood silently, the gun shaking slightly in his hand, arm outstretched.

"You robbed us of our dignity. Of our humanity," Derrick said, tears streaming from his eyes that were fixed on Audrey. "You killed Morgan and Grace. Left me, Emily and Xavier for dead, worse than animals. You threw us away. And why? Because we weren't ultimately *from* here? We were *slightly* different? Just for a way to satisfy the bloodlust of the ignorant people who kept supporting you? How do you live with yourself? *Any* of you? The fact that the shame of what you've done doesn't seem to affect you is all the more reason you don't deserve to be here. We've seen what you're capable of."

Derrick stepped closer to them, a few feet away now.

"Turn around," he said. "Hands behind your back."

"Think about this, Derrick," Audrey said. "Stephanie's right. You need to think long and hard about doing this. I've had plenty of—"

"Shut up! Turn around!"

"I'm not gonna turn around. If you're gonna shoot me, you'll have to look me in the eyes when you do it."

Stephanie watched on, unsure of what to do. She wasn't about to risk anything to save Audrey, but she didn't want the situation to get ugly.

One of the large men stood and ran toward Derrick. Stephanie wanted to shout out, but there was no time. Derrick quickly turned and fired, stepping aside as the huge man flopped on the ground next to him, a pool of blood forming beneath his chest. Derrick stood over the body, running his fingers through his hair, then looked up at the sky.

"You see what you caused?" Audrey pleaded with Derrick. "Can't we stop the killing? Put an end to all this now?"

Derrick closed his eyes and shook his head, looking down at the man's lifeless body. Then, without warning, he spun, walked straight to Audrey, raised the gun and released a bullet into her temple, the barrel no more than an inch from her when he fired. Audrey's body fell limp to the ground. Stephanie grasped her head with both hands, watching from several feet away as Derrick then moved to his right, pointing his gun at Audrey's other gargantuan man, not hesitating as he executed him as well, an unyielding bullet to the brain.

William and Andy both scrambled to their feet and started to run, stumbling down the side of the hill. William fell, and Derrick stalked up behind him, firing once into his back and then putting another into his head. Meanwhile, Andy was on all fours, trying to push himself up to his feet but struggling to get his balance, glancing back at Derrick, who started to stalk in his direction. Andy fell again, then rolled onto his back, staring directly into Derrick's eyes.

"Please," Andy said, shaking his head violently. "Don't do it. I can help you."

Derrick stopped and raised his gun, and Stephanie stood to watch.

Andy shivered, extending an open palm toward him. Those dewy mornings flashed back to Stephanie, Andy bursting into her tent, ripping off her clothes and raping her, knowing she had no recourse. Knowing that he held all the power, making her feel like something less than human, an animal he could do whatever he wanted with. She hated that she'd eventually become so passive about it, letting it happen so it would at least be quick, and she'd have fewer bruises to nurse. But the memories would always be there. They'd haunt her forever. The feeling of being owned, of being a willing victim. She was going to watch this happen, see him meeting his end. She hoped maybe it would calm the nightmares just a bit.

Derrick fired a bullet into Andy's forehead; he fell back, lifeless. Stephanie didn't smile. She wasn't sure how she felt in the moment. A little bit empty. Derrick put the gun away and turned toward her.

"What now?" she asked, shaking a bit.

"We sit here until this is over," he said. "Then we'll see what they want to do with you."

Another gunshot rang out from down the hill.

"The hell I am," she said.

"You're unarmed. You saw what I did to them. Don't think I'll hesitate to shoot you too."

"I don't think you'll do it."

"You *saw*—"

"That was them. I've never done anything to you. I was the one who let you in, gave you shelter, provided you with a place to live and a purpose. I certainly made some mistakes, but I never did anything to wrong you. You're no cold-blooded killer, Derrick. I know you well enough to know that. And I'm not gonna sit here and watch all this happen. My friends need my help. If you're gonna shoot me, fucking shoot me. But I don't think you will."

"Don't make me—"

Stephanie turned and started sprinting down the hill, and Derrick raised the gun.

52

"They've stopped coming out!" Leslie cried, her rifle resting on the ledge of the hospital roof, waiting for more men to stumble out the front door below. "I don't think that's all of them, is it?"

"No, not even close." Doctor Lawry was trying to fix a jam in his rifle. These hadn't been fired in years. "But they probably saw what happened to the other ones and are staying low, covering their mouths, and maybe huddling close enough to the building that we can't see them from up here."

"Do we have any idea who these guys are, or why they're here?" Leslie asked.

He kept fiddling with his gun, pulling a side lever back and forth, creating a *chick chunk* sound each time.

"No idea." He was getting frustrated with it. *Chick chunk. Chick chunk.* "I suppose they stumbled across our town and figured they could pillage it. Probably assumed there wouldn't be anyone left."

"But why the hospital?"

"All kinds of potential resources in a hospital. Or maybe someone told them about the cure."

Leslie peered down at the five dead bodies splayed out on the ground, the smoke becoming thicker as it billowed out through any opening it could find to escape the building. The first few men had been like fish in a barrel; she'd almost felt bad when they shot one of them, the bullet embedding in his back and fusing him to the earth. But all she'd had to do was look up to remind herself what they'd done to her town and to her neighbors who lived there in order to justify whatever they had to do to put an end to this.

She wondered how many people were still alive in Alessandra. How many had survived this invasion? Were the four of them on the roof the only ones left standing? Could they rebuild? They still had the walls around them, and the lake would always be a resource. What was the point, though? They weren't going to repopulate the Earth or anything. They'd be scraping by as long as they could until each of them died. And, eventually, there'd be only one of them left. Maybe the last human on the planet. And that person would have an extremely lonely and desperate existence.

Leslie didn't know what the future held, but she supposed it was worth hanging on for now, at least long enough to assess the damage. Maybe they could make the best of it.

Leslie heard one of Doctor Lawry's assistants gasp, and she glanced over to see one of them clutching her chest and collapsing. In that same beat, she heard a loud gunshot.

"Shit!" Doctor Lawry said. "Get down! Everybody, get down! Someone's firing at us. From where?"

He crawled over to his assistants and started looking for a pulse on the one who had been shot. The other one had removed her scrubs top and was pressing it hard against the wound, looking like she was on the verge of tears. Doctor Lawry began doing CPR, alternating chest compressions with mouth to mouth.

Leslie peeked over the ledge to scan the town. The shooter had to be out in front of them somewhere. How much shooting range could they realistically have? Leslie was far from a gun expert, but she knew there was only so far away from a target you could be and expect to hit with that sort of accuracy and impact.

She felt something zip past her head, like air being sucked into a vacuum next to her ear. Maybe two seconds later, she heard that same loud gunshot sound, and she fell back down, ducking beneath the ledge.

Holy shit. How close was that?

The bullet must have come within inches of taking her head off. A little bit to its left, and she'd have been dead before she even heard the sound, her brains splattered on the hospital's roof. They were pinned down by a sniper. She watched as they frantically tried to save the assistant's life, the scrubs pressed against the wound turning almost black as billowy clouds floated by carelessly overhead.

Stephanie knew a bullet could strike her at any moment as her legs churned forward, driving her down the hill toward the square. She was betting that she knew Derrick well enough to know what he was capable of and what he wasn't. And with every step, she got closer to being right.

When she reached the square, she ducked behind the stage, out of Derrick's sight even if he was still contemplating a shot. Now, she could focus on the sniper, crouched west of the square.

He fired another shot, and she could have sworn the sound made the ground shake underneath her. Now that she was this close, she could tell it was the sound she'd heard when she fired earlier; he was using the same rifle. She had been able to get off a few fairly accurate shots at a decent range, so she wondered what a more experienced shooter could do with it.

From where she was, Stephanie couldn't see if he'd hit anything, but he wouldn't be taking shots if there was nothing to fire at. She hadn't seen anybody on the hospital roof since that first shot; they'd most likely taken cover. The fact that he was still attempting to take them down meant someone must still be alive up there, and that gave Stephanie hope.

She peeked around the side of the stage and saw the sniper lying on the ground, the rifle pressed hard against his right shoulder, pointed toward the hospital. The air was thick with the stench of ash and soot, as black smoke lifted and began to blot out the sun, St. Francis still visible as smoke and flame filled up the lobby.

Stephanie wondered how long the hospital would hold up with the fire raging inside. Where exactly had they set it? If it was structural, she worried the building might crumble beneath her friends. They might not have much time. She needed to act.

Figuring she was about fifteen steps from the sniper,

Stephanie contemplated her next move. She had to be quick, but she also needed to be smart. She was no good to her friends bleeding out on a weed-covered lawn. His attention was focused into the scope, so that would work to her advantage. But if he saw any motion in his peripheral vision or heard her footsteps, it wouldn't take much for him to roll over and kill her at close range.

She wanted to get around to his gun side as quickly as she could, because she figured that eye would be more intensely focused forward than the other. Stephanie got low to the ground and crawled on her stomach around behind him, giving him a wide berth as she moved toward his right side.

A few feet from the stage, he started to move, and she froze, her heart pounding. Was this it? She closed her eyes and waited, holding her breath. In that brief moment, she wondered what death felt like. Something? Nothing? If a bullet pierced her skull, would the lights flip off, and that'd be it? The weirdest thing about death was imagining how the world could continue without you in it. In the abstract, everyone knew there was a history before they were born, so many people who lived and died, advanced civilization and achieved great things before there was even the possibility of imagining your existence. But the idea of the world continuing without you was so much tougher to wrap your mind around. How could you disappear? How could the power turn off?

Stephanie slowly opened her eyes and saw the sniper scratching his leg, then adjusting his position and focusing his gaze forward again. He hadn't spotted her. She kept moving to her right, a little bit at a time, aligned with his feet, then his right side, then the gun and on a bit beyond it. Let that rifle be a shield for her. Maybe it would give her enough of a block on his eyesight to allow her to survive this.

Her elbows scraping the ground, Stephanie started to inch forward, creeping toward the sniper, wanting to get as close as she felt comfortable before moving any faster. He hadn't fired in a couple of minutes; she didn't know if that was a good thing or not. She wondered how it was going on that roof. Had he already killed some of them? How many people were left in the town?

Now less than ten feet away from him, it was about time. She couldn't risk getting much closer in such a vulnerable position. She needed to push all her chips into the middle of the table. It would almost certainly be "Kill or be killed." There was no middle ground, and she was unarmed. Her only weapon was surprise.

Stephanie sprung from her prone position, her feet driving forward, took three big steps and then leapt toward the sniper, who noticed her and began to roll over, pointing the rifle in her direction as she landed on top of him. He didn't get a shot off as she smothered the rifle into his body, preventing him from pulling the trigger. She tried to grab at the rifle and wrest it away, but he had a strap wrapped around his right arm. The good news was that made it extremely difficult for him to use his right arm for much.

She landed a few punches to his face, drawing blood before he kicked her hard in the stomach, nearly knocking the breath out of her and pushing her body up enough for him to squirm away a bit. He pulled his arm loose from the rifle and swung it at her, striking her in the mouth and sending her twirling to her right, crashing on the ground as magnificent pain cascaded throughout her head. She could taste blood.

There was no time to nurse injuries. She knew if she hesitated, if she stopped for a moment to catch her breath, she was dead. Stephanie balanced herself with her hand and spun around to see him starting to raise the rifle. She pivoted and charged, lowering her head into his midsection and driving him backward, knocking him off balance and landing on top of him, the rifle jarred loose on the ground a few feet away.

He punched her in the face, but the ground prevented him from getting much leverage. It still hurt, but it was a punch she could take. Stephanie reared back and aimed for a hard punch, but he saw it coming and dodged a bit to his right. He writhed underneath her and brought his knee up, again connecting with her stomach and causing her to gasp, then landed a punch—much harder this time—to the side of her head.

He shoved her with both hands, and she rolled away to the opposite side of the rifle. He started to stand and scramble over to the weapon, but she was able to sweep her leg into his, knocking him flat on his stomach, and she pounced again, using all her weight to land a knee into his spine. He screamed when she did, instinctually reaching back with his right arm, and she grabbed it, pulling hard and twisting while rocking his body to the left. He was kicking, but not connecting with anything as his limbs locked up. Stephanie could feel the muscles tightening in his arm and shoulder, the pain palpable in the air as he gasped, his mouth agape, eyes pressed shut.

She felt something hard against her thigh, underneath his untucked shirt, between his body and the hard ground. She felt around, and immediately knew—it was a pistol. It must have been one of the guns they'd taken from Audrey and her crew on the hill. He had it tucked into the back waistband of his pants, probably to keep it out of the way while he laid on his stomach to fire the rifle.

Stephanie pulled up his shirt and reached underneath to grab the gun. She stood with it pointed at his head, the sniper still moaning and rolling on the ground.

"Pull that trigger, and I'll shoot you," Derrick said, from behind her. "I swear to god I mean it this time."

53

Her top covering the face of her friend, lying still on the hospital's roof, Doctor Lawry's assistant wiped a tear from her eye as she huddled against the ledge. It was heartbreaking for Leslie to watch. Leslie didn't know any of these people, but she was thrust into a perilous situation with them, and now one of them was dead. There was no time to mourn, though, with a sniper setting his sights on them and a fire raging below.

"I think I can see him," Leslie said, peeking her eyes just enough above the wall to see.

"The sniper?" Doctor Lawry said. "Where is he?"

"I'm not a hundred percent sure, but I'm pretty sure I see a guy lying down with a rifle not far from the square. Not taking a chance to look any closer than I did, though."

"Could we hit him from here?"

They both took a quick peek, then ducked back down again.

"With these rifles? I'm no expert, but I seriously doubt it," Leslie said. "No scope or anything. What do you think?"

"You're probably right." Doctor Lawry looked at his rifle and shook his head. "No way we could be accurate at this distance. It's wasting bullets and exposing ourselves."

Leslie heard a rumbling in the distance and could see a wall of dark clouds moving in their direction.

"What do we do now?" she asked.

"We're gonna have to get off this—"

Loud banging interrupted him, and Leslie didn't immediately know where it was coming from. She was sure it wasn't thunder, though. This was loud—and closer. It sounded like someone pounding on a door.

"Shit," Doctor Lawry said. "Did you hear that?"

"Yeah. Of course. What was it?"

More banging. It was coming from another part of the roof, behind them. He stayed in a crouch and ran a few feet away, looking around a corner. After a few seconds, the banging continued. Leslie and his assistant gathered beside him.

"Someone's trying to get through the door," he said.

There was another loud bang as Leslie watched the doors trying to open but being stopped by the rifle jammed in the handles.

"I think they're trying to kick it open," the assistant said. "Could it be a patient trying to escape? Was everyone accounted for?"

"George is the only one we didn't check on, but Leslie said …" Doctor Lawry trailed off, and they both looked at Leslie.

"Believe me, that's not him," she assured them. "That's at least *one* of these men who wants to kill us. Do you think they can get through?"

"I don't know. I guess if they kick at it enough, it might jar the rifle loose. I doubt they'll be able to break it, though."

"Wait…has the banging stopped?" Leslie asked. She hadn't heard any kicks against the door in what she thought was thirty seconds or so. "Maybe they gave up?"

"Or the smoke coming up the stairs finally overwhelmed them."

Leslie saw some motion out of the corner of her eye and noticed the doors were moving again, but weren't being kicked. They were being nudged open a little at a time until the rifle held firm, keeping the doors from opening completely. There was a crack, though. Leslie could see there was at least one man behind the door, but she couldn't tell much more than that. Whoever was there, it seemed they were trying to force the door as far open as possible. Could they get enough of an opening to slide through?

Something was coming through the crack between the doors. Leslie began to lean forward for a better look.

"Get back! Back!" Doctor Lawry yelled, throwing his arm around Leslie and pulling her behind a wall as a gunshot rang out from behind the stairway doors. "Are you okay?"

Leslie took a breath and tried to assess if she had any pain, with Doctor Lawry's assistant kneeling behind her.

"I banged my head a little when you knocked me back," Leslie said. "But, other than that, I think I'm fine."

"Well, it looks like they know we're up here."

"And they've got a clean shot at us," the assistant said. "Right along our exit route too."

"What exit route?" Leslie asked.

"There have to be at least two exits from any area of a hospital," Doctor Lawry explained. "The other roof exit is on the other side, past those doors, along the south side of the building. It's the fire-emergency stairs. Supposed to be smoke proof and even pressurized to keep it safe in case of fire, but I'm not sure if we have sufficient power to get the pressure up very high. Hadn't thought to test that in a while."

"But it's enclosed?"

"Right," he said. "It should be a hell of a lot safer than the stairwell that's behind those doors. And it dumps out near the loading dock in back."

"Great," Leslie said. "Now, I guess we need to figure out how to get there before the building crumbles underneath us, and without being shot."

"Let's not do this, Derrick," Stephanie pleaded, holding her gun firm on the man writhing on the ground. "If you were willing to shoot me, I wouldn't be standing here. Let me take care of my business."

"You weren't holding a gun on a man then. You weren't even armed. I don't *want* to shoot you, but you're on the verge of leaving me with no choice. I'm defending my crew, Stephanie. You have to understand that. Drop the gun."

"He killed my friends." She didn't know if this was true, but she knew Derrick didn't either. "He'll kill me if I give him half a chance. I can't let him walk away."

"I'm sorry, but you're gonna have to. This is the last time I'll ask you to drop the gun."

"Why are you siding with these people? What do you get out of this?"

"Protection. Belonging. Safety."

"Does this look like 'Safety' to you?" Stephanie held her arms out to gesture around at the town, the smell of soot, ashy and pungent, saturating the air. "Look at the hospital, burning with your men dead on the ground, unmanned horses running free. This man *right here*, taken by surprise and his weapon in my hands. If you hadn't come along, he'd be dead too right now. And what do any of you have to show for it? All this death and destruction, burning *my town* to the fucking ground, and what has been gained? What about this is attractive for you?"

Derrick's gaze moved past Stephanie, looking at the town the marauders laid waste to. It looked like he might be starting to cry.

"What do you *want* me to do, Stephanie? There's no certainty in this messed-up world. I thought I found a place to live somewhat normally here, and we all saw how that turned out. So, sure, I found this group enticing. Taking what they wanted, because who's gonna stop them? There are no laws anymore. You do what you have to do in order to make it to tomorrow. I tried living humanely, as a cooperative member of a community, and it got me left for dead, wandering through the forest alone. They gave me a second chance at life, and I took it."

"Well, here's your *third* chance. There's nothing left for you to defend. I don't know how many Alessandrans are left, but you're welcome here, whatever we can salvage of 'here' anyway. There's no more Audrey. And look at the hospital again. Take a good look at it. You know who's in there?"

Derrick shook his head, his eyes narrow.

"Leslie's in there, Derrick. I don't know if she's survived, but I know some people made it to the roof, and that's who *this* guy was shooting at."

"Why was she in the hospital? Was something wrong?"

Stephanie considered for a moment how much to tell him, but thought this wasn't the time to get into it.

"It's a long story, but she was fine. Healthy. There's a good chance she's alive, Derrick. We can help her. But not if we let this bastard get his gun back. He'll murder us all and walk away laughing. *That's* not your family. *We* are. Let's end this."

Derrick closed his eyes and sighed, then curled his lip and nodded slightly. Stephanie fired one shot into the sniper's head.

54

"There's a second rifle!" Doctor Lawry yelled, ducking back behind the wall as multiple shots fired from behind the door, narrowly missing them. "Well, now we know there are at least two of them in there. But damn it, we're pinned down."

"Any ideas?" Leslie asked. "We're never gonna be able to hit them through that small crack in the doors."

"Eventually, the smoke's bound to climb up the stairs, and they won't be able to breathe."

"Will the building hold up long enough for that to happen?"

Doctor Lawry shook his head. "Probably? Maybe? No way to know for sure. We don't even know how bad it is down there. There's a hell of a lot of smoke, though."

Leslie heard another clap of thunder and felt a couple of rain drops hit her forehead, then looked up and saw the sky flash with a streak of lightning.

"The roof of the tallest building for miles around doesn't seem like the place you want to be during a thunderstorm."

"We had a lightning rod up here for a while," he said. "But Audrey took it down because she said we needed the metal for supplies."

"One more gift from her, I suppose."

Leslie glanced across the roof, trying to stretch to see the spot where they said you could lift up the floor to reveal the emergency stairs. If she ran, could she get there? They could try to go one at a time, stay as far away from the doors as they could, run fast, and hope the men would miss. After all, it's not easy to hit a moving target, particularly when you're shooting through a small crack between two doors. And those didn't seem like rifles where they could get off several shots in rapid succession.

There was another shot, and Leslie saw Doctor Lawry clutching at his right shoulder as he fell backward, and rain began coming down more steadily. She and his assistant grabbed his coat and pulled him back behind the wall as more shots rang out, embedding in the roof's floor.

"Oh, shit. It *really* hurts." He was pressing a hand to his shoulder, and blood was starting to seep between his fingers. Leslie ripped some cloth from her shirt and handed it to his assistant, who moved his hand out of the way and pushed hard against his shoulder. He screamed, but she continued putting all her weight on it.

"What were you doing out there?" Leslie asked, mostly rhetorically; she knew he wasn't going to answer many questions in the shape he was in. "Damn it. At least it's the shoulder, though. He can still run."

"There's an exit wound. It's not too big," said his assistant, beginning to shiver in the chilly evening rain that was becoming a downpour. "Good that the bullet's not still in there. Biggest risk is infection. Wish we had alcohol to put on it."

"Yeah. Well, that's clearly gonna have to wait. If we can get off this roof and if there's anything left in the hospital once the fire burns out, we'll do everything we can to help him. In the meantime, what are we gonna do?"

Doctor Lawry started messing with the belt on his pants, trying to loosen it with his left hand; Leslie crawled over and helped him unbuckle it. He lifted it and stuck it between his teeth, biting down hard. It was hard to see anyone in that much pain.

She heard more shots and cringed for a second, then two more, and they echoed. That was a different sound. Those shots weren't being fired into the open of the roof. They were being fired *inside*. Into the stairwell.

Leslie looked, and the doors were fully shut.

"Did you hear that?" she asked, continuing to listen for more, cold water dripping down into her face. "They're firing at someone else. We're not alone."

"They're all dead," Derrick said, crouching down next to another marauder's body outside the hospital. "Or at least incapacitated."

"Several of them from bullet wounds," Stephanie said. "I'm guessing the ones who weren't shot found a horse and got the hell out of here."

She heard a burst of gunfire and ducked, her arms instinctually rising in front of her face.

"Shit," she said. "Where'd that come from, do you think? Are they firing at us?"

"I don't know. Definitely could have been the roof, though. And if so…"

"At least *someone's* still alive up there, yeah. And they're shooting at someone, which means they're in danger."

"Leslie…"

"I know." Stephanie nodded, then heard a loud clap of thunder. A couple of raindrops hit her on the arm, and the sky lit up. "We've gotta get up there."

"What about the smoke?"

The entire hospital lobby was engulfed in black smoke, but it didn't look like flames were quite as prevalent. Whatever was burning was giving off a lot of smoke, but Stephanie couldn't tell how much the fire itself was spreading.

"Visibility's about zero in there, but I've got an idea. We need to get to my office upstairs."

"Let's do it, then."

Stephanie tapped the door handle and found it was hot but not scalding to the touch. She pulled her shirt up to cover her mouth and nose; Derrick did the same. She nodded and pulled the door open, feeling her eyes start to sting and water as she did. She laid on her stomach, with Derrick again following her lead.

She crawled through the lobby to the stairs, and Derrick tapped her side to let her know he was with her. Going up the stairs wasn't ideal because smoke rose, so the second floor was even worse than the lobby, but this was the only way they were going to be able to make it through, especially if it was filling up the stairwell too.

Staying as low as they could, they crawled up the stairs, one hand continuing to hold their shirts over their face as a makeshift mask. She heard Derrick cough, and she wanted to reassure him, but she didn't want to waste the breath to do it. If he followed her, they could do this.

They reached the top of the stairs, and the smoke was so thick that it stung to keep their eyes open. Stephanie winced and shut them, feeling like it was sucking all the moisture from her pupils. She heard another pop, muffled this time, but still recognizable as a gunshot, and she tried to crawl faster.

She got to her office door and rose to her knees, turning the knob and pushing it open, thick smoke rushing in from behind her.

"We're here!" she said, as she fell into the room, coughing. "How ya holding up?"

Silence. She reached back and didn't feel him there.

"Shit!" She coughed again. In the moment, she wasn't sure if she should crawl back out there and drag him into her office with her.

Where was I when I heard him cough? Near the top of the stairs, I'm pretty sure. So he at least got that far.

No sense in making it all this way and not getting what they came for, she decided. Stephanie crawled behind her desk and opened a large bottom drawer, rifling through a box and pulling out two N95 masks, the same ones she and Michael used after the virus's first resurgence. After that, she'd stashed them in her office and always meant to return them to the storage closet downstairs. She never got around to it.

Sometimes, laziness and procrastination pay off.

Stephanie put hers on and pulled it tight; almost immediately, she could breathe pretty much normally again. She recalled that these masks filtered out about ninety-five percent of smoke particles. She still could hardly see at all, but at least she wasn't breathing in soot and whatever else was floating in the thick air.

Again, she dropped to her stomach because the visibility was much better low to the ground. With both her arms free, she was able to move faster, quickly crawling back toward the stairs. As she neared the top, she could see a shape in front of her. She couldn't tell for sure it was Derrick until she was almost face to face with him, his head lolled to the right on his elbows, half of his torso resting on the stairs beneath him.

"Derrick! Are you awake? I need you here." Stephanie nudged his shoulder, but he didn't move. She slapped him across the face, and he stirred, then coughed several times, his body jerking violently. "It's okay. You're gonna be fine. Put this on."

Stephanie pulled the strings over his head and placed the mask over his face, making sure it was a snug fit. His eyes grew big, and she could see him take a big breath.

"Holy shit," he said, then coughed a couple more times, a bit more lightly this time. "That's amazing. Is this what we were going up here to get?"

"Yeah. These will get us through the smoke. Still gotta stay low, though, but the stairs aren't far. Ready?"

They crawled down the hall, much more quickly this time, passing Stephanie's office and the patient rooms. She shivered a bit going past George's room, but didn't have time to think about that. Past Leslie's old room, Stephanie knew the stairs were just ahead. She veered left and touched the door, getting onto her knees to open it.

Once again, smoke rushed in, rising up through the stairwell, which had already been filling up. Visibility wasn't nearly as bad in here yet, though, so they stood.

"I think we can walk up," she said, pulling the pistol out from the back of her waistband, and Derrick doing the same. "At least for now. But let's be ready."

As they began their ascent, three shots rang out, echoing loudly, one bullet ricocheting off the metal banister where Stephanie had been about to put her hand. She jerked back, and both of them froze.

"Okay, then," Stephanie said, trying to control her breathing and looking up. "There's apparently someone else in the stairwell."

"They're firing down on us. That's not easy to avoid."

There were two flights winding up between each floor. The roof would take four flights to reach from where they were. Stephanie knew that whoever was at the top could fire down between the sets of stairs and potentially hit them, but the stairs could also act as a bit of a shield if they were smart.

"I think we can do this," she said. "Stick with me."

Stephanie stood up flat against the far wall, bending her back around the handrail and stepping sideways up the stairs, Derrick mimicking her as she did. Reaching the first landing, they stayed against the wall, pressed hard against it—head, shoulders, butt, and heels—shuffling around to the other side.

Shots continued to fire, and Stephanie flinched each time. Whatever had happened over the past couple of years, she still wasn't used to being shot at. She didn't understand how anyone could be. The noise was so mind-numbingly loud, and any one of those bursts could be the last sound you ever hear. It was all-consuming.

A voice in her head reminded her that they didn't have to do this. They could turn around, exit the building, take care of themselves, and hope whoever was on the roof could make it down. But so many people had died in such a short time. If she couldn't preserve as many lives as she could, and try to make this a place worth living in, what was the point? Why desperately cling to a life that wouldn't be much of a life anyway? She was going to keep climbing. Save the final shreds of Alessandra or go down along with it.

By the time they reached the second landing, there hadn't been any shots in several seconds. That bothered Stephanie more than the frequent shots had. She motioned Derrick to lean in close to her.

"They've realized they can't hit us from the top," she whispered. "They're gonna reposition, maybe come down a bit to get within range."

He nodded.

"Slow. Careful," she continued. "Keep your eyes moving and your gun ready."

Staying against the wall, they shuffled forward, a bit more

slowly now. Stephanie was looking out for any sign of movement. Anything at all. Footsteps. Echoes. Voices. Guns being cocked or reloaded. But there was nothing. How was that possible? Surely the attackers hadn't left the stairwell, not with Stephanie and Derrick right there, making their way up.

Hitting the fourth step on the third flight, Stephanie heard a deafening shot and then felt a searing pain in her side; she nearly crumpled to the floor before stumbling back to the landing below while trying to stifle a scream.

She sat down with her back against the wall, and Derrick scrambled over to her.

"What's wrong?" he asked quietly, looking back and forth between her and the stairs behind him. "Are you hit?"

Stephanie winced and looked at her right side, where there was a long tear in her shirt. She could see red skin through it and started to worry. If that bullet embedded itself deep into her side, it could not only damage internal organs but cause sepsis without adequate treatment, which she wasn't likely to receive in time. For a moment, she wondered if she'd bleed out and die right there.

She lifted her shirt and got a clearer view; her side was very sore and was going to bleed, but it looked like she'd been lucky. The bullet had skimmed her as it went past, creating a painful wound but nothing life threatening. Stephanie quickly yanked her shirt up and flipped it around backward, tucking it into her pants.

"Do you need something for that?" Derrick asked. "It could get infected."

"Yeah. Yeah, I do. But no time for that. At least now it's not on the side of my shirt with the big tear in it. Might buy me some time. Help me up."

Stephanie's side burned as she grasped his hand, and he pulled her up. She leaned against the wall and caught her breath.

"Go over there and find where the bullet entered the wall," she whispered. "Look at the shape of the hole. We may be able to tell where they're firing from."

Staying low, Derrick hurried back to the stairs and searched for the bullet hole. He quickly spotted an entry point in the wall and tried to examine it as well as he could without exposing himself. He stretched out his hand and felt it, sticking a finger inside to tell what the shape of it was. Then he scrambled back to Stephanie.

"I couldn't feel the bullet in there. It probably went all the way through. These walls aren't that thick, I don't think," he whispered. "But I can tell it created a tunnel going down and to the left, away from where we're standing now."

"How sharp an angle was it? Was it going closer to straight back up the stairs, or more deep into the wall?"

"Not quite parallel with the wall, but closer to that than going straight into it. Maybe fifteen or twenty degrees."

Stephanie's eyes scanned where the bullet hole was, then looked up above.

"Fifteen…or twenty degrees." She tried to do the measurements in her head. "We're not gonna be able to tell exactly, but that gives us a hint of where the shooter is. Or, at least, where he *was*. And that's almost straight above where we are now."

"He's probably got cover there. That wall goes straight up behind us. And he can pick us off pretty easily as we go up the stairs. Maybe we need to go back."

The smell of smoke was increasing, and Stephanie could tell the air was growing cloudier, visibility becoming worse. She looked at the stairs and the metal railing, searching it for possibilities. She needed a plan. Some way to get around the shooter. Derrick had a point, but there was no telling what might happen if they left. How many of their friends were on the roof? How much danger were they in? Right now, the shooters were distracted. If they could end it here, it might all be over.

"No, we've got to keep going forward," Stephanie said. "But I'm gonna need a boost."

55

Stephanie looked back at Derrick and tilted her head as if to ask, “Are you ready?” He gave a decisive nod, and she turned to face the stairwell’s center railing. She expected her side to hurt like hell when she did this, but there was no way around that. She needed some sort of antibiotic and a nice, large bandage, and the quickest way to get that was to take the shooter down.

She was glad Derrick was with her. This wasn’t something she could have done on her own, and she was going to take advantage of all those big bags of mulch Derrick had lugged around for years. His bulging arms looked like they could toss her up the stairs, but she wasn’t going to ask that much of him.

Stephanie took a deep breath and bent a bit at the waist, bracing herself as Derrick placed his hands on her waist. As he squeezed, the strength of his hands nearly took her breath away. It almost felt like pulling the strings tight on a corset. She tapped his right hand; she was ready.

He lifted her into the air, and her feet landed on the railing. She felt his hands shift to her back, pushing her upward as his hands slid down her butt and then let go.

As her head rose in front of the upper landing, she found herself for a brief second face to face with the rifle, poking through the openings in the vertical metal posts on the guardrail, a couple feet out over the stairs below. She moved right and pointed her gun at the man holding the rifle. She knew she’d only have a split second to react. She had to make this count.

She pulled the trigger from point-blank range, and the man’s face exploded in front of her, blood and brain matter splattered everywhere, painting the walls and her clothes. The rifle fell limply to the landing and then tumbled over down the stairs below Derrick.

The recoil on the gun threw off Stephanie's balance, and she started to fall backward. As she did, though, she noticed motion out of the corner of her eye—there was a second man standing up there, and he was raising his rifle. It felt like it was all going in slow motion, him pointing the rifle at her, her trying to get her bearings to fire back as she tumbled toward the stairs below.

He fired, the sound again nearly deafening in the closed space. Stephanie's ears rang as she pulled the trigger on her own gun, and then fell off the railing, with Derrick catching her and then carrying her quickly back to the landing beneath the shooter, laying her down on the floor.

"Oh my god, that's a lot of blood." Derrick was frantic, careful not to touch her now that she was safely on solid ground. "Where are you hit?"

Stephanie paused for a moment, trying to calm down so she could feel for pain. Adrenaline was a powerful drug that could overcome a lot. She'd seen case studies of men with broken arms lifting cars off the ground to free their child pinned underneath. Adrenaline could cover up most pain temporarily if the need was great enough. So she had to work past it.

"I don't think any of it's my blood," she said, her palm rubbing her forehead. "Nothing really hurts. I think he missed me."

"Thank god. How many of them are there? Two?"

"Yeah. Two. Or, well, there *were* two."

"Maybe there's zero," Derrick said. "You got off a shot at the end. Did you hit him?"

"I was…falling. I don't know. I really didn't see anything after I fired."

They both grew quiet and looked up the stairs. Stephanie could hear her heart, like a driving drumbeat; she was trying to hear anything else. Something to signal the other shooter was still there, lying in wait for them to get within striking distance again.

But there was nothing.

"He could be dead," Derrick said.

"He could also be lying there with his gun pointed at the stairs, waiting for us." Stephanie sighed, then turned to look at Derrick. "Like the other guy."

"Yeah. What do we do? Same thing as before?"

"No, that's no good. He'll be ready for that. We need to..."

"What?"

"Grab the rifle the other guy dropped," Stephanie said. "We may be able to use that."

Derrick picked it up and brought it to her.

"At this close range, I'm not sure it does us much good."

"Don't worry. We're not gonna shoot it."

She told him her plan; Derrick nodded and shrugged. She had the dangerous task, so he had little reason not to give it a try. And if she got killed, it was going to be time for him to retreat and find the emergency stairs.

Derrick carried the rifle to the stairs and went up two steps, short of a range the man could hit from where he was. He stood tall and extended the rifle vertically, high over his head, as far as he could reach, then waved it back and forth across the vertical metal posts above. When Stephanie had been up there previously —face to face with the barrel of the rifle—she'd noticed that the man had extended the rifle pretty far out through those vertical posts. So, first, this told them the man up there now wasn't doing that. And it was going to prevent him from doing so, giving Stephanie another step or two of space that could be really valuable.

She closed her eyes and sucked in a deep breath, mustering up one last burst of energy. This was likely going to be it—she had no other plan. She'd put herself in harm's way once more in the hopes of ending this now. She figured another step or two should give her enough room to see the man up there, and get off a quick shot before he could do much. If not, though, they were going to have to regroup. The smoke was getting thicker on the landing below, and she knew there was only so much time left before the shooter would get forced back onto the roof. If he did, Leslie and anyone else up there might not stand a chance.

One more breath, watching Derrick swing the rifle in an arc over his head, and Stephanie sprung forward, two steps at a time. She hit the fifth step and swung around, her shoulders rotating as she brought the gun up in front of her face, looking to see if there was a rifle lifting to point at her. If she'd miscalculated the angle, she knew she could be dead before she even got her gun ready. If so, she hoped it'd be quick. She didn't want to know what was happening. If it was going to end here, she hoped there was peace on the other side of this world.

Stephanie also knew she was no action hero or gun expert. Especially in a nervous situation where she'd be turning and firing in one motion, the odds of her missing him with the shot were uncomfortably high. But if there was ever a shot to hit, it would be this one. She hoped she had it in her.

As she swung around, she watched for any signs of motion, feet shifting, a rifle rising to get a better angle, anything. It was still. She stopped, her gun pointing up to the landing. Still facing that direction, she took one step backward up to the next step. Then another, onto the next landing now, Derrick's rifle still swinging back and forth.

Then she saw him, curled up on the floor, blood pooling in front of him. She held out her palm to Derrick, and he stopped swinging the rifle, setting it down and pulling out his pistol. She kept her gun trained on the man at the top landing, but continued on up the stairs, with Derrick a few steps behind.

Stephanie could see his eyes were still open, and he was shivering as she approached. He was holding his right hand against his chest; it was covered in blood, and it looked like at least two fingers were missing or badly damaged. He also appeared to be bleeding badly from the right side of his chest, below his shoulder.

"Is he alive?" Derrick asked.

"He's alive, but he's not in great shape. Looks like I did get him with that shot. Not exactly perfect aim, but I got his trigger hand. That was enough."

"Damn. Yeah. What do you want to do with him?"

"Cover your ears."

She pointed her gun and fired a bullet into the back of the man's head, wincing at one more deafening echo reverberated through the stairs.

"All right," Stephanie said. "Let's check on whoever's on the roof. Just be careful."

Stephanie pushed the bar to open the door, but it held firm, bouncing back at her.

"What the hell?"

Derrick tried the other door, and the same thing happened.

"Shit," she said. "They were trapped in here with us."

"Maybe the people on the roof barred the door with something."

"Smart if so. But we need to get—"

A shot fired, blowing a small hole in one of the doors, about six inches to Stephanie's left.

"Whoa." Stephanie's heart skipped a beat as she looked at the hole, then pulled her mask off her face and started banging on the door. "Stop shooting! It's me, Stephanie! Don't fire!"

There were a few seconds of silence. Stephanie was starting to think they might have to retreat when she finally heard a voice.

"Stephanie?" Leslie said, her voice almost startled and not too close to the door. "What are you doing here?"

"To fucking rescue *you*, that's what. And I've got someone with me you're gonna want to see."

"I can't believe you're alive, Leslie," Derrick said. "I didn't think I'd ever see you again."

"Holy shit, Derrick? Is that you? It can't…I don't understand."

"Let us out!" Stephanie said.

She heard frantic footsteps on the other side, then a rattling, and the door swung open. Derrick stepped through and threw his arms around Leslie, lifting her into the air as they kissed. She pawed at his face, like she couldn't believe he could actually be there, and she wanted to make sure this was real, the touch of her fingers a signal to her brain that this wasn't a dream.

Stephanie smiled and wiped a tear from her eye. In this world they lived in, a pure moment of happiness—of pure love—was so rare and fleeting that it could overwhelm you with emotion to witness it. Like a sliver of sunlight slipping into a room of pure darkness, you couldn't help but be drawn to it, to want to steal a little bit of it for yourself.

And it made her think of Michael. She'd had those moments with him. It had been a while, but they'd been there. The day of their wedding. When they'd bought their first house. Curled up in bed, feeling the warmth of his body, safely wrapped in his arms. It all came flooding back. She hadn't had time to mourn him, to properly remember what he'd meant to her all those years. His body was almost certainly still lying on that stage, lifeless, alone. He deserved something better. Something more. He'd been a good man. A man who, had circumstances worked out differently, could have been the father of her children.

It was going to be hard to let him go. There was no one who ever made her feel more loved or appreciated. No one who made her feel more beautiful. No one who made her feel more like a woman. She'd given her life over to being a doctor, to saving lives. It was a noble pursuit, and she wouldn't change anything about that. But Michael gave her something she couldn't find in her work, and it was a feeling she was going to miss dearly. She loved him. She always had. She could only hope that peace she had wished for herself could be passed along to him.

"There are more of us," Leslie said, stirring Stephanie from her thoughts. "One … dead. And Doctor Lawry needs help."

"Frank's here?" Stephanie said, shaking her head quickly. "Where?"

Leslie pointed her back around the wall, where they'd been seeking shelter. As she came around the corner and saw Frank's assistant attending to him, it dawned on her that the roof was covered in a layer of water, and everyone was soaking wet.

"What's wrong with him?" Stephanie asked.

"Took a gunshot to the shoulder," the assistant, Deborah, said. "I've been keeping pressure on it."

"Can I take a look?"

The assistant pulled back, and Stephanie assessed the wound.

"Clean exit. Doesn't look too bad, Deborah. You've been in good hands, Frank. I've got some stuff that can help back at my old house if we can't get to anything in the hospital. You ready to go?"

He nodded, and Stephanie motioned for Derrick to come over. He lifted Frank onto his back, draping his body across his shoulders and walking across the roof. Stephanie showed him where the emergency stairs were, and they started down, slowly but steadily.

She turned to Deborah and placed a hand on her shoulder.

"Leslie said someone was shot up here," she said. "Was it Theresa?"

She looked down and nodded silently.

Stephanie grimaced and shook her head, then wrapped her arms around Deborah, pulling her close to her chest and squeezing tight. They'd seen so much death over the past few years. Stephanie didn't ever want to become numb to it. They all mattered. She wanted to continue feeling something. Needed to.

Stephanie let go of Deborah and looked her in the eyes.

"I'll send Derrick back up here to get her once we've gotten Doctor Lawry squared away, okay? She's not gonna be forgotten. None of us are."

Deborah nodded slightly and then shuffled ahead to catch up with the group, Stephanie coming up behind.

"One more thing!" she called to Deborah, who stopped and turned. "Did we save the cure?"

Deborah smiled and dug into her right pants pocket, pulling out what looked like a half-quart bottle of liquid.

Stephanie smiled and motioned for her to go on ahead; Deborah stuffed the bottle back in her pocket and hurried to the stairs.

If this was their group, it wasn't a bad one. They'd search the town and assess what they had to work with. Maybe there were more survivors. Maybe they could find adequate shelter, and make the most of it. Stephanie knew nothing would ever be the same. Alessandra as they'd known it was no more. This was going to be a new place. A new beginning. And they'd start it together.

She didn't know what to expect, but there was a certain excitement to having a fresh slate. The world wasn't going to do them any favors, but they'd survived a hell of a lot to get here. Now, it was time to start over. Again.

EPILOGUE

Six months later

The winter is beginning to thaw, and it's been the longest cold season I think any of us has experienced. It's fair to say that Mother Nature has taken its toll, but we're continuing on. The world is a very different place than it was in the time of Alessandra. We've moved on as a community, but we'll never completely forget. How could we, with these walls still mostly standing around us?

We don't call this Alessandra anymore, though. It doesn't feel right. The people who made it what it was, so many of them are gone now. Those of us who are still here try to carry on their memory as best as we can. After we escaped the roof of the hospital, we quickly saw the inside of the building was going to be a total loss if the whole place didn't collapse, so Derrick carried Frank to my house—fortunately, one of a dozen or so homes that survived, perhaps because it was empty—where I had some turmeric and rubbing alcohol to help prevent infection in both of our wounds. Unfortunately, he had some nerve damage and has never quite recovered full use of his arm. I still have occasional pain, but I'm mostly fine, though I have a scar that reminds me of that day.

Once we got treatment, Frank and Deborah stayed in my house while Derrick, Leslie, and I tracked down horses because Derrick wanted to check on the women back at the marauders' camp. We approached with guns drawn, expecting some resistance, but they all immediately threw their hands up in surrender—two men who fled Alessandra when the tide turned against their group and eight women in impractical vintage dresses all gathered around a fire. One of the women was Emily, who I was especially happy to see return to the town.

When we did, Deborah greeted us alongside three women and four small children—I guessed they were between five and eight years old, but no one had been keeping track—who had been living in the back house of the compound behind the mansion. Along with Walt, Lucas, and a few others, that left us with twenty-six people remaining in our community. It wasn't much, but it was better than three people rubbing sticks together and trying to keep each other warm. We had enough shelter if people shared, we had our best gardener back, and we still had the virus cure that Deborah smuggled out of the hospital before setting the fire. It was a start.

There was so much cleanup to do. Not just the burned-out houses—most of which are still husks, and work reasonably well for breaking off wood for fires—but all the dead bodies scattered everywhere. We knew we couldn't bury them all, so I suggested we each choose two people we wanted to receive a proper burial. Frank picked Victor and his neighbor, Lucas. Deborah chose her assistant friend, Theresa, and didn't have a second. I didn't hesitate in choosing Michael and Nick.

We all helped to dig those graves, and then said some words about each of them—what they meant to us, the legacy they'd leave behind. In its own way, it was beautiful. For a while, I didn't think I'd ever stop crying. But, eventually, you run out of tears. You have to move on, or life moves on without you. We were sad, but reasonably optimistic about the future.

So much disappeared with the hospital, though. Our ability to treat infections and sickness became even more primitive than before. Most of our solar panels were at the hospital, and they were damaged during the fire. It was good we had some trained medical staff—including myself—but there was only so much we could do with basic items we had on hand. The flu swept through our community about the time the leaves fell off the trees, and it was incredibly hard to contain when we lived so closely to one another. It started with one of the women from the marauder camp and quickly spread to three others, including Deborah.

We tried to keep them warm and as hydrated as we could, but our ability to mitigate the effects of the virus was extremely limited, and influenza is very contagious in that sort of environment. Eventually, we cordoned the sick off in another part of the town. Frank and I made the decision, and we knew it was probably a death sentence for those who left for the quarantined area, but we were all going to die if we didn't. We lost eight people, leaving us with thirteen.

Not long after that, Walt died. He'd been deteriorating physically for some time, and it was no surprise when he didn't show up for breakfast that morning, and the bed check confirmed that he was dead. He was a good man who had seen a hell of a lot from his perch at that bar. But, at some point, death just becomes a part of the spectrum of life. Can what's inevitable ultimately remain tragic?

So we told a few stories of Walt and buried him with the others, then went on with our days. Emily has done fairly well with some of the other women in keeping the garden sputtering along with winter vegetables, at least enough for us not to starve. They did a second planting of turnips and radishes, both of which I'm getting incredibly tired of, but you take what sustenance you can get. Emily says we've got to get through the last frost before we start planting some spring crops—beans, eggplant, okra, tomatoes—and I can't wait to see those go into the ground. I think we could all use a change of pace into the warmer weather.

Turning to the warmer weather, though, is another sign of time slipping past. The days seem long, but the months and years feel short. None of us is going to live eighty years. Walt was sixty-five, and he could barely get around on his own by the end. Would we even *want* eighty years living like this? We feel like organisms, feeding off the earth, without even the basic motivation to procreate. Everything is hard. There's no relaxation. There's a sense of community, and camaraderie. We depend on each other. No one's in charge. We all know our role, and we play it every day. But even twenty more years of this seems like a lot.

So, time is going to beat us, if this world doesn't. We each make a choice every day when we wake up to do everything we can to make it to the next. Without this community to push me, I don't know that I'd have the strength to go on, but I do, because the collective will drives me to. As long as they want to forge ahead, I have a responsibility to continue on alongside them. There's no mission other than to live. No objective bigger than tomorrow. There is no more Alessandra, only today. Here. Moment to moment. Meal to meal. We'll find our way, as best as we can.

ACKNOWLEDGMENTS

I finished the initial rough draft of this novel (and, well, the complete three-book series) and sent it to my beta-reading team on March 8, 2020. At the time, we had some inklings that an actual pandemic might be on the horizon, but I don't think hardly anyone really expected the events that unfolded soon after that.

Three days later, I took a scheduled work flight to Greenville, S.C., and the world somehow changed from the time I boarded the plane to when I landed. An NBA player had tested positive, and everyone was panicking. I went out to a downtown bar, but quickly wondered if that was something I should be doing. Was this safe? What's going to happen?

I write this almost seven months later, as I get prepared to put this book out into the world, and so much has changed. Mask wearing is practically assumed everywhere I go. Terms like "Flatten the curve" and "social distancing" are such accepted parts of our lexicon now that it's hard to imagine they weren't always there.

It's been pointed out to me on multiple occasions in those ensuing seven months how eerily prophetic *A Greater Evil* and the larger *Alessandra Chronicles* seem to be when it comes to the true pandemic we're now living through. I truly hope this is the closest I ever come to actually living out the plot of one of my books, because my books don't tend to be pleasant places to be.

If a reader picks up this series a few years after 2020, will they assume it was written looking back on the pandemic rather than plotting out what the research indicated might happen? Will they think the rings are metaphors for masks? Will they think Audrey was actually right—or, at least, had a point— regarding social distancing, and have a more sympathetic view of her actions?

It's like the world has shifted beneath this story and changed the very foundation of the world on which it was built, which is both intriguing and troubling. It makes me wonder what the next seven months have in store for us. And the seven months after that.

In retrospect, I'm very glad I got the writing on this done before the world went completely crazy, because I wasn't productive at all for the first couple of months of quarantine. Fortunately, Emily Landers was far more productive than I was, delivering tremendously helpful feedback as a beta reader, and really helping me to get a fuller picture of how my story would play to eyes that weren't my own. The book you read would have been far different—and worse—without her help.

The same is, of course, true of my editor Julie Tibbott. She's been with me for three books now, and I don't know how I'd be able to get to the finish line without her. Her keen eye for detail and immense patience with my writing foibles is exactly what I need to coax the best out of these stories that rattle around in my head. Meanwhile, Monica Haynes (The Thatchery) again outdid herself in somehow finding a way to create a cover image that evokes everything about the book so perfectly. I sincerely don't know how she consistently does it.

And my wife, Jamie, is always my first reader. Always my best fan, and most critical eye on everything I write. She's the essential element to everything I do. She's the person I can talk through plot points with, commiserate with when I'm struggling with where to go with a story next, and count on to always push me to be a little bit better. I couldn't do any of this without her support and desire to see me succeed.

Thanks, also, to you. I like to think I write for me and not for readers in general, but that's never entirely true. I want people to enjoy diving into these crazy worlds that come pouring out of me. Knowing you're out there makes me want to deliver again, to come back with something better next time, to keep learning and improving as I go. Thank you for following me on another journey.

BUY MORE BOOKS BY JEFF HAWS

Novels

Let the Devil In (Book 2 of The Alessandra Chronicles) — Michael will work alongside his ex-wife if it means the town's survival. With the settlement still recovering from a bloody massacre and the defeat of their tyrannical leader, he struggles to help develop a democratic society. But he fears their peaceful utopia will crumble before it's created when their ragged band suffers a series of brutal murders. With power mongers using scare tactics to promote panic, Michael knows he must uncover the killer's identity to regain citizens' confidence. But with the return of a sinister figure from his past, a viral outbreak at the gates, and suspicions surrounding his ex, he's not sure who to trust. Can Michael dig up the truth before humanity's last colony tears itself apart?

The Solitary Apocalypse (Book 1 of The Alessandra Chronicles) — Along with the rest of a North Georgia town that survived a deadly worldwide plague, Michael's forced to wear a steel ring around his waist wherever he goes. He's seen cohabitation banned. Marriages dissolved. Families torn apart. But he's a good soldier, supporting the leader's draconian policies — until he learns an explosive secret about her that threatens to destroy the delicate balance they've achieved between safety and order. Now, Michael must enlist help to confront the awful truth about the town of Alessandra, and the fate of what may be the last human colony on Earth before he's silenced by the people who don't want anyone to know what they've done.

The Little Tragedy — For the past twenty years, every child has fallen into an endless coma on the night of their 10th birthday. Families are broken apart. Society is forever altered. And now, the human race itself is marching toward extinction. Until Kevin Fraser wakes up. With one Fraser child awake and the other rapidly approaching his 10th birthday, his family -- and the world -- holds its breath. Is this the sign of the plague finally ending, or will the walls start closing around the Frasers as the burden becomes too heavy for them to bear?

Killing the Immortals — Would you murder for god? Would you stand in the way of those who would? Cain and Hannah have to decide what side they're on in this fast-paced thriller about the dangers of fanaticism in a world where people are living indefinitely.

Novellas and Short Stories

Tomorrow's News Today — When Walt suddenly discovers that anything he writes at his small newspaper job will come true, he believes he has the power to reshape his crumbling marriage and career. But he also has the tools for his own destruction. Which path will he choose?

The Slingshot — Taylor's a typical geeky teenager who just wants to fit in with the cool kids for once. But soon, events spiral out of his control, and his moment of mischief threatens to tear apart his life, and his family's along with it. His older brother is the only one he can trust to save him.

FREE WITH NEWSLETTER SIGNUP

The Trolley Problem — Andrea will do anything for her son. She wants what's best for him, so she's doing her best to work a custody arrangement with her husband, and juggle a relationship with her new boyfriend. But now her ex wants to cut her out of her son's life, and she has to decide how far she's willing to go to keep her boy in her life.

* * *

REVIEW AND RATE *A GREATER EVIL*

Now that you've finished *A Greater Evil*, please consider posting a review and rating on Amazon and Goodreads. This serves both as invaluable feedback for the author, and as social proof to other readers that this book is worth their valuable investment of time to read. Also, if you liked what you read, follow Jeff on Amazon and Goodreads to interact, and be among the first to know when he writes something new.

ABOUT THE AUTHOR

Jeff Haws is a long-time journalist who has turned his writing eye to fiction. This is his fifth published novel and seventh published book. The first novel in this series, *The Solitary Apocalypse*, was published in 2017. Over the past 20 years, his writing has appeared in the *Washington Post, Atlanta Journal-Constitution, Miami Herald, Arizona Republic, New Orleans Times-Picayune*, and many other publications. He lives with his wife in Atlanta, Georgia.

SIGN UP FOR NEWSLETTER FOR UPDATES: jeffhaws.com/newslettersignup

TWITTER/FACEBOOK/INSTAGRAM: @ByJeffHaws

www.ingramcontent.com/pod-product-compliance
Lightning Source LLC
Chambersburg PA
CBHW052029240626
47153CB00006B/2011
* 9 7 8 1 9 4 5 7 6 8 1 2 5 *